The Husba

or

Bev's Book

WHAT IS A HUSBAND BENCH?

" 'The husband bench' refers to the ubiquitous seats all over malls and grocery stores where ostensibly patient husbands, with little else to take up their time, wait for their wives to finish shopping. Typically, MacDougall invests this with telling irony."

From the foreword by Ann V. Norton

Beverly Colby Lambert has always fascinated readers of the best-selling *The Cheerleader* and its sequels, *Snowy* and *Henrietta Snow*. In *The Husband Bench or Bev's Book*, told from her point of view, she reveals the convoluted and absorbing depths beneath her beautiful surface.

Both longtime fans of The Snowy Series and those new to it will relish learning "What happens *next?*" to Bev and Snowy and their friends, the former high-school kids who are still growing up together.

Bev's complex love life becomes even more intricate as *The Husband Bench* explores love in various forms, from pure to complicated—selfless, selfish, serious, comic.

"A Favorite Book"
The Cheerleader

This best-selling novel about growing up in the Fabulous Fifties, in the years of ponytails, pajama parties, proms, and "parking," is a coming-of-age classic that has become a "favorite book" for countless readers.

> "Rereading it is like snuggling into a blanket or drinking a warm cup of cider, and I think that's what a 'favorite book' should be."
>
> —EMILIE CLARK, *Synthesis*

> "One of the truest portraits of an American girl ever written . . . Everything works in MacDougall's book. She captures the times, the attitudes, the emotions with the authority of one who was once there and knows the route back by heart."
>
> —*Detroit Free Press*

> "A devastatingly accurate portrait of the '50s."
>
> —*Library Journal*

> "If future historians and sociologists are ever impelled to find out what it was like to be a high school student in America at mid 20th century, they will need go no farther than *The Cheerleader* for documentation and enlightenment . . . Utterly honest, accurate, and sympathetic."
>
> —*Kansas City Star*

> "It's heartbreaking at times, hilarious at others, and she's got it all down beautifully."
>
> —*Philadelphia Inquirer*

> "A classic."
>
> —*Publishers Weekly*

"Girlfriend Novels"

Snowy

"MacDougall's novel opens during a freshman year in the 1950s at Bennington College where Snowy, 'a New Hampshire hick' whose real name is Henrietta Snow, meets her glamorous California roommate, Harriet, and pulls some antics that would make today's students proud. Snowy's term as student employee in a Boston publishing house finally brings her back into contact with her two closest high-school friends . . . The three maintain their friendship as they marry, raise families, lose their parents, and face the 'fragility of our forties.' MacDougall's sexy, painfully true story illuminates what an endless process growing up is."

—Booklist

Henrietta Snow

"Her Snowy may be getting on in years, but Ruth Doan MacDougall's eye is as fresh and lively as ever. And best of all, MacDougall's perspective—then and now—is generous, accepting and forgiving. Fans of *The Cheerleader* and *Snowy* will love catching up with old high-school buddies Snowy, Bev, Puddles, Tom, and Dudley. Their marriages may have busted up, their waistlines spread, their chins doubled, but their loyalties remain through trials, tragedies and triumphs. New readers, especially those of us who are unapologetically middle-aged, will welcome a 'girlfriend novel' for our cohort. Funny, sad, unsentimental and wise, *Henrietta Snow* is a delight."

—REBECCA P. SINKLER,
former editor of the *New York Times Book Review*

BY THE SAME AUTHOR

THE LILTING HOUSE
THE COST OF LIVING
ONE MINUS ONE
THE CHEERLEADER
WIFE AND MOTHER
AUNT PLEASANTINE
THE FLOWERS OF THE FOREST
A LOVELY TIME WAS HAD BY ALL
SNOWY
A WOMAN WHO LOVED LINDBERGH
HENRIETTA SNOW

With Daniel Doan

50 HIKES IN THE WHITE MOUNTAINS
50 MORE HIKES IN NEW HAMPSHIRE

Editor

*INDIAN STREAM REPUBLIC: SETTLING A NEW
    ENGLAND FRONTIER, 1785-1842,* by Daniel Doan

The Husband Bench

or
Bev's Book

A Sequel to
THE CHEERLEADER
SNOWY
HENRIETTA SNOW

Ruth Doan MacDougall

FRIGATE BOOKS

At the author's Web site, www.ruthdoanmacdougall.com, items of general interest such as discussion guides, background information, and photographs are available.

THE HUSBAND BENCH, or BEV'S BOOK.
Copyright ©2007 by Ruth Doan MacDougall
Foreword Copyright © 2007 by Ann V. Norton

Cover photograph: istockphotos.com © Dave White

Cover design: hannusdesign.com

Loon drawing by Laurie Sutherland
Courtesy of the Loon Preservation Committee, PO Box 604, Lee's Mills Road, Moultonborough, NH 03254; www.loon.org

Library of Congress Cataloging-in-Publication Data
MacDougall, Ruth Doan
      The husband bench, or Bev's book / Ruth Doan MacDougall
                  p.cm
            ISBN-13: 978-0-9663352-5-5
            ISBN-10: 0-9663352-5-2

            1. Women—New Hampshire—Fiction
      I. Title II. Subtitle: Bev's Book
      PS3563.A292H87 2007
      813.54—dc.21

                                          2007900139
                                          CIP

12345   11 10 09 08 07

To Sally Burnham Smith Barrett

FOREWORD

The Husband Bench or Bev's Book begins on New Year's Day 2000 and thus takes up just where *Henrietta Snow* left off: Tom and Snowy are devoted lovers but unmarried, and Bev and Roger have decided to renew their vows after living separately for more than ten years. Like the first three books of (what has become) Ruth Doan MacDougall's quartet, this novel incorporates a character's memory to provide exposition and context, and—also like its predecessors—it's as much about the triumvirate of Bev, Snowy, and Puddles as friends and representative women of their generation as it is about their relationships with husbands and lovers. Yet unlike the other books, this one covers a very short, particular time—from January to June—and it stars Bev, Snowy's beautiful, dramatic best friend. It's also about life at sixty as the twenty-first century begins and the triumvirate copes with older bodies, adult children, and retired husbands.

"The husband bench" refers to the ubiquitous seats all over malls and grocery stores where ostensibly patient husbands, with little else to take up their time, wait for their wives to finish shopping. Typically, MacDougall invests this with telling irony. Roger at sixty-two has the same energy and ambition that catapulted him through high school and into Dartmouth and law school, and, to Bev's exasperation, he automatically assumes he will wield the same control he had when she was "home" with the children. But Bev's dozen years as a real-estate saleswoman, home owner, and essentially single woman have given her an independence she relishes, and the book's tension comes from Bev's indecisiveness: does she really want to "return" to life as a wife? Can they maintain their individual lives but live together?

Like all intensely realized characters, Bev is both unique and archetypal. Stunning at any age, effortlessly stylish, a "man's woman" who expects and receives worshipful attention, she has served as Snowy's foil throughout their shared saga. In *The Husband Bench* we see Snowy through her eyes as a "worrywart," someone who fruitlessly agonizes over the inevitable; Snowy's fears about global warming, or driving while talking on a cell phone, are merely "tiresome." We also get to enjoy Bev's conscious calculations—planning exactly the right outfit to achieve just the right effect for each person from whom she wants something—and watch her sometimes hilarious rationalizations (buying $400 "strappy sandals" for one event saves her the trouble and expense of finding shoes for the next). Yet while Bev relishes her looks, she no longer enjoys the envy they inspire in women; plus, she knows that people still assume beauties must be "dumb." And Bev's too self-aware not to realize that her original wedding dress would look absurd on her now. Her rueful sense of her "old-lady hands" reminds her that it's been many years since she was queen of the prom.

Bev has grown through marriage, and the novel acutely portrays its constant compromises and calculations, highlighting how successful couples choose the practical act that will cause the least damage. Bev can now control her reactions—for instance, to avoid manifesting "haughty hurt" when she realizes Roger is not listening to her every word, knowing not to sweat the small stuff. Likewise, Roger has learned to apologize when he realizes that he has assumed his agenda will take precedence over hers. She also lacks the jealousy her teenage self would have felt; she finds the fact that Roger has had other lovers "titillating," objectively hoping this will enliven their sex lives more than fearing it spells the end of the marriage. There are, frankly, some secrets they just do not need to share; both accept this. Bev's moral code might confuse those with traditional sensibilities, but as always MacDougall presents without judgment the difficult choices adults face in a world where customary authorities have lost their bite. Most importantly, we—and Bev and Roger—hope they survive mutual infidelity, spats over furniture, and disagreements about their children to enjoy what's important about their marriage: as Bev describes it, "their history together and their hot-and-bothered love . . . "

However, Bev has one big secret from Roger, about a matter that many people would consider Roger's essential business.

Bev's armor is not impenetrable, as Snowy has always known, and here we see Bev's anguished self-questioning as we never have before. MacDougall repeatedly, and effectively, employs what literary critics call "free indirect discourse" to emphasize that Bev is not always so sure, so secure, as she may seem: the point of view shifts from the narrator's direct representations of Bev's thoughts and actions to Bev's voice itself as she tries to take "the long view" her mother Julia taught her to seek. For instance, Bev refuses to pass judgment on the love life of her younger son, Leon, asking herself, "Am I the epitome of virtue?" And with heartbreaking poignancy, she longs for her parents, especially the father whose death at Iwo Jima haunts her even now: at confident sixty she contains the deeply hurt child suffering still this primal loss.

The family tensions connected with Leon showcase MacDougall's deadly accurate mix of humor and realism, her perfect ear for dialogue, and her uncanny ability to convey characters' wry self-knowledge. A true child of the 1970s and 1980s as his parents are of the 1940s and 1950s, Leon completely lacks his father's ambition and work ethic and "lives at home" without guilt, like many young adult children in this day of soaring real-estate prices and fierce job competition. Bev loves him regardless but must constantly negotiate his relationship with Roger, who simply can't understand a man who hasn't become a patriarch and breadwinner. In this MacDougall again highlights American sociological history, which shows that men have been at some level "liberated" as well as women, for better or worse.

Bev in fact has followed a recognizable trajectory. The attractive, fashionable housewife turned real-estate agent employs the skills she learned about managing and decorating homes—and the human manipulations she acquired as chief cook, chauffeur, nurse, and foreman of a family—to good financial use. Here MacDougall stresses a point feminists have made for hundreds of years: that "housework" and parenting are full-time, difficult jobs too often taken for granted in a world that respects mostly the acquisition of money. While Bev may find her daughters' word "empower" too strong for her tastes, she nevertheless understands that this verb describes her current life, and she relishes the fact that she's past "playing wife and mother while [Roger] climbed the ladder of success to his own firm."

Once again, we see "the Gang" at their next phase of life, and the book joyfully shows that life at sixty is pretty damn good: hot sex, new professional challenges are possible. The triumvirate endures despite petty annoyances and some discreetly withheld opinions. When MacDougall wraps up this segment of the ongoing saga, we're left with the sense that there's more to come. As the current generation of cheerleaders might say: Bring it on! We always want more. Like Snowy and Bev, we fans of the Gunthwaite gang treasure site fidelity.

ANN V. NORTON
Saint Anselm College

The Husband Bench

or

Bev's Book

1

"**THE TOURNAMENT OF ROSES,**" said Roger, walking back into the bedroom in his old maroon woolen bathrobe after his morning shower and glancing at the tuned-low television set. "The Rose Parade. That's decorating-the-gym taken to the extreme."

Bev was watching the parade from the depths of the king-size bed, once their bed, now his. This had become truly a "master" bedroom downstairs in the big old white colonial in Ninfield, Connecticut. Until three nights ago, she hadn't slept in this house since early June 1987, which meant, today being the first day of the year 2000, it had been twelve years and six months ago. She laughed, enjoying the sight of him, her tall and handsome husband. His bathrobe smelled like wet wool, like mittens. She said, "Decorating the gym? Crepe paper? Kleenex carnations?"

He stroked the mustache that he'd grown years ago when his hair started to recede. That hair, formerly dark brown, almost black, was now a good iron gray, as was his mustache. "Because of Dick's wedding and everything, I don't even know who'll be playing in the games."

"Leon probably does." Their younger son, Leon, and two of their other children had also driven back to the Ninfield house last night—early this morning—after the big wedding at the North Congregational Church in Woodbury and the reception at the Highfield Country Club. She and Roger were together

1

again, in a house full of all their children except their older son, Dick, who was now in New York, starting off on a Bahamas honeymoon with Jessica, his bride.

Roger opened a bureau drawer. "Leon will probably sleep through the parade *and* the games."

Bev didn't point out that she and Leon would be driving home this afternoon, having driven down here together from Waterlight, her home in Gunthwaite, New Hampshire, for the wedding. She plumped up the pillows behind her. The mattress was new since 1987 and also the bedclothes, boring plaid, a male choice, so Roger's girlfriend Amanda hadn't redecorated his bed during her two-year tenure. Bev almost wished she had. That might be something fun to be jealous about, and it would add an extra zing to make love in bed linen picked out by Amanda for a torrid romance with Roger. Instead, Bev said, "I've been trying to remember the name of an old movie—from our youth— about the Rose Bowl. Starring Diana Lynn, who was a favorite of Snowy's, but of course I preferred movie stars who were redheaded." Snowy (Henrietta Snow), her best friend, was a blonde, like Diana Lynn. Bev's hair, red in her childhood, then auburn, had turned completely gray, then white, in her thirties. She was now sixty and Roger was sixty-two, which seemed utterly impossible. They had been high-school sweethearts back home in Gunthwaite. How quaint! How complicated. "Snowy and I saw that movie when we were ten or eleven, and it was about the Rose Bowl beauty pageant and who would win," continued Bev, picturing herself winning, just as she had imagined the triumph while watching the movie fifty years ago. She had grown up to become Queen of the Junior Prom at Gunthwaite High School, but that didn't get you a ride on a float of flowers. You were only the cynosure of all eyes in a crepe-papered gym, and the only real roses were in your crown and wrist corsage.

Roger said, "Mmm."

He wasn't listening. For once, she could rise above her automatic reaction, a swift withdrawal into haughty hurt. She

2

snuggled deeper in the bedclothes and relished watching his routine, his familiar ways of taking underwear out of his bureau, dropping the bathrobe over a bedroom chair, unself-consciously naked, the high-school basketball star who still played a lot of tennis to keep in good shape. Despite that, she'd been worrying about his working too hard at the law firm he'd founded years ago. They had come to Ninfield because an established firm here had made him the best offer when he graduated from law school at Boston University; in Ninfield she had created a whole new life for herself, with Roger and with the children, playing wife and mother while he climbed the ladder of success to his own firm. She'd been fearing he was a prime candidate for a heart attack or a stroke, Roger Lambert the overachiever, Roger the hotshot insurance lawyer. But last night he had told her that he was ready to retire. Would he really? He stepped into a pair of Jockeys and adjusted the contents. She'd always wished he wore boxers so she could buy him exotic or amusing pairs, but with Jockeys she was limited to making puns about lawyers and briefs. She used to choose all his clothes as she did the children's when they were young, dressing everybody like paper dolls. Dressing! She remembered that the first time they'd gone to a tailor for his first really expensive suit, she had overheard the tailor asking him in a whisper, "On which side do you dress yourself, sir?" Roger had looked at him blankly. But Roger hadn't been an A student for nothing, and while Bev was still wondering what on earth the tailor was talking about, Roger whispered back, "I wear Jockeys. Neither side." Bev had given thanks that Snowy and their other best friend, Puddles (Jean Pond Cram), hadn't for some strange reason been there with her and Roger or else these three best friends, the triumvirate, would have been rolling in the aisles.

Roger said, "You could Google and find the title," and pulled on a T-shirt, went to the closet, took out an old pair of jeans.

"What?"

"The name of that movie."

He *had* been listening! And now she herself heard other things, clattering noises from the kitchen, and she smelled coffee. At least one of the children was up. Bev threw aside the bedclothes. "Time to get the show on the road."

Roger said, "Wish you could stick around through the weekend."

She was wearing a sweet flannel nightgown suitable for New England winters, white and virginal with embroidered doves adorning the chaste neckline. It had elicited the desired reaction from Roger. She said, "I've got that appointment tomorrow."

He zipped up the jeans and reached for a dark brown Shaker-knit sweater, one she didn't recognize, which matched his eyes. "Wish you hadn't had to make that appointment. Showing a house on a Sunday."

She felt anger flare. She damped it down. Toeing around under the bed for her white slippers, she said, "That's what they wanted, and the customer is always right, especially when they've got as much money as this couple apparently does. Anyway, I often work on Sundays. You'll have to get used to it."

He came over to her and kissed the top of her head. She liked being tall, five feet, seven inches (well, shrinking in recent years to five six, another joy of the aging process), but she also liked feeling petite beside his six two. He said, "Sorry."

He'd apologized! She slid into his so-familiar—yet still new—arms. When he'd been going out with Amanda, his aftershave had changed to something unfamiliar, no doubt a gift from Amanda. This Christmas Bev had given him, in addition to a briefcase, the simple old English Leather she'd begun giving him after they got married, and this was now what she inhaled, against her will thinking of other men's aftershaves and colognes, Frankie's Ralph Lauren Chaps, Geoff's Christian Dior. After she'd got married and the children began arriving, she had lost her interest in perfume and never regained it later; nowadays she wore none at all. But she took pleasure in men's fragrances. She said, "I'm sorry too."

"I'll make my special pancakes and we'll tell the kids the news over breakfast."

She smiled up at him. He had never been useful around the house, except with cars, but occasionally he'd liked to make breakfast or preside over steaks on the barbecue grill. It was funny to see him now doing everyday chores in the kitchen, where she felt like a guest.

Unfortunately he added, "With the exception of Leon, no doubt. He'll be absent, sleeping in."

Bev stepped back. "Roger, you must stop harping about Leon's fecklessness. He is thirty-three. He's not going to change." Back when Leon had refused to go to college, Bev had been very distressed and Roger had wanted to toss him out. Bev had become resigned, but Roger, who'd been voted Most Likely to Succeed in his high-school yearbook, never had.

"Sorry," he said again, yet this time he didn't sound as if he meant it.

Apologies, she thought, draping over her shoulders the holly green cashmere robe Roger had given her this Christmas. (When she had opened the gift, she had been pierced by the memory of childhood Christmas mornings and her mother in a blue flannel bathrobe, which Mother called by the old-fashioned name of wrapper.) She went into the next-door bathroom. Apologies. Last night at the wedding reception Roger had finally apologized for something he'd done in 1987, the action that had made her leave him: After she had taken the Connecticut real-estate exam, she had waited in vain to receive the results, berating herself for having flunked, but then at the wedding reception of their older daughter Roger had presented Bev with the certificate, which he had found in the mail; he had hidden it, waiting to bestow it upon her, framed, in front of the audience of wedding guests.

Hanging the bathrobe and nightgown on the bathroom door's hooks, she didn't recognize her hands, an old woman's hands. On her left ring finger were her engagement ring and wedding band from 1959. Over the past twelve years and six months away from Roger, she had worn these rings, describing her new relationship with him as a "bi-state" marriage. For a long time she had gloried in her new life of independence, her businesslike affair (to take care of those urges) with Geoff Plumley, the owner of the real-estate agency she worked at, and the holidays when Roger would drive up to Gunthwaite and stay with her for marital reunions. Conjugal visits!

Roger had been too busy at work to get involved with anyone else until recent years, and when eventually she realized he must be learning new bed techniques from other women, she found it titillating. "Does that make me kinky?" she had asked Snowy, who looked shocked. Jealousy didn't strike until Gretchen, a Ninfield friend, had informed her that Roger's latest girlfriend was Amanda, another friend from Ninfield days with whom she used to play tennis. Amanda wasn't some bit of fluff; Roger got serious about Amanda. Luckily, Amanda grew tired of waiting for him to "make a commitment," according to Gretchen, and Amanda didn't have the sense not to push him toward a decision. As he and Bev became involved in the elaborate preparations for Dick and Jessica's millennium wedding, they'd felt closer to each other than they had in decades, remembering their own wedding, looking through their old white-satin wedding album at the photographs of their young selves, and reliving all the years together.

And last night at the wedding reception, after his apology Roger had asked her to marry him again, to renew their vows. She had said yes. They had begun making plans, Roger thinking out loud about handing over the Lambert and Lambert law practice to Dick and the associates, Bev thinking to herself about what to wear. Roger had produced his PalmPilot to study the calendar; together they had settled upon a date for the renewal-of-vows ceremony.

She looked at the flannel nightgown and wondered what to choose for a second wedding night on a second honeymoon. Frilly or svelte? And the dress for the ceremony? She had saved her wedding dress all these years. It must still be up in the attic of this house. Should she wear it again? She had always thought in terms of a gorgeous new dress if she and Roger finally got divorced and she remarried. As she walked past the mirror over the sink, she made her old-crone face and waggled her old-lady hands. She had never outgrown loving to make faces. Then she sighed. She might weigh the same as she did in high school, thanks to torture on the treadmill, but it was distributed differently and there were all the other increasing signs of age, which were bound to get worse, especially since Puddles, a nurse practitioner, had told her and Snowy to cut their hormone dosage in half for safety's sake. If she decided on that 1959 wedding dress, she would have to have it altered. She couldn't even be saved by her "shapewear," which Mother would have called a girdle.

In the shower, the soap was Dove, the same brand she'd bought when she lived here. Roger had just kept on buying it, not bothering to experiment. Or did he use Dove because it reminded him of her?

Suddenly, she was scared. She hadn't shared a bathroom or a house with him for so long! Would he expect her to be home to make dinner when he wanted it? But if he truly retired, then *he* would be the homebody!

And what, she thought, will the children think? How will they react?

"Your attention, please," Roger said, standing up from the round pine table and holding aloft his coffee mug decorated with a caricature of Rumpole of the Bailey. "I have two announcements."

7

Bev, dressed in a black ski sweater and jeans, gulped Gevalia and wondered who had given him that mug. One of the children? She and they were sitting at this table in the big kitchen whose decor looked more minimalist than was intended, because when she had decided to stay in Gunthwaite she had had all of her antique pine-cupboard collection moved there, and he hadn't replaced it with anything. She glanced nervously around at her brood. Today Mimi, age thirty-seven, had gone back to wearing her usual granola grunge and her brown hair in a long braid, after rising to the occasion yesterday, putting her hair up and donning the nice dress Bev had insisted upon, which Mimi had enhanced with one of her lovely handwoven shawls. Etta, twenty-four, was the baby of the family, a surprise (Bev having been forgetful about birth-control pills), and although now a Mount Holyoke graduate working for an equestrian magazine, she would always be the baby. And since babyhood Etta had always looked like Bev, a genetic duplication that astonished and pleased Bev, but Etta had never worn her auburn hair short, the way Bev had; it cascaded in thick waves over her shoulders and, like other young women with long hair nowadays, she combed her long bangs diagonally across her forehead and bobby-pinned them underneath at the side. This bangs style annoyed Bev because it was so unattractive, but she'd been biting her tongue and not saying anything, hoping it would soon go out of fashion.

Leon, thank God, had dragged himself out of bed in time for Roger's buttermilk pancakes and Roger's announcements. Her younger son had grown up tall, dark, and handsome, and lacking an ounce of ambition.

Lloyd, Mimi's husband, sipped coffee in his serene way, his mind seemingly elsewhere. He looked like a just-clipped hedge; Mimi had made him have his rampant frizzy black hair and beard trimmed for the wedding.

Roger continued, "Dick's wedding took place yesterday, in the last century, though of course there are those who think that the millennium won't officially start until next year. Be that as it may, in June there will be our first family wedding of the twenty-first century."

Bev caught Mimi and Etta exchanging an apprehensive look. Bev hadn't told Mimi and Etta and certainly not Leon anything about her affair with Geoff Plumley, which in any case had ended in 1997 when Geoff took up with little Caitlin Perry, a young—very young, winsome, and nubile—salesperson in the agency. Nor had she told them that the reason she'd been making trips to Santa Fe wasn't just for the change of scenery but to see Frankie Richardson, an old boyfriend she'd met at her fortieth high-school reunion, also in 1997. However, they must have guessed something. What did they know about Roger and Amanda? Were they expecting Roger to announce that he and Bev were divorcing and one or both would be remarrying?

Unperturbed, Leon poured New Hampshire maple syrup. Bev had always felt guilty about his carefree behavior. When she was growing up, her own goal had been to have lots of fun, and had he inherited this attitude? But her other goal had been to marry a millionaire, which was sort of ambitious. She had gone to Katharine Gibbs secretarial school in order to become a secretary to a millionaire. Back in those days, the so-called Fabulous Fifties, it hadn't occurred to her that she might become a millionaire herself. She had ended up marrying Roger after graduation because she realized she didn't want to wait to find her millionaire, and anyway, Roger as a brilliant lawyer might become one. She hadn't been able to keep tabs during these years apart, but she guessed he might be. And she herself was doing exceedingly well in real estate, after a setback a few years ago. Her worth wasn't that of Roger's, not yet, but it wasn't peanuts. Whenever she thought about her independence and her success, into her mind crept one of those words that Mimi and Etta were apt to use but which she didn't really understand or trust: *empower.*

"I have asked your mother," said Roger, "to marry me again

in a renewal-of-vows ceremony this June on the forty-first anniversary of our wedding."

Mimi's and Etta's heads swiveled from him to Bev, who was reminded of tennis spectators and how she had hated to play with Roger because he was so competitive.

Leon asked, "Got any bacon?"

Roger ignored him but summed up, probably more succinctly than he'd planned, "And your mother has done me the honor of saying yes, as she did forty-one years ago." He raised Rumpole in a toast. "Thank you, Beverly Colby Lambert!"

Etta cried, "Oh, wow!" and jumped up to rush around the table and hug Bev, then Roger.

Slowly Mimi stood up, more restrained, having opinions about marriage. Bev still considered it a miracle that Mimi had married Lloyd instead of cohabiting. But if Mimi had acquiesced to convention in the matter of marriage, she had stuck to her guns about not producing children. So Bev was pinning her grandchildren-hopes on Dick and Jessica. Mimi said cautiously, "Mother, Dad, this is great news," and gave Bev a hug before asking, "Will you still be, um, maintaining separate households?"

"That," said Roger, "is the second announcement."

Bev saw Etta and Mimi hold their breaths. Leon yawned, but at least he covered his mouth. Sometimes he remembered the manners she had drummed into him.

"Most of us," Roger said, eyeing Leon with parental loathing, "work hard. My father worked all his life at Trask's factory. I started helping in my uncle's grocery store when I was too small to see over the counter. I worked hard at the store after school, and I worked hard in school."

Here it comes, Bev thought, the up-by-his-own-bootstraps speech about Roger's French Canadian background, about how he was the first in his family to go to college, about his scholarship to Dartmouth, his law degree, the way he'd slaved to support his wife and children and start his own law firm—

"Dad," Etta said, "please, please, cut to the chase."

Yes, Etta would always be the baby and would always be able to twist her father around her little finger. Roger smiled at her. "Okay," he said. "The point is, I've worked long enough. I'm going to retire."

Etta hugged him again. "Neat. I never thought you would."

Mimi asked, "Where will you retire to?"

"My hometown," Roger said. "Good old Gunthwaite. If none of you kids wants to buy this house, your mother and I will put it up for sale. Your mother is, of course, a real-estate expert."

He had Leon's full attention now. Leon asked, "Where in Gunthwaite?"

There was a peculiar mixture of satisfaction and wariness in Roger's voice as he answered, "Your mother and I will be sharing her house. The beautiful Waterlight house."

"You're shitting me," said Leon.

Up in the cold attic shadowy beneath the ceiling's bare bulb, Bev stood getting her bearings, remembering how Betty Furness on the *Today* show had once displayed some of her vintage dresses and hats and said, if Bev recalled correctly, that the best thing she'd ever done was to marry a man with an attic. Betty had saved *everything.* But of her own apparel, Bev had only stored the wedding dress up here, having given her clothes to Goodwill when she tired of them. She'd left some special high-school and college items such as prom dresses in her mother's attic, but by the time her mother and stepfather moved to Florida she had no sentimental attachment to them anymore so Mother had disposed of them someplace. Leave it to Roger to have saved his Gunthwaite green-and-white athletic jacket and his letter sweater all these years!

11

Hurry, she told herself. Leon's comment had sparked a tirade from Roger, not that Leon stuck around to hear it. Bev had found him upstairs in his old bedroom, stuffing clothes into his duffel bag, but he had at least hung his best-man tailcoat, waistcoat, and trousers back up neatly in his garment bag. She had said, as if nothing had happened, "I'll finish my packing and meet you in the car." Pale, Leon hadn't replied. She had gone out to the hall to the linen closet, turned on its light, and found it much the same as when she'd left it, shelves stacked with towels and sheets and clean rags from old T-shirts and such. Grabbing a rag, she had opened the door to the attic stairs and climbed.

Although she'd given away her own clothes, she had saved some of the children's, and now she saw her young wife-and-mother handwriting on the cartons closest to her on the left under the eaves. The lettering was large enough so she didn't need her reading glasses. Mimi's Baby Clothes, she had labeled one; another, Dick's. Leon's; Etta's. Young, young.

Growing up, she had joked to Snowy and Puddles about having six children and a nanny to take care of them, but she had never really imagined herself in the role of mother. Well, she certainly had flung herself into that role as soon as Mimi was born. She should have won an Oscar.

These cartons weren't where she remembered them. She realized that things had been shifted around to make room for many boxes labeled in Dick's handwriting. School papers, not the precious ones from the children's elementary-school years that she had saved, but his high-school papers, Yale undergraduate, Yale Law School. Boxes of his books. Of course! He had been using this attic as a storage unit while living in his condo, the way Etta, who lived in an apartment in Amherst, Massachusetts, was using Waterlight's huge attic (the size of which Snowy had made Bev feel guilty about by remarking that it could house a million homeless people).

Hurry! Keep Roger and Leon apart from each other!

As she moved between the cartons and the accumulated clutter—lamps, stacks of old LP records, her grandmother's whatnot she'd forgotten about—she felt as if she were drowning, her past flashing before her eyes. There was the old wedding-present electric frying pan she'd used so much in the early years when she and Roger set up housekeeping in the basement apartment on the wrong side of Beacon Hill and then their first house in Ninfield, a new ranch house all fresh and hopeful, before the two bigger and bigger ones that led to this colonial with its swimming pool and lawns and gardens. She had also kept their first television set, and here it sat. To turn it on or off, you pushed or pulled its button, which made a soft secret click she'd always liked. Why get weepy over a damn black-and-white TV? Because it looked like a time machine? Did the things that had happened since she last watched shows on it really happen?

She spotted the long white box. Label: Wedding Dress. No time to open it to see what condition the dress was in. Just take it back to Gunthwaite. Swiping the dust rag across the surface of the box, she suddenly remembered that she used to lift the dress out periodically and refold the layers of white satin and tulle so that the creases wouldn't set in the same places.

Then she saw nearby a carton she had labeled: Bev, High School. This had escaped the Florida move; she vaguely remembered finding it amid the cartons of other things Mother had passed along before the move, mostly books. She hesitated, then dusted the top and unlocked the folded flaps. After the Junior Prom, Mother had pressed her crown of red roses to preserve it, but all these decades later it was just wire and brown crumbs in a plastic bag. The bag and her Junior Prom trophy lay on top of a scrapbook with a handwoven green-and-white cover. Woven by Mother, from whom Mimi had inherited the talent. Bev didn't open the scrapbook, but she remembered how Mother had collected items about Bev's starring roles in Gunthwaite High School's Dramatics Club plays, her prize-speaking awards, clippings and photos and publicity posters. Beneath

13

it was a maroon leatherette scrapbook, the high-school "Roger Scrapbook" in which Bev had kept clippings about his successes, basketball and prize speaking and debate and Boys' State. She had forgotten about these two scrapbooks back when she'd had Roger bring all the photo albums of the children to Gunthwaite after she bought her first house there and was obviously going to stay. Those photo albums had been in a bookcase down in the living room here, along with the wedding album that Roger had also brought, intentionally or unthinkingly.

Hurry! Balancing the carton on the wedding-dress box, clutching them, she rushed back to the door, blinding herself to everything else in this haunted attic.

Down in Roger's bedroom, she quickly finished packing her one suitcase. One, but a big one. She took out of the closet the garment bag containing her spectacular mother-of-the-groom dress, tinsel-silver with a flocked green pattern, and draped it across the bed. Mimi or Etta could fetch these. She carried the box and carton into the kitchen.

Roger was loading the dishwasher and Mimi was sponging off the table. Leon, Etta, and Lloyd were nowhere to be seen, here or in the pantry. Then out a window Bev saw her dark green Subaru Outback pulled up to the back door, Leon in the driver's seat.

Mimi asked, "What've you got there?"

"Oh, odds and ends," Bev said, remembering how Mimi and Lloyd had been married atop Mount Pascataquac in Woodcombe, New Hampshire, the town where Snowy lived, and Mimi had worn a simple white muslin dress that she had designed and sewn herself. Bev would have preferred a wedding that didn't involve a hike, but Mimi had looked beautiful. "Could you go get my suitcase and garment bag?"

"Sure," Mimi said.

Bev ran outdoors to put her attic gleanings in the back of the car. She said to Leon, "Just another minute."

He didn't reply.

14

Indoors, Roger poured detergent into the dishwasher and began, "On your drive back, make it plain to Leon that I expect—"

Bev gave him a warning look.

He sighed. "Okay," he said. He dried his hands on a dish towel and placed them on her shoulders, drew her to him, and kissed her.

Bev and Leon headed back up I-91, Leon at the wheel, still white and silent. Into the CD player Bev slid some generations-compromise music, one of the country-and-western CDs that she'd begun buying after the reunion with Frankie, though of course Leon didn't know that was why. At least she assumed he didn't; one fault he did not have was snooping. He hadn't inherited from Roger the curiosity that, Roger had told her with pride, had made him in his boyhood hunt for and find the Christmas presents his mother had hidden, unwrap them, investigate, and then do up the packages and retie the ribbons so cleverly that nobody ever knew his surprise wasn't genuine on Christmas morning.

"You ain't woman enough," sang Loretta Lynn, "to take my man!"

In 1995, when Bev bought Waterlight, a big old year-round brown-shingled lakefront cottage, Leon had moved into it with her from the first house she'd rented upon moving to Gunthwaite with him and Etta, a ranch house she had eventually bought. He had left that first house for a year to live with one of his girlfriends, and later he had left Waterlight to live with another, but he had moved back two years ago and she knew he considered Waterlight his, which to a certain extent it was because he was the caretaker, the handyman, and understood the details of its care and feeding better than she did. He looked after some summer places as well and did some freelance carpentry, but his main job was Waterlight; its maintenance was his responsibility, from granite cellar to cedar roof. He did the yard work too. She worked in the gardens if she had time, but he had finally become a competent gardener, though like most men he preferred digging to weeding. He also took care of Waterlight's boats: the sailboat and two canoes that had come with the place, and the old wooden Chris-Craft she'd bought and learned to drive, to impress people when she was showing island property. His work at Waterlight earned him room and board and five hundred dollars a month, an amount she had never mentioned to Roger.

She said, "Waterlight is a big house, Leon."

Finally he spoke. "Not big enough." His words echoed Loretta Lynn's.

Although the heater had warmed the car, and the heated seats had warmed her back and bottom, she pulled her parka closer around her. Would Leon move out when Roger moved in? Well, maybe that would be best. But could he survive without Waterlight? Her baby boy. He had been the baby of the family for nine years before Etta arrived, but he had never resented her usurpation. Roger had been an only child for four years before the arrival of two sisters and two brothers, and, he'd told Bev, he had been none too pleased by these attention-hogging babies. She thought of the need for a guest list for the renewal-of-vows ceremony. Would Roger want to invite his sisters and brothers? Would they want to come? Pauline lived in Atlanta; Claire in Indianapolis; Joe in Houston; Skip in Melrose, Massachusetts.

Bev asked Leon, "Are you ready to stop for a break?"

He shook his head.

Bev looked out the window at the bleak cloudy day, the boring turnpike north through Connecticut, western Massachusetts, the

16

gray roadside scenery mostly bare of snow. What a way to waste January 1, 2000! Why on earth hadn't she told her customers that she would be away all weekend, attending her older son's wedding? Because she had been afraid of this return to Ninfield. She had feared being trapped there amid the memories of who she was when she left to go to Mimi's wedding and didn't return. The memories. Her mother had just died then, committing suicide before the stomach cancer could kill her. By making the appointment to show a house tomorrow, Bev had guaranteed herself an excuse to escape.

She hadn't known she'd get a remarriage proposal!

They were passing Amherst now, but instead of thinking of Etta working and living here, she thought of her father, Richard Colby, going to Amherst College while her mother was nearby at Mount Holyoke. Her parents had grown up together in Bedford, Massachusetts. After college they had tried working in Boston for two years, Mother as a secretary, Daddy at a stockbroker's, but they had both realized that city life was not for them, so when they got married they embarked on the Great Depression adventure of chicken farming, buying with their parents' help a run-down farm in Gunthwaite. On Bev's birth certificate, Daddy's occupation was listed as "poultry farmer." There was no line for an occupation for Mother; it was assumed a wife wouldn't have one.

Farmer. In addition to the nasty chickens, there had been a cow, huge and terrifying to Bev despite the dainty name Mother had given it: Clover. Mother did most of the milking, a twice-daily chore that Daddy found tedious. Bev had once overheard him reciting to Mother a bit of doggerel that extolled the merits of evaporated milk, and she'd immediately memorized it because it had made Mother laugh. When she'd piped up with it later at supper, she made them both laugh at their precocious little daughter, but Mother explained that it contained a couple of words that weren't polite so she'd better not ever recite it again.

17

Therefore Bev never forgot it:

No tits to pull,
No tails to switch;
Just punch a hole
In the son of a bitch.

Turning down the CD player, Bev took her cell phone out of her shoulder bag (a Christmas present woven by Mimi) and pressed Snowy's numbers. The general store that Snowy owned and ran in the postcard-pretty town of Woodcombe was closed on New Year's Day, so Snowy would probably be relaxing in the apartment she shared with Tom Forbes, the high-school boyfriend with whom she'd renewed the romance after her husband died in 1987. The apartment was down the main street from the store, upstairs in the barn Tom had converted for his business, North Country Coffins, where he built pine coffins. If Snowy was working on a poem in her office in the apartment, Tom would answer.

"Hello?" Snowy said.

"It's me. Are you busy?"

"Hi, are you home already? We just got back from a walk. Cocoa time."

"Leon and I are on the road, heading home."

"I hope he's driving, not you?"

Bev knew that Snowy the worrywart disapproved of drivers using cell phones. "Don't fret, I'm the passenger. Snowy, this morning I was watching the Rose Parade and I couldn't remember the title of that movie with Diana Lynn."

"*Peggy*," said Snowy. "The name of Diana Lynn's character."

With Snowy around, you didn't need to Google certain subjects. Bev said, "And this morning I found my wedding dress in the attic." Bev had phoned Snowy last night from Dick's wedding reception in the euphoria of the moment and the champagne, to tell her about Roger's proposal and retirement, to invite

18

her to their renewal-of-vows ceremony, and to ask her to call and tell Puddles.

"Your wedding dress!" Snowy said brightly. "Renewing your vows! What a milestone!"

Bev and Snowy had been best friends since second grade in elementary school, so during last night's phone call Bev suspected and right now she knew that Snowy was being overly enthusiastic and really thought the whole thing was funny, if not downright asinine. She remembered that Snowy had confided last year that Tom had proposed but Snowy had decided marriage wasn't necessary. Irritated, Bev asked, "Did you get hold of Puddles?"

"Yes, she was still up, celebrating the millennium with her cat, Guy having gone to bed. She said she'll come if the timing doesn't interfere with the cheerleading championships."

"When are those?"

"In February."

"Oh, whew, that's okay then, we're planning June, on our wedding anniversary. Well, not precisely on that day, June twentieth, because it's a Tuesday this year and we don't want a weekday. So we've decided on the following Saturday, June twenty-fourth."

There was dead air from Snowy. Bev held the cell phone out and looked at it, then looked at Leon's stony profile. Vows. Had everyone taken a vow of silence? Then suddenly Bev remembered that June twenty-fourth was Snowy's wedding anniversary, June 24, 1961, when she married Alan. "Oh Snowy! I forgot!"

The anguish in her voice made Leon glance over at her.

Snowy said, "It's all right. It's great. Unless, now that you've remembered, it bothers you, a jinx or something. But it wouldn't really be. We had a happy marriage, except for the end."

In May 1987, when unbeknownst to Snowy the general store was on the verge of bankruptcy, Alan had drowned himself in Woodcombe Lake.

Bev said, "It's really all right with you?"

"Yes," Snowy said firmly.

"I'll give Puddles a call and officially invite her and Guy."

"You know how Guy is about not traveling up from South Carolina to New England. He'll think he'll freeze to death even in June. Puddles wondered if she might bump into Norm Noyes if she comes to Gunthwaite."

Bev said, "Leave it to Puddles to undo her vows at my renewal of mine!"

When they hung up, they both were laughing. And that last comment of hers had made Leon, at last, grin.

He said, "This Puddles, she's the crazy one you and Snowy went down to see last year? Because her husband had had a heart attack but when you got there he hadn't?"

"One of Puddles's little ploys. She'd been inviting us to South Carolina for years." Not wanting to think about the real reason Puddles had tricked her and Snowy into making the trip, Bev looked out the window and registered that they were almost in Vermont now. Even here, there was hardly any snow. December had been mostly rainy, causing Snowy to carry on tiresomely about global warming. Bev remembered an old adage: A green Christmas makes a full churchyard. She shivered and said, "Roses. If this open winter continues, we're going to lose some rosebushes."

"You always think we're going to lose some."

"And sometimes we have." Bev knew she was about to repeat herself, but she didn't mind doing so when she was quoting her mother. It kept Mother alive. "Your grandmother used to say that in New Hampshire roses should be treated as annuals."

Leon lapsed again into silence, perhaps wondering if Roger would invade the gardens as well as the house.

The thought bothered Bev, too. To avoid it, she lifted the phone to call Puddles, who *had* been a nag with invitations to South Carolina ever since she married Guy and moved there in 1960. But what had galvanized Puddles into inventing his heart attack was the end of the friendship between Bev and Snowy. The memory of this made Bev's stomach go sick and her face muscles flinch into a grimace.

"You okay?" Leon asked.

"Let's stop at the rest area."

It was right ahead, over the Vermont line, and Leon pulled in and found a parking space. Inside the post-and-beam building filled with exhibits of Vermont products and arts and crafts, they headed for the restrooms. Bev couldn't help thinking of the rest areas she and Snowy had stopped at on the long drive down to South Carolina, a drive during which they'd hardly spoken at first, Bev at the wheel, Snowy studying the map. What had really brought them back together? Sausage gravy at a truck-stop breakfast on the second day. Snowy had never tasted any before, so that's what Snowy had ordered, sausage gravy and biscuits and scrambled eggs. Bev had laughed over this, laughed for the first time on the trip and then, remembering how good sausage gravy was, scooped up a spoonful. So thus they'd been sharing food again.

Bev examined her face in the ladies' room mirror. She didn't look evil. In fact, modesty aside, for her age she looked quite presentable. Ever since she was little she had known she was very pretty, the evidence of mirrors being confirmed when she overheard Mother saying to Daddy, "Bev is going to be a raving beauty just like your mother, Richard. We're going to have our hands full!" Bev had memorized these lines, as she would later memorize her lines in the Dramatics Club plays. Daddy had laughed. And then he had gone off to war and been killed at Iwo Jima.

Being pretty had its drawbacks, especially for a business-woman. People automatically thought: beautiful but dumb. Both men and women tended not to take you seriously, and some women were envious. She had, however, proved herself, despite the face she saw in the mirror. Business. Real estate. She didn't look evil, wicked, contemptible. Yet Snowy had

21

thought she was an unscrupulous money-grubbing opportunist, all because Bev had planned to develop the farm Snowy loved, although it had once been *Bev's* home, the place where *Bev* grew up, owned by *Bev's* mother and Fred, *Bev's* stepfather, so what right did Snowy have to act as if developing it were the end of the world? Okay, Mother and Snowy treasured the place far more than she ever had. But Mother did leave it, Mother and Fred sold it and moved to Florida because of his health, so it wasn't totally precious to Mother. Not that Mother and Fred could have afforded to keep it for a second home to return to in the summers, so Mother had no choice. Earlier, after Daddy's death, Mother had sold that first farm and moved into town. Round and round Bev's thoughts went as usual when she got into this rut. Snowy's Bennington roommate, Harriet Blumburg, had ended up buying Mother and Fred's place, so the property wasn't developed after all, but still Snowy wouldn't relent. For a year they didn't see each other. Then last May came Puddles's call for help.

And by the time they'd reached Puddles's house on Hilton Head, their friendship was healing. Upon arrival, finding Guy hale and hearty, they were united in their outrage at the trick Puddles had pulled. Then they'd had a wonderful visit, and on the drive home they had tacitly agreed to ignore the rift, to pretend the rupture hadn't happened.

Still, Bev tried never to mention the real-estate business, which was difficult to do. It was her career, her challenge; it had replaced romance in her life, providing the excitement, the thrills.

Back in the main room, she found Leon eating Doritos he'd bought from a vending machine and contemplating a display of handwrought hardware. She asked, "Ready to leave?"

He nodded and held out the Doritos bag. "Want some?"

"Thank you." She took one, and they started for the door, but she halted at a pottery display. When she and Roger got married, Snowy had given them a set of Bennington Potters mugs. Broken long ago. Careful Snowy still had most of the set of Bennington Potters dishes that had been one of the wedding presents Mother and Fred had given Snowy and Alan—that is, Mother had given Snowy the money to buy it, Snowy being there on the spot in Bennington, at Bennington College. Snowy had chosen to go to college in Vermont where, it was a well-known fact, the cows outnumbered the people, while Bev had headed for Boston and Katharine Gibbs and Puddles went to Boston and the Mass. General School of Nursing. If you renew your vows, Bev wondered, do you get to renew your china? But she'd bought new china many times since 1959.

I am sixty years old, she thought. I shouldn't be thinking shallow thoughts about a new china pattern. My mind should be on a higher plane. I should always be taking what Mother used to call the long view.

The long view ahead of Roger's retirement?

Leon said, "Maple syrup and cheddar. The Vermont image. It's really New Yorkers, white wine, and Brie."

Bev laughed, and they went outdoors to the car. She asked, "Would you like a nap and I'll drive?"

He shook his head and said, "I'm good," and got back in on the driver's side.

As they continued up I-91 toward White River Junction, where they would cross into New Hampshire, Bev pulled her cell phone out of her shoulder bag again, but just as she was about to tap in Puddles's number, it trilled. A customer? Roger? She checked the caller ID. Frankie, from his Santa Fe condo. She said, "Hello."

"Happy New Year," said Frankie. "How did the wedding go?"

"Perfectly," she said. He knew about Dick's wedding, but he didn't know that she'd planned to stay with Roger at the Ninfield house while in Connecticut. Now that she was re-engaged, so to speak, she'd better tell him about Roger and end things. She pictured Frankie in his sexy Western clothes, his beautiful boots.

Frankie Richardson, a cute boyfriend from their junior-high and high-school years, had become a handsome older man, balding, tanned. He was a widower, his wife having died of breast cancer six years ago. Bev hadn't been to Santa Fe since November, and she always wondered if he dated during her absences; although she'd never found any evidence in his condo, and the only photographs there were of his wife and their children, she felt she should assume he had a girlfriend or girlfriends about whom he was discreet. She said, "I'm on my way home to Gunthwaite now."

"I wish you were on your way to New Mexico."

She shot a look at Leon, who was watching the turnpike. His mind on Waterlight? She couldn't tell Frankie about Roger, not with Leon right beside her. "My schedule is jam-packed."

"Maybe I could fly to New Hampshire."

This was the first time he'd suggested leaving his beloved Southwest to see her in Gunthwaite. She said hastily, "But my schedule—there would be absolutely no time." Frankie certainly ought to understand this, for they were pretty much in the same business, real estate. He was a developer of exclusive "spec" houses.

"You should give yourself a vacation," Frankie said. "Remember in November when we were sightseeing here per usual and you said you'd like to see Sedona instead sometime? Why don't we meet in Phoenix and drive up there, what do you say?"

Temptation pounced on her. "Oops, sorry," she said, "you're fading, breaking up. I'll be in touch." She pressed the phone off and put it back in her shoulder bag, suddenly feeling unable to talk to Puddles. To Leon she said unnecessarily, "Business."

He grunted.

Closing her eyes, she saw glowing travel-magazine pictures of the red rocks of Sedona.

The Plumley Real Estate Awards Conference was next weekend in Eastbourne, on New Hampshire's seacoast. The prize for selling the most properties, for being the top producer, was always a trip. In 1994 she had won a trip to Telluride, which she took with Geoff; in 1996 she'd won a trip to Montreal, which she took with Roger and Leon, to teach Leon about his paternal roots (he hadn't paid any more attention than he had during childhood trips to visit Roger's mother, who had moved to Montreal to live with a sister after Roger's father died and had stayed there until her own death). Last year she had won again, a trip to San Francisco, where Frankie had joined her. She hadn't been able to tell Snowy about that, because at the time they weren't speaking and afterward because of her policy of not mentioning real estate to Snowy. This year's prize was a trip to Orlando. Snore! From her estimate of the other agents' sales, she guessed she would win it, but she'd been often to Disney World when the children were young, when she and Roger and the children were visiting Mother and Fred in Port Salerno. She wished she could skip the awards ceremony.

Where should she and Roger go on their second honeymoon? To Maine, where they had spent their first at the Camden hotel where she had waitressed two summers? For Mimi and Lloyd's honeymoon, Roger had given them a hiking trip in Europe. Bev had never visited another country except Canada. Neither, as far as she knew, had Roger. But Snowy, who didn't have much money, had been to Britain twice! (Well, the second trip had been a present from Harriet.) Bev began to picture Snowy's descriptions of Stratford-upon-Avon, Anne Hathaway's Cottage, and Warwick Castle, but they blurred into those red rocks she'd seen in Westerns. Sedona. She might pretend to laugh at New Age stuff, but the possibilities did intrigue her. In Sedona she could have her fortune told—and could she via a medium, a channeler, speak to Mother and Daddy?

25

Bev awoke as they were driving through Leicester, Gunthwaite's neighboring town. It was dark out now, the streetlights were on, and the dashboard clock read 6:15. Leon was humming to her Willie Nelson CD. Was his mood better? She knew about moods. Especially, of course, her own. "Sorry," she apologized. "I dropped right off." She stretched as much as she could in the seat belt.

Leon hummed, "On the road again—"

And as the road neared Mimi and Lloyd's house, she leaned forward to see if they'd got back yet. Mimi had said she and Lloyd planned to leave Roger's soon after Bev and Leon did. The windows of the old farmhouse were dark. The car's headlights illuminated the sign out front: Weaverbird. Mimi's shop with her looms and woven wares—from ponchos to scarves, place mats to bookmarks—filled the front rooms, and Mimi and Lloyd lived in the back and upstairs. Lloyd, a graphic artist, worked for the Leicester newspaper. Probably along the way home Mimi and Lloyd would make a lengthier stop than a rest area; probably they'd dally over a meal.

Still, the constant worry of children, even grown-up children, weighed upon her.

She thought of Tom's daughter, Libby. How many years would it be this year since Libby had been killed by lightning while hiking with him and Snowy? 1990? Ten years.

Between Leicester and Gunthwaite the road no longer ran through woods, passing only a trailer park and some houses that looked just as insubstantial and temporary, though they'd been there ever since Bev could remember. First, trees had been cut down for a Wal-Mart. Then came Staples, Home Depot, a strip mall, car dealerships. These were all in Leicester, and Snowy maintained that Dudley, a classmate who'd become the mayor of Gunthwaite, would not have allowed them in Gunthwaite, which already had plenty of malls and messes from earlier years of uncontrolled growth. Bev admitted the new stores were an affront to the eye, but come on, be reasonable, be practical.

Snowy was particularly boring about Wal-Mart, at which she refused to shop because of the National Writers Union and solidarity or some such futile gesture. When the old stationery store in Gunthwaite closed recently, Snowy did finally have to break down and go to Staples.

Seeing Applebee's, Bev asked Leon, "Do you want to stop or shall I cook a frozen pizza?"

"I don't care. Whatever you want."

"I'd just as soon get home. It seems as though we've been away longer than since Wednesday. I've got some homework to do tonight for tomorrow's appointment."

"Okay."

If only, she thought again, she didn't have to waste next weekend at the Holiday Inn in Eastbourne, attending the seminars and discussions that led up to the awards banquet. When Geoff had ended their affair (or let it taper off), during the ensuing awkwardness (and her anger and hurt, which she hadn't expected to feel) she had decided not to leave Plumley Real Estate to work for another agency, because she had a better chance of continuing to sell properties if she stuck with a situation she knew. She had held her head high; she had reestablished her independent-contractor relationship with him and could act professional with ease in the office. But in the semisocial atmosphere of those Plumley Real Estate Awards Conference weekends, he got a rueful look when he talked with her over drinks and she automatically was tempted to flirt, if nothing more. Her instincts told her that his romance with young Caitlin Perry was fizzling out now instead of heading toward marriage. How old would he be in 2000? Sixty-seven? He definitely didn't seem to be thinking about retirement.

Leon veered up onto the bypass skirting the residential and downtown sections of Gunthwaite, the old mill town that Dudley had saved with his various projects of revitalization. The latest was getting it on a list of "Walkable Small Cities," which reminded Bev of all the walking she and Snowy and Puddles had done in their youth, to and from schools, to and from Main Street. Whereas with her children, she'd spent hours chauffeuring them around Ninfield to lessons and friends' houses, everywhere. As Leon took the lake exit, she remembered his trumpet lessons and his Little League games.

Down on the main road, she felt like a queen making a triumphal progress through her realm. She knew every place they passed. If she hadn't sold it herself, she knew who at which agency had. She'd sold apartments in these condo developments, sometimes twice over during these past twelve years; she had sold house after house after house, the prices rising the closer the places got to the lake. I am one damn good real-estate agent, she thought.

And into her mind came the realization that in this first year of the new century she could leave Plumley Real Estate and Geoff Plumley and start her own agency.

Leon turned off onto Lakeside Road.

The broker's exam! Oh God, she wailed inwardly, in order to start an agency she needed to get her broker's license, which meant taking the broker's exam, another horrible harrowing ordeal, as bad as or worse than taking the Connecticut sales exam and then the New Hampshire sales exam! And what if she flunked?

There were no lights in the houses on Lakeside Road. These were summer cottages, closed for the winter. In her youth, they used to be called camps. They crowded together, each hoping for a glimpse of Lake Winnipesaukee, but not until the road neared East Bay and the lots and cottages became bigger were there views, unseen in the dark. In the headlights were only the silhouettes of pines.

Leon turned at the mailbox that said Waterlight and drove down the narrow drive to the arc of the gravel sweep.

Startled, she saw a car parked in front of the cottage's big hulking shape. An old pale Volkswagen bug. From within the cottage emanated a glow of light brighter than the night-lights

28

that automatically came on throughout the place. The kitchen lights—

She gasped, "Burglars! Don't stop!" She groped in her shoulder bag. "I'll phone the police."

"Fuck!" Leon said. He parked behind the VW and jumped out.

She cried, "*Leon!*"

"For Christ's sake, don't phone the cops." He ran up the broad front stairs to the screened porch that wrapped the entire house.

She was on his heels. "*Leon! Don't you dare go indoors!*"

"It's okay, I know the car, I know who's here." On the porch, he opened the front door.

She clearly remembered locking it when they left Wednesday. "Who? Leon, did you give somebody your key to Waterlight?"

He didn't reply, switching on the hall light, hurrying across the big hallway decorated for Christmas with poinsettias, mistletoe, swags and garlands of evergreens. She followed him past the two-story living room where the tall Christmas tree loomed, its bulbs dark, on down the hall to the right, past the dining room, into the kitchen. The track lighting showed her pine-cupboard collection against the walls she'd painted white. She had also painted the soft green cabinets and the pale blue and green vintage cottage furniture. She knew that she had switched off these lights before her departure on Wednesday.

Bev's flesh crawled. She said, "Leon—"

He continued along the hall toward the back bedroom, his room. The door was open. Transfixed in the middle of the room stood a small but sturdy young woman in jeans and a flannel shirt under a parka, a knitted navy watch cap pulled down to her eyebrows. In her left hand she held a duffel, and over her left shoulder was a tote bag decorated with teddy bears dancing ring-around-the-rosy. In her right arm slept a child swaddled in a baby blue snowsuit.

29

"Mother," Leon said, "this is Trulianne Hughes."
He remembered his manners in such a crisis?
"And this," he said, "is Clem."
Clem slept on, looking just like Leon at age two.

2

BEV GRABBED ONTO THE door handle and stayed upright. She said, "How do you do?"

The young woman—Trulianne? What kind of name was Trulianne?—glanced at Leon. She was maybe in her early thirties, pretty with the slight overbite that Bev had heard was intriguing to men, and she wore her straight brown hair in long strands that fell below her shoulders. The shock eased from her face, and when she spoke her voice was crisp. "We had a nap and overslept. We'll be going now."

"Okay," said Leon, taking the duffel.

Bev found herself stepping aside. No! She stepped back and stood her ground, blocking the doorway. She demanded, "Who is Clem?"

Both Trulianne and Leon looked at the little boy. Neither answered.

Years ago Bev had joked to Snowy that she might unknowingly already be a grandmother, thanks to Leon's liaisons. She had not really believed this. Her mouth was dry. She swallowed and said, her voice now almost a whisper, "It's obvious he's Leon's son. And you're his mother?"

Trulianne said, "His name is Clement Hughes."

Bev repeated, "Clement Hughes."

Trulianne paused, then explained, "My mother's maiden name is Clement and I always planned to name a son that."

31

Bev's knees began to buckle. She had never ever fainted, except on cue in plays performed by the Dramatics Club and the Ninfield Players. She had once had what was thought to be a heart attack but turned out to be a potassium deficiency caused by diuretics. Astounded, she announced, "I think I'm going to faint."

Leon dropped the duffel, seized Bev, lifted her up, and lugged her down the hall to the kitchen and propped her in the old bentwood rocker. She felt dizzy. She felt robbed, as if the house had indeed been burgled; she felt robbed of nine months of anticipation and shopping, robbed of that new type of party, a grandmother's baby shower. She felt an overwhelming desire to hold Clem, to stroke the same light brown curls that Leon had had at that age before they began to darken.

She burst into tears. In Dramatics Club plays she had learned she could weep at will, but these sobs were involuntary.

"Oh Christ," Leon said, sticking a glass under the sink faucet. Then obviously deciding she needed something stronger than water, he yanked open the liquor cupboard and poured Courvoisier.

But before he could give her the glass, Trulianne placed the little boy in her arms and then, with a practical gesture that reminded Bev of Puddles, handed her a Kleenex. Clem still slept on, warm and heavy.

"He's worn out," Trulianne said. "This afternoon we were playing in your backyard just before we were going to leave. Out of nowhere came this animal who went sliding down the bank into that open water around the dock." She asked Bev, "I'm guessing an otter?"

Bev nodded, blotting her eyes, cuddling Clem.

"Well, while I was watching to see where it would come up, Clem ended up in the water. He'd tried to chase it. His walking is more like staggering at this stage."

Leon gulped the cognac he'd poured for Bev, who held Clem closer. The child could have drowned! Clem could have been torn to pieces by the agitator that kept the ice cleared away from the dock!

Trulianne said calmly, "So I fished him out, but we both got soaked in the process, so we had a hot bath and what was supposed to be a quick nap while our clothes were in the dryer. We were just leaving when you arrived. We'll be on our way." She reached out for her son.

Bev hung onto Clem. "Wait. Wait! Who *are* you, where do you live? Leon! Leon, tell me what this is all about!"

Leon began to laugh. Then he flopped into a kitchen chair, put his arms on the table and his face in his arms.

Trulianne said, "Leon's pickup truck broke down. In Eastbourne. It was flat-bedded to the garage where I work. I'm an auto mechanic."

Bev stared. Auto mechanic? Eastbourne? What had Leon been doing at the seacoast?

Trulianne said, "So we met and . . ." She shrugged.

Although it was plain what had happened next, Bev would brook no evasions. She said, "And?"

Trulianne looked toward Leon.

As Bev expected, he didn't help her out. His head remained down, face hidden. Bev persisted, "And?"

Trulianne sighed. "And then we saw each other a lot."

Bev asked relentlessly, "*And?*"

Trulianne said, "Clem wasn't a mistake. I'd decided it was time to have a baby. I was thirty then. I wanted to be a single mother. I had a secure job and—"

Leon snorted.

Trulianne's self-sufficient air vanished. She dropped into the chair beside Leon and ripped off her watch cap and twisted it around in her hands. Like Etta, Trulianne wore her bangs pulled diagonally across her forehead and bobby-pinned. Trulianne blurted, "When there are layoffs, the female mechanic is the first to go, but the garage was doing so well I hadn't expected there would ever be layoffs. It's taking a while to find a job at another garage. Like, discrimination, you know? After all my training, I don't want to work at a McDonald's instead. When my unemployment ran out, I had to give up my apartment and go back home. But things are kind of crowded in my parents' house. Leon, he offered me his room here while he was away at a wedding, so Clem and I could have a little millennium vacation." She dragged the cap back down over her head, over the skull that suddenly seemed as young and vulnerable as that of the grandson lolling against Bev's breast.

Bev said, "You must stay here, Trulianne. Welcome to Waterlight."

Then she thought: But isn't Leon dating some other girl, that Heather somebody?

Then she thought: What do I tell Roger?

Leon raised his head.

Trulianne looked at Clem, not at Leon, as she said reluctantly, "Clem's all off-schedule now. And it *is* getting late. We'd better spend the night. Thank you."

After Bev gave Leon orders to settle Trulianne and Clem into what was called the suite, a downstairs bedroom with a bathroom and a small sitting room (at the opposite end of the house from Leon's bedroom), she went into the room beside it, which the previous owners had used as a TV room, complete with La-Z-Boy recliner. Most of those owners' Waterlight furniture had been sold to her with the property; she had got rid of the worst, including that recliner. She had had the sofa and chairs in this room reupholstered, and it remained the general TV retreat room although there were other television sets throughout the house.

She was searching for a toy. Finding nothing here, she went on along the hall to the living room.

This room was so big it might intimidate a little boy. Sometimes when she looked up at its three-sided second-floor balcony, she felt the thrill of being onstage. Drawn across the back wall of French windows facing the lake were curtains woven by Mother for the Ninfield house (last Wednesday she'd seen that Roger *had* bothered to replace those, with very ordinary drapes from a home-decorating store). Above the enormous fieldstone fireplace the massive antlered head of a moose stared out across the expanse of sofas, armchairs, her dear old wing chair upholstered in blue toile de Jouy, bookcases, houseplants in the wicker plant stands and wicker tea cart she'd found in antique shops (how funny her acquisition of wicker here, the way she'd collected pine cupboards in Ninfield!), with varied oriental rugs on the wide-board floor. On the white walls were paintings of the lake by local artists. She plugged in the Christmas-tree lights to make the room festive for Clem when he awoke from his late nap. She wanted to heap little-boy presents underneath. Would the moose frighten him, even though she had as usual swathed the huge neck in the lengthy red-and-green scarf Mimi had woven for the first Waterlight Christmas?

Inside the window seats were stored Monopoly and other games and jigsaw puzzles, but these were too old for him. On one window seat sat a plush black-and-white loon, with two fluffy brown babies riding on its back courtesy of Velcro. Aha! This could be a toy, and she placed it under the tree.

Hurrying on toward the kitchen, she glanced into the dining room. The seats of the six dining chairs had been woven by Mother. Clem's great-grandmother. Over the sideboard hung a painting of Waterlight done by Harriet, Snowy's roommate, whose work was internationally known so thank heavens it was a gift from Harriet and she hadn't had to pay a fortune for it. Stored in a compartment of the sideboard were Mimi's and Dick's and Leon's and Etta's silver baby cups, silver porringers, silver spoons, all engraved with their names. She could give Leon's to Clem. No, she warned herself. Not yet; take it easy.

And no, she decided, she wouldn't serve supper in the dining room, which seemed suddenly too formal for this occasion not covered by Emily Post.

But instead of sticking a frozen pizza in the oven, she launched into making a spaghetti dinner, complete with garlic bread. She checked Leon's ice-cream supply in the freezer, for dessert, and hoped Clem had inherited his partiality for chocolate chip. I'm a grandmother, she kept thinking, setting the kitchen table with plastic place mats showing loons afloat on a lake. I really am. She had been surprised at herself when the yearning for grandchildren had grown on her. Snowy apparently didn't understand this desire, but Puddles did, Puddles the grandmother of twelve-year-old Little Guy and seven-year-old Jean. Being a grandmother scared and horrified some women as a sign of old age, so why didn't it bother her? Well, hadn't she accepted her prematurely gray hair, deciding not to color it then or when it became prematurely white? Besides, even though her white hair wasn't so striking as auburn, it *was* flattering. I am a grandmother.

And she threw herself into the new role, unfolding a big linen napkin for Clem in case Trulianne hadn't packed a bib. Could he manage a glass, or had Trulianne brought a sippy cup? Should she get a stack of books from the living room for him to sit on? No, probably Trulianne would hold him on her lap. Would Trulianne permit her to hold him again? What should her grandmother-name be? During these years of hankering for a grandchild, she had tried to decide on a name. Her children had called her mother Nana and Roger's mother Grandma. She had called her mother's mother Nana and her father's mother Grandmother. Her own name, Bev, might be the easiest for a child to say.

The kettle of water for spaghetti having come to a boil, she ran to the suite to announce that supper was imminent—and to make sure she hadn't gone mad and imagined the existence of Clement Hughes, grandson.

Leon had been a sunny-tempered little boy. Clem, awake, demonstrated that he'd inherited the trait, undismayed by Bev cooing at him in besotted grandmotherly fashion. Trulianne permitted her to carry him into the living room, where he was delighted by both the moose and the loon toy. In the kitchen as he sat on Trulianne's lap, smiling a Leon smile, wearing the Winnie-the-Pooh bib Trulianne had brought, he happily ate chopped-up spaghetti and mushed the ungarlicked bread Bev had put aside for him and handled a grown-up glass of milk with nary a spill (well, so far only occasional suspenseful sloshing that Trulianne corrected).

Bev asked, "Just how old is he?"

Trulianne said, "Two years and two months. This is good spaghetti sauce, Mrs. Lambert."

"Thank you. It's Paul Newman's." Adoring Clem's little face smeared with marinara, Bev did math. Shocked, she figured out that he had been conceived and born during the year Leon was living with his girlfriend Elisa, a divorced young woman who worked at a Gunthwaite brokerage firm and had a house and a small son from her marriage. Bev took a gulp of Chianti and slid a glance at Leon, who was concentrating on his plate. She had used her fun pasta dishes, white with hand-painted sprigs of parsley, oregano, and basil around the edges and different hand-painted vegetables in the bottom, and as he coiled spaghetti en route to the hand-painted eggplant below she was reminded of the way he looked as a child when eating his cornflakes to get to the dinosaur at the bottom of his cereal bowl. Why, she chided herself, should I be shocked by Leon's morals? Am I the epitome of virtue?

She said to Trulianne, "Please call me Bev, not Mrs. Lambert. And what will Clem call me? What does he call your mother?"

"Gram," Trulianne said.

Bev was about to suggest he call her Bev, when it dawned on her that suggesting a nontraditional name might make Trulianne think she felt the baby was illegitimate (oh God, he was!) and unworthy of a legitimate grandmotherly name. "Illegitimate" must be a politically incorrect concept. Bev gave up the dilemma, leaned toward Clem, and cooed, "I'm your grandmother, your grandma, your granny."

"Gaga," he said.

Enchanted, Bev cried, "Eureka, that's it, that'll be my name!"

When they reached dessert, she learned that Clem loved chocolate chip.

And when Roger phoned to make sure she'd arrived safely, she didn't say a word about the unexpected guests.

But she did have a private word with Leon, while Trulianne was readying Clem for bed and Leon was supposedly loading the dishwasher but instead was mostly standing with a dish in his hand staring blindly at the old pine jelly cupboard.

"Tomorrow," Bev said, "take them shopping. Some places are bound to be open on Sunday as usual, even if it's the day after New Year's. Make sure Trulianne gets whatever she needs. A booster seat. A crib—or does Clem have a bed now? Buy a toddler bed. I'll cover your credit-card costs."

He protested, "But Mother, they aren't moving in for good, they're just staying overnight!"

Within her surged a Roger-type lecture about responsibility, about the consequence of actions. She began, "Now that I know they exist, I want to become acquainted with them and I want them to feel at home here—" Exhausted, she broke off and asked, "Could you bring up my things from the car to my room? In all the excitement, I forgot."

He grumbled.

"By the way, Leon," she said, "what were you doing down in Eastbourne? A hankering for fresh seafood?"

She knew he wanted to reply: None of your damn business. He said, "Now and then I go see the ocean, here and Maine."

"Oh." Then she took a breath and asked, "Are there any more surprises like Clem?"

38

He gaped at her in stupefaction. "Holy fucking shit, of course not!"

Trulianne permitted Bev to read to Clem from the Dr. Seuss in Trulianne's teddy-bear tote bag until he fell asleep in the suite's king-size bed. As Bev closed the book and got quietly up from beside him, she whispered to Trulianne, "Please, won't you stay here a few days, have a little more of a vacation?"

"You're a really good reader, you know that? He's zonked."

"I've had a lot of practice." Bev plunged ahead. "Er, has Leon told you about our family? There are four children; Leon has a brother and two sisters, and that's where I got my practice."

"Leon's brother's wedding was yesterday?"

"Yes. Er, do you have any brothers or sisters?"

"Three brothers. One older than me, two younger."

"Ah. Is that how you came by your interest in cars?"

"I guess." Trulianne smoothed the duvet over Clem. "I was better at fixing them. My dad would do his own car repairs on weekends, and I was the one who liked to help, not my brothers."

"Um, you mentioned that things are a bit crowded at home?"

Trulianne looked around the suite, and Bev saw the wide open spaces through her eyes, the bedroom with its crewel-covered wing chair drawn up near the fireplace, its blue love seat and window seat, its bureaus and dressing table, steamer trunk and television set, the private bathroom, the sitting room with a daybed and the secretary-type desk at which Snowy used to write when she had lived here before moving in with Tom. Trulianne burst out, "Everybody's back! Travis, the youngest, he never left, he's still living at home. Michael and Justin, they're back after their divorces. There's one bathroom. It was bad enough when we were kids!"

"Oh." Bev tried to think how to proceed from here. "Speaking of bathrooms, you've done a great job with Clem."

Trulianne said proudly, "Had him toilet trained at eighteen months."

And Bev pleaded again, "Please do stay as long as you like."

"Well," Trulianne said, "maybe tomorrow."

Bev didn't push further. "Goodnight to you both," she said, "sweet dreams," and she made her exit out through the sitting room into the hallway, where she tiredly climbed the beautiful staircase to the balcony hall overlooking the living room. In her bedroom, the largest of the four upstairs bedrooms, she found that Leon had deposited there her suitcase, garment bag, and the carton and wedding-dress box. She stood gazing around the room she had decorated as a safe haven, safe harbor—blue rag rugs on the pine floor; white walls; airy organdy curtains for the lake view; photos of the children on the fireplace mantel; the wicker settee upholstered in pale green chenille; the white duvet on the king-size white-painted bed, the blue pillows patterned with black-and-white loons, at the foot a folded green cotton throw with more loons (she had indeed gone loony upon her return to the Lakes Region); the television set; the jewelry box on her bureau in which reposed, half-forgotten, the little gold basketball Roger had given her when they started going steady; one of Mother's bookcases on which stood photos of Mother and Daddy, Mother and Fred, and Roger's high-school and college graduation photographs—and she thought how everything had changed since she left it on Wednesday.

She went into the bedroom next-door. She had turned it into a home office with another bookcase, her antique slant-top desk, her white Pottery Barn modular computer desk and filing cabinets, her computer. It was also her gym, equipped with her detested treadmill, a pair of hand weights, another TV, and a stack of exercise videos. There was a sofa bed too, for guests, just in case Waterlight's other bedrooms couldn't accommodate everyone. On the bookcase were more family photos. Could she snap some pictures of Clem? Could she set a framed photograph of her grandson on her desk in the Plumley office for all to see and carry a smaller one in her wallet?

At the slant-top desk she ignored the property listing she should go over before tomorrow's appointment. She looked at the telephone. She and Snowy and Puddles had begun to communicate via e-mail, but they all still preferred the phone. And the Clem news demanded the telephone. She lifted the receiver, intending to call Snowy. Instead, she tapped in the number of Puddles's Hilton Head split-level house with plenty of curb appeal under Southern pines.

"Hello?" said Puddles.

Bev said, "I know it's late—"

Puddles interrupted with her usual forthrightness. In their youth her face's pale delicacy and her fragility (now an arthritic stiffness she fought with tai chi) had made people think she was a shrinking violet—until she opened her mouth. "So," Puddles said, "you're going to tie the knot again! That takes guts. If Guy and I ever tried to renew our vows, I'd add a zillion stipulations. And Guy would say, 'I don't.'"

Bev tried again, "I hope I didn't wake you—"

"We're just getting ready for bed. Guy's in the bathroom. So you're going to have Roger as a full-time bedmate again!"

In her mind's eye Bev saw Puddles at the telephone in the bedroom decorated New England style in rebellion against the heavy dark furniture inherited from Guy's Southern family that dominated elsewhere. White chenille bedspread, white ruffled curtains, braided rugs, and, heaven help us, on one wall the Gunthwaite High School pennants with which Puddles had decorated her teenage bedroom in the house on Gowen Street. Puddles and Snowy had been cheerleaders, rah rah rah, and nowadays Puddles was the head coach at Broughton High School on the mainland in addition to her work as a nurse practitioner at Palmetto Family Medicine on Hilton Head. Bev said, "I hope you and Guy can come to the ceremony. It won't interfere with the cheerleading championships.

41

It's going to be as close to our anniversary as we can get, June twenty-fourth."

"Then put me down as RSVP'd yes. Forget about Guy. He won't budge. Not from his golf and not from Dixie. Are you going to have orange blossoms and the whole works?"

Bev heard in Puddles's tone the same note of controlled mirth that had been in Snowy's. Bev said frostily, "I didn't have orange blossoms the first time around." She had been on the brink of telling Puddles about Clem, Puddles who would understand. Now she knew that no matter what, she must tell Snowy first. Sometime. "So, anyway, Happy New Year and I'll be in touch."

"Happy New Century!" said Puddles.

The next morning, Bev wanted to cancel the appointment to show the estate to the couple from Massachusetts eager for waterfront on Lake Winnipesaukee. The weather was glum, with rain in the forecast, *rain* again, not snow, although the thermometer said twenty-four degrees. Awful weather for showing a property, though that didn't normally cramp her style. Today, however, she wanted to stay home with Clem. But after her pre-breakfast granola bar and treadmill session in her office-gym, during which she donned her silver-framed glasses and refreshed her memory reading the details of the listing she hadn't read last night, and after her shower, she went into her walk-in closet and chose working clothes, a white shirt, black wool slacks, black leather boots, and salt-and-pepper tweed blazer. Dressed, she surveyed the effect in the closet door's full-length mirror. Okay. She carried the boxes from the Ninfield attic into the closet and set them on the floor, thinking: What and when do I tell Roger?

Down in the kitchen, Leon hadn't yet put in an appearance, but Trulianne and Clem were there and, to Bev's relief, were making themselves at home. Trulianne let Bev hold Clem on her lap and help him with his Cheerios while in the laundry room off the kitchen Trulianne started a wash-load of their clothes. So they would indeed at least stay today? Bev didn't inquire aloud. When Leon came wandering in from his bedroom, he was showered and presentable in jeans and a sweater, though he'd begun another growth of designer stubble after the ordeal of remaining clean-shaven throughout the Ninfield visit.

Bev mouthed at him, "Booster seat!" and when Trulianne emerged from the laundry room she said, "Leon will take you and Clem to lunch."

"What?" Trulianne had apparently just noticed the magnet that held Bev's grocery list on the refrigerator. A present from Snowy during the time Snowy lived here, it showed a woman in a pageboy, wearing a decorous shirtdress, proper hat and gloves, pushing a shopping cart, and it said Fuck This Fifties Housewife Bullshit. Looking from the magnet to Bev in some surprise, Trulianne actually giggled.

Bev repeated, "Leon will take you and Clem to lunch," and added casually, "I'll concoct my famous meat loaf for supper."

"Oh," Trulianne said. "Oh, okay."

Hooray! Bev made her Shirley Temple face at Clem and tore herself away from him, ran upstairs and rebrushed her teeth and reapplied Chanel lipstick, then hurried downstairs to the hall closet and slipped into her new white wool coat, which she belted dashingly around her waist as she ran outdoors, across the porch, whose narrow-board ceiling was painted a traditional blue, and down the front stairs. She stopped, then walked slowly around and around Trulianne's old Volkswagen, in daylight a faded yellow with a child's car seat in back.

She was always charmed by the sight of new Volkswagen beetles; they were so shiny cute and brought back memories of a few college dates in the old version (not with Roger; was it the boy from MIT?). VWs hadn't exactly suited her style, but their lack of a gas gauge had been exciting. However, the sight of this old VW and the thought of Trulianne's unemployed state nearly broke her heart. The car looked particularly small and basic in front of the subdued elegance of Waterlight's mass of dark brown shingles with dark green shutters and trim, and the car seat looked too tiny and brave.

Above the porch door hung a sign that had come with the place: Welcome to the Lake.

Finally Bev walked on to the brown-shingled two-car garage for her Outback. She drove downtown trying to wrench her mind from grandson to real estate.

The Plumley Real Estate office was at the end of the Miracle Mile, past the malls and McDonald's and Burger King and Kentucky Fried Chicken, where there were spared trees and nicer places, a wine-and-cheese shop, a florist's greenhouse, an oriental rugs showroom. She parked in front of the sand-colored art-nouveau building, curvy, wavy. When Geoffrey Plumley, a Massachusetts real-estate agent, had come to New Hampshire after his divorce, he had chosen to have this architectural whimsy built because it amused him and was distinctive. It certainly did stand out from Gunthwaite's other real-estate offices, which were either in rehabbed older homes or prefab buildings indistinguishable from a million others.

If she opened her own office, where would it be? In Waterlight?

The broker's exam. Another god-awful exam. She made the retching noise she'd perfected in high school and then she said, "Feh!", the satisfying exclamation that Harriet had taught her.

As she slid out of her car, she noticed that the BMW parked beside Geoff's Range Rover had Massachusetts license plates. Her customers? Were they so eager they were early? Hell and damn!

She stepped into the big room with its blond desks set on

44

gray wall-to-wall carpeting and saw that Geoff had seated them at her desk, had supplied coffee in Plumley Real Estate mugs, and was sitting in her chair making small talk about the joys of living on the lake (which he himself did in a tidy bachelor condo), looking as usual lovably rumpled, like an absentminded professor, and exceedingly trustworthy with that widow's peak in his tousled gray hair. None of the other salespeople had come in yet, not even Lorraine Fitch, Bev's competition in the top-producer contest over the years, old-pro Lorraine, Bev's bête noir, her archrival for the crown.

Geoff rose and said, "Here Bev is now."

"Hello," Bev said to Mr. and Mrs. Starling. "I'm Bev Lambert, and I'm sorry I'm late."

"No, no," they said, "we're early," and Sumner Starling got to his feet. He was the one she'd spoken to on the phone, when he had called last week from Weston, Massachusetts, to say they had seen her ad for the property in the *Boston Globe* and on the Plumley Web site and were interested. He said, "This is my wife, Lynne."

They must be in their early sixties. Both very fit, in sweaters and slacks and boots, parkas hung over the backs of their chairs. Sumner was bald, while Lynne's coiffure was the color of Clem's Cheerios.

"How do you do," Bev said, shaking hands with both Starlings. To Sumner, she added, "Please, sit down." She took off her coat, hung it on the coatrack, and sat in the chair warmed by Geoff, cozier than the Outback's heated seats, a brief distracting reminder of their intimacy, such a well-kept secret—or so she'd thought. She and Geoff had never gone out in Gunthwaite as a couple, to protect their business relationship and to maintain a semblance of propriety; she was, after all, still married, and she knew that Geoff had been glad about the wedding ring on her finger, at that stage. They used to meet elsewhere, usually at a motel in Manchester, a very nice motel so she felt more discreet than tawdry. How clandestine! How silly. Probably everyone in the Plumley office guessed. Their affair started out simple; dinner and bed, with initially the bed part strange—he was the first man she'd ever slept with besides Roger—and later fun, she a wife and mother playing at being a hoyden, a courtesan. Then she realized he was getting serious and thinking of proposing marriage. But then young Caitlin had joined Plumley Real Estate.

Sumner was explaining what he'd already told her over the phone, that they owned a seacoast cottage in Maine but now that their family was growing with grandchildren, they had begun thinking about the benefits of lakes over the Atlantic Ocean, which was freezing cold even in August. They were realizing that the grandchildren—he called them grandkids, a word Bev hated—would have so much more fun at Lake Winnipesaukee. And in winter there was skiing nearby. He sounded as if he had made up his mind. Laughing a staccato laugh, he said, "Now that I'm retired, I'm ready for a new adventure!"

Some adventure; the asking price for the place that had caught their eye was $4,500,000. But Bev understood such adventures, though she had bought Waterlight at a bargain price, $750,000, because of her inside knowledge about the owners' need to unload fast in the midst of a divorce battle.

Putting on her glasses, she went over her listing with them. An Adirondack-style house with eight bedrooms, a fully applianced kitchen with granite countertops, a whirlpool room. A guest cottage, three-car garage, clay tennis court. On four acres with six hundred feet of water frontage, a sandy beach, two docks. Western exposure—sunsets! She hesitated about mentioning that it was located on a no-Jet-Ski cove. She certainly wished Jet Skis were outlawed on East Bay. But maybe the Starlings were itching to zoom around making a horrible racket. She pried, "At the ocean, do you sail?"

"Oh yes," Sumner said. "We'd be bringing our sailboat to the lake."

In her experience, people with sailboats detested Jet Skis. So she mentioned the restriction, which they applauded.

"Well, then," she said, "let's go see the place in person. Would you like to ride with me or follow in your car?"

Sumner said, "We'll follow."

"Sweetheart," said Lynne, "why don't I ride with Bev so we can do some girl talk about furnishings and decorating?"

He looked taken aback. He protested, "I'm interested in furnishing and decorating too." Standing up, he held Lynne's parka open for her to put on. "We can talk about it there."

Bev saw a desperate expression dart across Lynne's face and improvised, "Lynne could give me the general idea of your tastes on the drive over, and then we could discuss things further when you've seen the place."

He said plaintively, "Oh, all right."

In the Outback, as Bev drove off Lynne sagged into the passenger seat and said, "He's retired."

Bev said, "Mmm?"

Lynne asked, "Are you married?"

"Yes," said Bev, keeping it simple.

"Has your husband retired yet?"

"He's planning to this spring."

"I can't get away from Sumner," Lynne said. "He is home all day. I like to cook, but I like to do it on my own. Nowadays Sumner joins me in the kitchen and asks why don't I do this or that a more efficient way. After dinner he corrects me about which containers I should put the leftovers in. He wants to go everywhere with me. I can't even go to the Estée Lauder counter to buy a damn lipstick without Sumner tagging along. He won't even sit and wait on a husband bench."

"A husband bench?"

"You know, those benches where men wait while their wives shop." Lynne closed her eyes. "If you don't mind, I'll pretend I'm alone now."

Oh my God, Bev thought.

And the freezing rain began.

But the Starlings loved the place so much, even in this

weather, that they made an offer on the spot. It was one that Bev knew the owner would grab at.

On the trip back to the Plumley office, Lynne rode with Sumner.

In the office, after Bev phoned the owner who did accept the offer with alacrity, after all the paperwork was done and the colossal deal made, Geoff congratulated Sumner and Lynne, while the other salespeople (including munchkin Caitlin) who by now were in the office watched enviously, except Lorraine Fitch, busy with her own paperwork, biding her time. Over the years Lorraine, who must have reached her midsixties, had changed from Cassius's lean and hungry look (when she'd been Bev's predecessor in Geoff's love life, Bev had belatedly realized) to a well-upholstered look. In either form, Lorraine could certainly sell. But Bev had triumphed today.

Lynne whispered to Bev, "I was so glad to see the lock on the whirlpool-room door!"

When the Starlings left, it was Bev's turn for congratulations from Geoff. He went on at some length.

"Thank you," she said modestly, "but the place sold itself."

"No, it didn't. You got the listing and you made the sale. Would you like to go out for a drink to celebrate? How about the Gunthwaite Inn?"

He was suggesting their first drink together in public in Gunthwaite. Bev sensed Caitlin's eyes on her. Caitlin was younger than Trulianne but she'd been carrying on with a man old enough to be her grandfather! If Bev stole Geoff back, she would be doing Caitlin a favor. She said to Geoff, "Thank you, but no." Putting her coat on, she heard herself continue, "Oh, I'm sorry, I'm not going to be able to attend the awards conference this weekend."

"You're not *what?*"

She didn't have to give him a reason. "I'm sorry."

He lowered his voice. "You've got to be there. You're the top producer. You've won again this year."

Never before in all these years, not even when their affair was at its most intense, had he ever told her ahead of time who had won.

"That's wonderful," she said and twinkled at him. "I'm delighted. But alas, I still can't be there. It's a family emergency."

The thought of her family, particularly Leon, had always put him off. "Well," he said. "That's too bad."

She hurried out to her car.

Stopping at the Dilly-Dilly Deli to buy a take-out turkey wrap and coffee, she drove to the Gunthwaite Mall, parked, washed her hands with the bottle of Purell she kept in the car, and then ate the wrap ravenously as she made a shopping list. Then on her cell phone she tapped Snowy's phone number. Snowy's store was only open until noon on Sundays, so she would be back in the barn apartment.

Tom answered the phone. "Hello?"

"Hi. Is Snowy writing?"

"I just heard a big guffaw in her office, but that's apt to happen when she's writing as well as when she isn't."

Although some of Snowy's poems were funny, Bev had a feeling Snowy might even laugh over those that weren't. "I was wondering if you two could come to supper tonight."

"I'll get her. It's Bev, Snowy."

Snowy asked, "More news about the renewal of vows?"

"Even bigger news," Bev said. "Can you and Tom come to supper tonight? I know it's short notice, but there's a to-die-for little boy I want you to meet."

"A little boy?"

"Oh Snowy, Snowy, my grandson! I've been a grandmother for two years and two months and I didn't know it!"

An A student like Roger, in a flash Snowy cried, "Leon?"

"Yes! And Clem is the image of him, that's his name, Clement, and the mother is from Eastbourne, she's an auto mechanic who has been laid off. Snowy, he doesn't call me Grandma, he calls me Gaga, isn't it perfect?"

49

Snowy shrieked, "How did this happen? Tell all!"

Bev loved telling stories. She told all, with Snowy silent, absorbing it.

When Bev finished, Snowy asked, "What about Roger?"

"I've got two weeks to figure that out. He's coming up on the fifteenth for the long weekend, Martin Luther King Day. We're going skiing, if there's any snow. Roger hates skiing on man-made snow."

An unfortunate comment, because it set off Snowy's "This global warming—"

Bev cut in, "Can you come for supper?"

Snowy started laughing. "We'll be there with bells on."

"It's just going to be meat loaf. Comfort food for a little boy in strange surroundings."

Snowy said, "You make a great meat loaf, Bev."

Which was true, Bev knew.

Snowy asked, "What time do you want us?"

"Early, little-boy time. Five o'clock."

"See you then."

Usually after a big sale, Bev rewarded herself with a new item of clothing. (Well, sometimes more than a measly single item.) This afternoon in the mall, she spent a delirious time in the children's store buying little boys' clothes and then reveled in a spree in the toy store. Then she went into Shaw's Supermarket. She ignored the husband benches everywhere.

Not until she was driving back to Waterlight did she permit herself to think of Lynne Starling seeking solitude.

During the old-fashioned meat-loaf dinner with peas and mashed potatoes, Bev admired and appreciated Tom's ease with

Clem, who had the place of honor at the kitchen table in his new booster seat, the one item Trulianne had let Leon buy. Tom, grandfather of three, was used to grandchildren. Leon's behavior improved, probably thanks to Tom's behavior—and to the day spent with Trulianne and Clem? Leon was actually talking to his son, carrying on what could pass as a conversation about riding in Leon's pickup today when Leon and Trulianne and Clem went shopping. Boys and trucks. Snowy seemed to be enjoying Clem in a fascinated but detached fashion. And typically, Snowy was the soul of tact, chatting with Trulianne about how years ago she'd lived in Eastbourne, telling an anecdote about working as a tour guide at the Ruhamah Reed House in the restored section called Old Eastbourne and almost being fired for eating an unhistoric slice of pizza in public. (Bev had heard it before and knew that she herself could have told the story more entertainingly, but she laughed merrily.)

Then Tom mentioned that he and Snowy had made a New Year's resolution yesterday to go to Scotland in April, before the general store's busy season began. David, Tom's son who worked at his coffin factory, would handle North Country Coffins.

Snowy asked Bev, "Will you and Roger go on a second honeymoon?" Then she flushed, obviously remembering that Leon and Trulianne hadn't gone on a first. So much for tact!

"Yes," Bev said. "We haven't discussed where yet, but just now I made *my* resolution. I want to see Stratford and swans and Anne Hathaway's Cottage. Speaking of seconds, how about some more meat loaf, everybody?"

Clem nodded eagerly, and Trulianne said, "Yes, please. It's terrific."

Carving more slices, Bev explained, "My secret is pork sausage, half a pound of pork sausage to a pound of ground beef. The rest is some chopped onion, a can of tomato soup, a cup or so of bread crumbs, an egg, and some milk if you like it really moist—"

Trulianne jumped up and grabbed the memo pad and pencil

off the counter under the wall phone. She sat back down and scribbled.

Tickled, Bev served Clem a slice, then Trulianne. "Cook it at three hundred and fifty degrees for an hour and a half. If necessary, pour off the fat after an hour, but if the sausage is lean you don't have to."

Snowy added, "The cold leftovers taste like pâté. Delicious."

Bev knew that nowadays Snowy made meat loaf with ground turkey and wheat germ, disgusting, so she put a big slice on the plate of poor long-suffering Tom without his having to ask.

After the chocolate pudding, Leon went off with Trulianne to help give Clem his bath. Wonder of wonders! Bev shooed Tom out of the kitchen, telling him to take a second cup of coffee into the living room and see the toys Clem had opened under the Christmas tree this afternoon. In the kitchen, as Bev and Snowy did the clearing up, Snowy oohed and aahed properly over Clem's attributes and then said, "Imagine deliberately choosing to raise a child on your own. Why did Trulianne come to that decision?"

Snowy's daughter had been sixteen when Alan died. There had remained, Bev knew, a lot of raising for Snowy to do by herself. Bev said, "She was working in a man's world. Maybe that convinced her to go it alone."

"Maybe she's a lesbian who didn't want to make a withdrawal at a sperm bank."

Strangling the sink sponge in horror, Bev stared at Snowy, with whom she didn't have to bother about political correctness. "A lesbian? Oh my God!"

Snowy looked contrite. "Just speculating. But it feels hetero, doesn't it, Trulianne and Leon."

"Yes!" said Bev.

Snowy held up Clem's Pooh bib. Was her expression now wistful? "After you phoned, it occurred to me that if she would consider an auto-mechanic job around here, not down in the Eastbourne area, Dudley and Charl's daughter Denise married

52

the Huntington Garage, so to speak. Remember? Denise married Kevin Huntington. If he doesn't have an opening there, he might know of a lead."

"Snowy, you're a genius! But eek, how do I explain Trulianne's relationship to me?"

Snowy pondered. "Just say she's a friend of the family."

"The family. Roger. Mimi, Etta. Dick. How do I tell them there's a new family member?"

But Snowy had no suggestions about this.

That night, Bev was tormented by one of those nightmares about forgetting to take an exam, and she awoke sweating. She could not face another exam, the broker's exam.

Then during her treadmill session and during her shower, she thought of being her own boss.

If she didn't try, she wouldn't fail. That had been the reasoning behind her decision not to try out for cheerleading. With the Dramatics Club plays, there was always another play, another role, another chance to star. Cheerleading was too life-or-death. It meant too much; she had pretended to be above such nonsense, but she wasn't. Had any girl been, back in the Fabulous Fifties?

In later years, it had dawned on her that not trying could be failure. So she had tried. Because she had lived in and coped with four houses in Connecticut, she had thought she knew real estate. She hadn't realized until she took her first course that she would have to know about fiduciaries, amongst other bewildering things. But real estate was a business a woman could make money in, and the schedule could be flexible enough to accommodate Etta, still living at home then, so she had persevered. She had found that selling real estate was like acting, the career she hadn't dared try, and just as tough. But she had succeeded!

Going into her closet, she pictured herself her own boss with her own office. In Waterlight's suite?

No! Suddenly she comprehended that Roger would be here,

would really be here in this house, day in, day out. To keep her independence and her sanity, hadn't she better rent an office elsewhere? *If* she took the exam and *if* she passed it?

She deliberately switched her thoughts to clothes. What to wear today? She didn't have any appointments to show a place or get a listing or go to a closing, but usually she went to her desk at Plumley's no matter what, to drum up business one way or another. This day she would stay home. So she put on jeans and a loon sweatshirt. Should she order one of those wonderfully schmaltzy grandmother sweatshirts with Clem's name on it? But could she officially acknowledge him?

As she sat down to breakfast with him and his Cheerios, with Trulianne and Leon, she thought: How can I not acknowledge this little boy, this flesh and blood?

But what about Roger? He had hidden her real-estate certificate from her. Could she hide a grandson from him?

The day was sunny, and according to the weather report the temperature might break records. If it did, she'd never hear the end of it from Snowy. She asked Trulianne, "Has Clem ever been to Disney World?"

"No," Trulianne said cautiously.

Bev said, "I've won a trip for two there. I'm too old for Disney World, no matter what they say. Why don't you and Leon use this prize and I'll pay Clem's expenses. Don't answer now. Just think about it."

Trulianne said, "Mrs. Lambert—"

"Bev," said Bev.

"Bev, Clem and I should be going home. We can't be going to Disney World."

Leon said, "Mother, I've got that job at the Eatons' place."

"I know, Leon," Bev said. He was remodeling the Eatons' garage into a guest cottage. "But please, both of you think it over—" She cut short her entreaty, hearing the clatter in the hallway that signaled the arrival of Miranda Flack, the young woman (well, age forty-five, long divorced, mother of two) who

54

tackled the cleaning of Waterlight once a week. Bev stood up from the table, caressed Clem's cheek, and said, "I have to make a phone call. I'll be back in a few minutes."

Trulianne asked, "Do you like selling real estate?"

Disconcerted by her interest, Bev said, "Yes, I do. The main trait you need is patience, which I didn't think I had but I developed it. And it's fun to put people and places together."

Trulianne volunteered, "My mom is a desk clerk at a hotel. My dad, he works for a roofing company."

Bev said, "He must have a good head for heights."

"Oh, he does."

"I envy that. I have a fairly good head, but not for roofs. I can paint ceilings. I can even paint houses; I've got a picture that my husband took of me up on a twenty-four-foot extension ladder painting our first house."

Trulianne asked, "Why wasn't *he* painting it?"

Leon gave a shout of laughter.

And the question surprised Bev, coming from a woman of Trulianne's generation. "Painting was my thing," she said. "He was busy with other things." She added, "Please, think about taking Clem to Disney World," and left the kitchen.

Miranda, scorning Bev's equipment, always brought her own vacuum cleaner and a plastic tote crammed with cleaning supplies. She had deposited them in the hall and was hanging up her parka in the closet, her wire-rimmed glasses halfway down her nose as usual. She was wearing a new chambray shirt and fashionably holey jeans. Her brown hair had grown out enough to be pulled into a jaunty ponytail. "Hi, Bev, how did the wedding go?"

When Miranda had asked what Bev would be doing on the millennium New Year's Eve, Bev had worried over telling her about Dick's wedding because Miranda's June wedding last year had been canceled when the new Mr. Right had backed out, unable to cope with her breast cancer. "It went perfectly," Bev said, hoping she didn't sound abrupt. The problem to worry

55

about now was an explanation for the presence of Trulianne and Clem.

Miranda said, "Any priorities today?"

"Nothing particular. Don't bother with this hall and only do the minimum in the living room, if you would. I'll be taking down the decorations this week and Leon will be lugging out the tree, so things will just get messy."

"Then I'll make the hall and living room my priority next week."

"Great. And, ah, no need to bother with the suite, either. Unexpected guests, a friend of the family, I'm not sure how long they'll be staying."

"Okay," Miranda said, picked up her equipment, and headed for the dining room.

At her slant-top desk upstairs, Bev phoned the big Victorian painted-lady house on Water Street where Charl and Dudley lived. Charl answered, listened, and said, "I'll give Kevin a call and inquire. An auto mechanic! Your friend must be so smart! I wish I knew more than just how to turn the key in the ignition. I'll call you right back."

Bev put on her glasses, swiveled to her computer desk, and looked up details about broker's exams. She would sign up for the one held in May.

The phone rang. Charl reported, "I'm sorry, but Kevin doesn't have an opening and he hasn't heard that anybody else is hiring. I'm afraid he didn't think much of women mechanics."

Damn damn damn. "Well," Bev said, "this was just a starting point. Thanks for your help, Charl."

"I wasn't any help. But listen, at least I've got a tip for you."

Over the years, Bev had received occasional real-estate tips from Charl and her twin sister, Darl, both of whom had many connections in Gunthwaite. Although there was never anything political involved, Bev suspected that Dudley disapproved; he strove to be squeaky-clean and above the fray.

Charl said, "I was talking with Arlene last night."

56

Arlene was another of Charl and Dudley's twelve children. Although Charlene and Darlene had had shortened nicknames since childhood, and Darl's daughter Marlene was called Marl, Arlene had remained Arlene. Was a consonant necessary?

Charl continued, "Her in-laws have decided it's time for Ivythorpe."

"That's a hard decision." Bev recalled the big brick house out on Elm Avenue whose official name had been the Harris Home for the Aged but which was known to everybody as "the old folks' home." In the 1960s it had begun expanding, and gradually an entire neighborhood had been bought up and razed for the creation of Ivythorpe Health Care Center, a complex of nursing home, apartments, condos, and townhouses for the varying needs of one's golden years.

"It's an *awful* decision!" Charl exclaimed. "I hope and pray Dudley and I never have to make it. I want to live out my life right in this house and leave it feet first."

Bev shuddered at the thought of retirement homes, nursing homes. Shrink-wrapped old people. "Are they going into an assisted-living condo?"

"Doesn't 'assisted living' sound horrible? Yes, they are. And of course they'll be putting their house on the market."

The tip. "Thank you, Charl."

"Well, I hope your auto-mechanic friend finds something. Bye."

Suddenly atingle with lust, Bev sat picturing Arlene's in-laws' white house on Pleasant Street. The Morgans' home was handsome, dignified. She could imagine an elegant sign out front: Beverly Lambert, Realtor. How completely satisfying! Could she afford to buy the house and turn it into offices, keeping the best for herself and renting the others? Would her accountant throw a fit? And Roger—would he weigh in with an opinion, now that he was going to be a real husband again?

She took off her glasses, stood up, and walked to the windows. Down on the brown lawn Leon was giving Trulianne and Clem

57

a tour of the back gardens, which weren't much to look at right now, only humps of salt-hay mulch and bare shrubs. In his blue snowsuit, Clem was lurching from an azalea to a lilac. Oh God, that open water around the dock, where he might have perished Saturday! Could Leon fence it off somehow? In the summers, Tom's son David occasionally came here with his wife and two daughters, for a change from swimming in Woodcombe Lake at the town beach, and Bev kept a lifeguard's eagle eye on the two girls, but that caution was nothing like the pure fear that gripped her heart now. Come summer, how could she fence off her entire lakefront?

Assuming Clem and Trulianne would ever return to Waterlight.

But Trulianne had written down her meat-loaf recipe. Didn't that establish a relationship?

Clem. Adorable Clem. The need to hug him, hold him, treasure him. She grabbed her real-estate Polaroid out of the desk and flew downstairs. At the hall closet she pulled on her parka, slung the camera strap over her shoulder, and then rushed out the kitchen's back door, slowing on the porch to regain an appearance of composure. She went down the steps to the soggy dead grass of the lawn. The breeze off the lake was almost balmy.

Clem caught sight of her and shouted, "Gaga!"

I'm in love, Bev thought, swinging him up in her arms. I'm gaga and in love.

Leon was saying to Trulianne, "The rhododendrons always look like hell in the winter and Mother always thinks they won't recover, but they do. I spray them with an antidesiccant every fall."

He was showing off!

Trulianne said to Bev, "I've been doing what you asked. Thinking about it. But I've got to get home today, back to job hunting. I can't fool around at Disney World, not even for Clem. But thank you anyway, Mrs. Lambert."

THE WEATHER CONTINUED IFFY during the next two weeks, and Bev found herself hoping that the lack of snow would keep Roger in Connecticut for the long weekend of Martin Luther King Day. She was too busy! But was she too busy with the wrong things?

Roger e-mailed her often. He reported on Dick and Jessica's doings after their return from their honeymoon; Jessica worked for a public relations firm in New York, and from her Manhattan apartment Dick was commuting back to work in Ninfield at Lambert and Lambert. Roger went into high gear about the trip to England she had told him she wanted for their second honeymoon, sending her URLs for Web sites to look at, "The Beauty of Shakespeare Country" and that sort of thing, but she couldn't think about Stratford anymore. He wrote, "We should get to work on the guest list for the ceremony." She e-mailed back, "I'm too busy now, but when you're here we could make a start." She tried to put the whole subject out of her mind to concentrate on real estate. And on Clem.

But Etta e-mailed her, "May I help with the renewal-of-vows plans, even from afar? I know you believe it's never too early to start planning events. :)"

And Mimi sent an e-mail that got more specific: "How can Lloyd and I help? Would you like him to design the invitations? Would you want them decorated with a little swatch of weaving, the way we do with our line of greeting cards? If so, what colors? Will you have a color theme for your dress and the flowers and the decorations (if any) and the cake, etc.? Will you have a general theme à la 'theme weddings'? I'm assuming it will be held at Waterlight. Outdoors, or don't you want to risk rain? What time of day are you thinking of? What about a caterer? I recommend Indulgences. As you may recall, they made my wedding cake and the hors d'oeuvres. Tourtière, too, though of course it wasn't so good as yours. What about music? If you want live music, we have friends who play flute and guitar professionally and do so at weddings and other events. Better book now!"

Staring at Mimi's letter on her computer screen, Bev felt hectored, harassed. She hadn't even *begun* to plan!

Bev e-mailed back to Etta, "Thanks so much for your offer, darling, but I'm still fiddling around with ideas." To Mimi she e-mailed, "Yes, the ceremony will be at Waterlight, but I haven't yet decided if it'll be outdoors or in. I'd love to have Lloyd design invitations with your weaving. I'll let you know when I decide colors, etc. Too busy right at the moment."

Too busy. She had listed Arlene's in-laws' house. The price, $350,000, a price the Morgans wanted (and would probably get), brought her back to her senses and her business sense, so she didn't even broach the subject of buying it to Christine, her accountant.

First things first, she told herself, and signed up for the broker's exam in May, learning to her horror that she would have to take it not on good old-fashioned paper as she had the other exams back in the 1980s but on a computer. Gritting her teeth, she also signed up for a cram course held just before the exam. This on top of the courses you had to take anyway, to keep your real-estate license! Then there were the closing details for the Starlings' purchase, all the paperwork, other places to show other customers, and the weekly sales meetings—

And always there was the image of Clem in the crowded house in Eastbourne. As the days passed, her concern increased and her fevered imagination pictured him in some hovel on a savage seacoast raked by howling gales. The images she had photographed, of him in his blue snowsuit, she hid in her slant-top desk inside an old real-estate folder of notes she'd scribbled at some of those tedious licensing courses, "Real Estate Ethics" (lots of jokes about oxymorons), "Risk Management," "Real Estate Finance." Roger would never be curious enough to open that folder.

After looking at the photos of Clem, she often wandered back into her bedroom and looked at the photographs of her father on the bookcase. Snapshots of him and Mother, of him and Mother and little Bev; a formal photograph of him in his Marine uniform. In 1955 when her Girl Scout troop had made a trip to Washington, D.C., the Iwo Jima Memorial had just been put up the previous year. But at planning meetings for the trip she hadn't asked that it be inserted into the sightseeing schedule, and when they were there she didn't ask one of the troop leaders to escort her on a private side trip to it. Had she even known of it? Had Mother spoken of it and she hadn't wanted to hear? Not until their children were old enough to understand did she and Roger take them on an educational trip to the nation's capital to see the memorial amongst the other sights. As when she and Roger took the children to the Gunthwaite cemetery where Daddy was buried, Roger was the one who had explained to them that their grandfather had died so that the American flag could fly over a little Pacific island, the point of the sacrifice being to acquire a place where American bombers could land, this stop-over site eventually enabling bombers to reach Hiroshima and Nagasaki with their atomic-bomb cargo.

Because she hadn't had her own father in her life since the War, was she excessively upset by Leon's behavior toward Clem?

She remembered how she used to worry that Roger would die when the children were young, especially when they reached age five, her age when Daddy died. Fathers die. Husbands die. Mother had told her, "Daddy is dead," and had held her tight.

But goddamnit, Leon was alive and should be part of Clem's life!

In the attic she hid the booster seat.

Over the phone Snowy inquired sympathetically, "There's nothing you can do but wait and hope?"

Bev thought: I'm pinning my hopes on a meat-loaf recipe. She said, "I've phoned Charl again and asked her to ask Denise's husband to keep an ear open for any mechanic's job. I don't know what else to do. If I push Trulianne, ask her to come here to visit or, if she won't, ask if I can visit her and Clem in Eastbourne, I might ruin everything and never see Clem again—" Bev heard her voice tremble. "Snowy, I *crave* him."

"Oh Bev," Snowy said, full of sympathy, yes, but no help whatsoever. Bev paid scarce attention as Snowy changed the subject to politics, the upcoming New Hampshire presidential primary and her son-in-law's plans to run for the U.S. Congress, and then to the plans for her trip to Scotland with Tom in April. Snowy was very excited about this trip, even though she'd been to Scotland once before. That had been with Ruhamah, her daughter; this was with Tom. Bev envied such excitement as Snowy babbled on about the Macleods that her genealogical research had unearthed on her father's side of the family, which gave her the excuse to include Macleod territory in the itinerary. Snowy said, "I'm reading *Scotland's Highlands and Islands* and in it there's the story of how in the sixteenth century the Macleods were at a church on Skye when the Macdonalds set fire to the place, but one woman got out a window—Bev, she had to cut off a breast to be able to squeeze through! She alerted the rest of the Macleods, who waylaid the Macdonalds and killed them."

Bev started to say that she and Snowy wouldn't have had to take such drastic measures, but then she sensed Snowy was too impressed by her ancestor's action to be in the mood for flat-chested jokes. Instead, she said, "I should be reading up on Shakespeare country. I will. I'm just awfully busy right now."

During dinner one evening when Leon was home instead of

at Heather's, she tried to talk to him about Clem. "Your son will be changing by the moment, growing and changing. Aren't you the least bit interested in seeing this?"

He finished his Chicken Dijon before replying, "That was the deal. No strings."

She wanted to scream at him that he wasn't a stallion, standing to stud. That *couldn't* be all Trulianne really wanted of him. She asked, "Has Trulianne found a job yet?"

He shrugged.

"Her training," she said. "I assume she went to one of the New Hampshire technical colleges. Probably the one in Eastbourne?"

He grudgingly nodded.

Briefly she let herself hope that if she told Roger, he could convince Leon to insist on assuming some responsibility for Clem. What were the legalities? But Roger persuading Leon to do anything? How absurd!

At Plumley Real Estate there were stacks of out-of-town telephone books. Bev carried the Eastbourne area phone book to her desk and looked up Hughes. As she expected, she found over a column of them. But one was Hughes, T. That must be Trulianne, and the address was the apartment she'd had to give up. At her parents' house, Trulianne would probably just be using her cell phone, if she had one and if she could still afford the monthly charges. How to find out her parents' first names and thus their phone number and address? Bev turned her gaze to her computer and wished she were a geek.

Then she flipped to the yellow pages. Day Care: See Child Care. Child Care—there were twenty-nine places listed. Twenty-nine. If Trulianne had been taking Clem to a day-care center while she had a job and still dropped him off while she job hunted, he was a needle in a haystack. No. It *wasn't* impossible. Bev could phone every one of those day-care centers. Probably, though, they weren't allowed to give out names. She jumped up, took the phone book over to the photocopier, copied the Child Care page, and put the photocopy into her shoulder bag, just in case.

Was she going crazy?

That evening, Frankie phoned from Santa Fe. "Has life settled down since the holidays? Aren't you ready for a change of scenery? Sedona?"

Oh, she was tempted. But she said, "It's just too hectic here right now," and distracted him with the story of the big sale to the Starlings.

The Thursday evening before the long weekend, as Bev was making dinner for herself and Leon, Roger phoned. He said, "They're predicting snow on Sunday, so we can get some skiing in on Monday. I'll be up Saturday afternoon." Then he asked, "Okay? You don't have an appointment?"

"No. That's great."

His voice was suddenly sounding uncertain. "I thought that maybe Saturday we could do a nostalgia tour of Gunthwaite. The old haunts. I haven't done that for years. Just taken the bypass to see you. We could drive around, then get some supper."

She wished she'd lied and told him she had an appointment with customers. She had been living here since 1987; she did not need a trip down memory lane. Was he having misgivings about returning to his hometown for good? In high school, Roger had been as eager as she to leave Gunthwaite behind, maybe even more so because he wasn't attached to his parents the way she was to Mother and, yes, to Fred. She tried to change his mind about the tour by asking, "Will you want to do more driving, after that long drive up?"

"It's a different kind of driving. For that matter, you could drive."

In all the years of their marriage, whenever they were in a car together he drove. Taken aback, she said, "Well. Fine, I will."

"We could have supper at Hooper's."

She wanted to suggest someplace newer, such as the Riverside Pub, which had only been around for maybe fifteen years instead of forever—

He asked anxiously, "Hooper's *is* still there?"

"Like the Rock of Gibraltar. Okay, Hooper's."

"Then that's settled." Sounding his usual confident self again, he added, "I've got some news you'll be very interested in. I'll tell you this weekend."

Was Jessica pregnant already? But wouldn't Jessica and Dick not just tell Roger; wouldn't they also tell the grandmother-to-be? She said, "Give me a hint."

"Nope. I want you on pins and needles."

Roger, playing games, unaware of the news she could spring on him. Feeling oddly pitying but benevolent, she said, "I'm all agog."

During dinner with Leon, Bev managed not to mention Clem, but while they were doing the dishes afterward she said, "I wonder if Trulianne is still job hunting. I hope she's found a job by now."

Putting a plate in the dishwasher, Leon surprised her by supplying information. "She's kind of waitressing."

You could always get a job waitressing. Bev wanted to ask where, what restaurant, and how had Leon found out, were they in touch by phone or e-mail, but she decided that as usual it would be wisest to go at things somewhat obliquely. "I hope she can choose her hours. Such as if Clem is in day care, she could work a shift that would match. Her mother can't be babysitting while working full time at the hotel job. Or maybe her mother works nights there?"

Leon shrugged.

Bev pressed on, "I doubt if Trulianne would rely on her brothers as babysitters."

"Yeah," said Leon vaguely.

"I suppose this is just a stopgap until she can find an auto-mechanic job."

"I suppose."

Bev wanted to strangle him.

Saturday was sunny and zero-cold. When Roger arrived that afternoon, Bev still hadn't decided whether or not to tell him he was already a grandfather. For heaven's sake, she couldn't even decide if she should tell him she was going to try for a broker's license! She'd concentrated on choosing clothes, the ski togs for Monday, and today the Berber fleece vest she was wearing over her teal turtleneck sweater and jeans. He kissed her, carried his duffel up to her—their—bedroom, then in the kitchen sat down to the tea and brownies she'd set out. She tried not to feel invaded.

He laughed. "Boy brownies."

"Of course." She'd always had to keep two kinds of brownies on hand in their household because he and Mimi liked theirs with nuts while the rest of the children insisted on plain. Bev liked both. In those olden days, she had made brownies from scratch. "These are from Indulgences, the bakery that's run by a friend of Snowy's."

"No more Vachon's Bakery? No more Vachon's chocolate doughnuts, the best in the world?"

"Alas, Vachon's is gone."

He said, "So many new places to learn."

She hoped he wasn't going to pop out with the obvious Thomas Wolfe quote about you can't go home again. A decision occurred to her. "Let's have Indulgences cater our ceremony."

"Okay, but we haven't discussed the menu yet."

"We'll get to it. What's the news you were going to tell me?"

"Ah," he said, "you'll have to ply me with more than boy brownies. A cheeseburger at Hooper's."

She sighed. "Shall we start on the tour? Since I'm driving, we'll take my car."

"Where's Leon?"

"I don't keep track, Roger. He's all grown up."

"That's a matter of opinion."

Bev began to feel exhausted. A headache stabbed, and the long weekend with Roger had only just begun.

Outdoors, she saw that he hadn't driven here in his old

pampered black Porsche. They walked past his latest SUV, a Toyota Land Cruiser with his skis on top. As they got into her car, suddenly she was roused by the strangeness of having him in the passenger seat, sitting there fastening his seat belt, fingering the leather upholstery, studying the dashboard. Things *could* be new and fun, she thought, steering up the gravel driveway. She could start doing wheelies and terrify him, if she knew how to do wheelies.

He fished a stack of her CDs out of their cubbyhole and asked, "Since when are you a fan of country-and-western?"

Pitfalls everywhere, how exciting! "They amuse me," she said. "Where do you want to start the tour?"

"Anywhere," he said.

She chose back roads into town, crossing over to Worm Hill and North Main Street, driving past the middle school that would always be new to her, although it had been built in the 1960s. On Main Street she took State Avenue and kept straight past the turn onto Chestnut Street, where she had lived in the yellow house to which she and Mother had moved from the chicken farm when she was seven years old, where they had lived four years until Mother married Fred and they moved to the other farm. Farms, the perfect places for Mother—and the wrong setting entirely for Mother's only child! At least at Mother and Fred's farm there hadn't been livestock. Fred had worked as the head teller at the Gunthwaite Savings Bank. Mother worked at her looms in the old Cape's dining room, which had become her workroom, making the place mats and pocketbooks that the League of Arts and Crafts sold. During spring, summer, and fall, Mother tended the vegetable and flower gardens; year-round, on weekends Fred either chopped and stacked fireplace wood, a chore he inexplicably loved, or he tinkered with his dreadful Jeep.

Bev hadn't met Roger until high school, so he had never been inside the Chestnut Street house and had probably forgotten that she ever lived there. He didn't protest her not driving past it or Snowy's house on nearby Emery Street, Puddles's on Gowen Street.

As they neared Trask's, the big brick factory in which Roger's father and most of Gunthwaite's population had worked until times changed and industries closed or moved elsewhere, she turned onto Mill Street and drove into a neighborhood of mill houses, some of them duplexes. The concept of upscale rehabbing hadn't reached this spot, though there were more tidy homes than run-down. She had sold a couple of the better ones. She slowed at the bright blue house with yellow trim. Along the roof edge hung an unlit fringe of those icicle lights that had become so popular at Christmas in recent years.

Roger said, "I don't think this was the greatest idea I ever had."

"Whoever's living there now, they're keeping it up."

He laughed. "'Nasty-neat French,' as it's called." He looked awhile at the house.

Bev thought how different his life here had seemed when she first encountered it, but not *that* different because many other kids came from the same background. She, more than he, had accepted it. Fascinated by his mother's accent, Bev had had to struggle not to start imitating the rapid lilt during conversations, for fear his mother would think she was making fun of her. (His father never said much of anything.) After she and Roger were married and the children were appearing on the scene, she was the one who had insisted on naming their first daughter after both their mothers, so Mimi was Julia Marie, then naming their second son after Roger's father as well as her stepfather, thus Leon Frederick. The names for the other two children, the redheaded children, came from one person each; Dick of course was named after Daddy, Richard William, and Etta after Snowy, Henrietta.

Roger said, "Well, we're here, so let's see the store."

She herself hadn't seen the store in years. Curious, she drove into the cross-hatching of streets to the neighborhood grocery store that had been owned by his uncle, where Roger had worked growing up. There was no longer a Lambert's Market sign or a sign with the subsequent owner's name. Indeed, the little building was no longer a store at all. The plate-glass windows, where canned goods had been displayed and placards had advertised specials, had been replaced with siding and regular windows; it was converted into a house that looked to be in the throes of an identity crisis.

"For God's sake," Roger said. "A house. Somebody's living in Uncle André's store. And you told me Trask's is a convention center now?"

"The Gunthwaite Conference and Convention Center." Bev turned the car around in a driveway. "If you went to any of your reunions, they're probably held there now, the way our fortieth was."

"If I recall correctly, you yourself never went to any reunion until that one."

"Your forty-fifth will be coming up this year."

After a pause of calculation, he said, "Holy shit, so it will."

Bev backtracked to State Avenue and drove slowly past the transformed Trask's building atop the sloping winter lawn. White trim emphasized the cleaned brick, and the window boxes were fluffy with evergreen boughs.

Roger didn't say a word. Because Fred had worked at the bank instead of at Trask's, she had none of the associations and emotions accumulated by Roger—and Snowy and other children of Trask's. So she didn't say anything either and kept driving along State Avenue.

Then Roger said, "The only time a job in that place tempted me was during the War when it stopped making gear cutters and became a defense plant. My father making bombsights seemed a big deal to me, though not so big a deal as being a soldier."

Working at Trask's had kept his father from being drafted. Snowy's, too. But, Bev thought, her own father had enlisted.

"Varney's," Roger said.

He was looking at the self-service gas station where the old one had been, Varney's, *the* high-school hangout for guys, who spent more time working on their cars than pumping gas for customers. Bev remembered how terrified Snowy used to be whenever she and Snowy walked past Varney's, with boys whistling at them. Bev had pretended to hate this gauntlet too, but she'd really relished sashaying past all those eyes. Ah, such youthful panache!

Roger had no idea that the mother of his grandson was a mechanic, probably a very professional one compared with the boys at Varney's.

He said, "Remember the Heap?"

His 1941 Ford in which they used to go parking. In which she had lost her virginity on New Year's Eve 1957, her freshman year at Katharine Gibbs. "How could I forget?" Bev replied.

He laughed, reached over, and pinched her thigh. "This is enough of a tour. Let's have an early supper, an early night."

But to turn around, she drove on to the high school, into the parking lot that covered part of what used to be an entire expanse of lawn. Between the two brick buildings (the original building, which had included the junior high, and the Practical Arts building), a piece of peculiar architecture had been added to serve as a connector; in the old days you crossed back and forth in an underground tunnel.

Roger said, "Four years in that place. Seemed like a lifetime. Now, four years go by in a blink."

He had attended St. Mary's, the parochial elementary school and junior high. Bev said, "I was here *six* years, counting junior high. From age twelve to eighteen. What a lot of growing up! No wonder it felt so long." She drove back out onto State Avenue, back to Main Street where telephone poles were still festooned with big wreaths and garlands, and Christmas decorations still adorned the buildings saved by Dudley's projects. Automatically she glanced at the window display in Yvonne's Apparel and saw mannequins attired in the resort-wear into which they had changed from New Year's Eve party dresses. To go to Sedona . . .

Back in their youth, Hooper's Dairy Bar had been a small white clapboard building with a horseshoe-shaped counter, *the* place where teenagers went after dates and *the* place where families bought ice-cream cones. The ensuing years had brought a barn-board exterior and a wing with booths. After

Bev parked and she and Roger went inside, walking past the counter where together they had sat so many times during dates, a waitress seated them in one of these booths and handed them menus. Bev opened hers. Instead of just ice cream and burgers and sandwiches, nowadays it offered a full "family" selection complete with senior-citizen meals that even included that really revolting golden oldie, liver and onions.

Roger wasn't looking at the menu. He gazed out the window and asked, "How the hell do you live with this around you all the time? There's no escape from the past."

Bev was deciding on the grilled chicken Caesar salad. "Did you ever read Snowy's poetry collections I've given you?"

"Mmm," he hedged, picked up his menu, and studied it.

"When I read her *Tapestry Granite*," Bev said, "I finally realized New Hampshire is in my bones." She added, "Living in your hometown can be eerie, upsetting, but it can also be kind of comfy."

He glanced up at her and repeated mockingly, "Comfy?"

She would not let him make her feel stupid. "Yes, comfortable, like bunny slippers."

"Since when did you own bunny slippers?"

Well, not since she was approximately nine years old. To her relief, the waitress returned, and instead of seeking a rejoinder for Roger, Bev ordered her salad, dressing on the side, and an iced tea.

He didn't order a cheeseburger for old times' sake, after all. From the senior-citizen selection he chose the pot-roast dinner, a dollar cheaper than the same dinner on the main menu. For that bargain price of $6.50 you also got your choice of beverage and a small dish of Hooper's ice cream.

Bev realized she was staring at him incredulously.

When the waitress left, he grinned at Bev and said, "Now that I'm going to be retiring, I have to watch my pennies."

"Is this Dutch? Or I can pick up the tab." Bev wished she had Snowy's appetite so she could order the most expensive dessert on the menu, Hooper's super-duper banana split, six scoops of ice cream, three toppings.

"Just kidding around," he said. "Remember Russell? We used to play doubles with him and his wife? He's been lying about his age for five years so he could get the senior discount at the movies. The opposite of when we used to pretend to be younger than we were, to get the children's tickets."

"Speak for yourself. I paid full price when I turned twelve or whatever age it was."

"You couldn't have got away with lying. By high school you looked more grown-up than the other girls and according to your mother's photo albums you always did."

Never, she reminded herself, never argue with a lawyer.

The waitress brought his coffee and her iced tea.

Lifting the mug, Roger took a sip and said, "Now, my news. You know how none of the kids wanted to buy the house? Well, after this spell of living in Jessica's apartment, Dick and Jessica have changed their minds. They say it's too good to pass up. Dick mentions"—Roger gestured around Hooper's and at Main Street out the window—"memories. And Jessica likes the idea of a base in Connecticut, with her roots over in Woodbury. So Jessica will do the commuting."

Bev felt swept by delight. She had thought she'd said good-bye years ago to that house and all her projects there, decorating, gardening, her labors of love. But now it would stay in the family! "We'll arrange things so they can afford it?"

"What are parents for?"

They smiled at each other, and he reached across the table for her hand. Holding hands in Hooper's, as of yore.

But not during the night together (Leon evidently wasn't coming home, was spending the weekend at Heather's, so they could carouse to their hearts' content), nor the next day of snugly reading the Sunday papers that Roger braved the predicted snowstorm to drive out and buy (when he'd finished with news, he brought up the subject of the guest list, and they did make a start on it until Bev found a basketball game on TV to distract him), nor Monday skiing at the Gunthwaite Recreation Area (Bev announced she couldn't stand the loudspeaker music anymore so she was going to change to cross-country skiing), never throughout the long weekend did she tell him about Clem. She didn't even tell him about the dream of her own real-estate agency.

She didn't tell Puddles, either, when Puddles phoned the next week in a dither about the upcoming cheerleading championships. Yet the phone call and Puddles's problems with teenage girls made her recall how Puddles had been a great believer in snooping in your children's bedrooms. Bev herself hadn't ever exactly snooped, but back when Leon was in high school she was tidying his room one day, tidying and sort of checking around, and she had found marijuana there, in a Baggie in one toe of a pair of foul sneakers she wouldn't have touched with a ten-foot pole if she hadn't been—well, snooping. When Leon had come home, she'd had a little talk with him. Then she had never checked his room that closely again. Cowardly! And she'd never told Roger what she'd found. Never.

Would she be keeping Clem a secret from Roger forever?

The next weekend, which Leon also spent at Heather's, on Sunday morning she went into his room and searched for an address, a phone number. She found that he had an address book in his laptop with some actual addresses, not just e-mail addresses; after Trulianne's name he had typed a different street address and phone number from those in the Eastbourne phone book, so these must belong to Trulianne's parents. Then she clicked on the mail section, desperately trying to retain her self-respect and not read anything more than was absolutely necessary as she scrolled. Eureka! There was a message from Trulianne a couple of weeks ago, with "Update" in the subject line:

Hi Leon,
You can stop worrying. Got a job at the
Kitchen Garden. Finally decided I had
to compromise. But meanwhile, I'll keep
looking.
Love,
T

So Leon and Trulianne were in touch! Leon wasn't the uncaring lout he'd been pretending to be; he was concerned about Trulianne's plight. Maybe he'd even offered financial help, not that he had much to contribute. And Trulianne had signed her message with "Love."

Bev reread it, hoping for overlooked clues, noting that Trulianne hadn't used computer shorthand or any of those faces made from parentheses and colons that Etta couldn't resist. She also noted that Trulianne did not give Leon any news bulletins about Clem, although with a child there would be news every day about his progress, his doings.

Kitchen Garden. Last year a Kitchen Garden had arrived at the Mall of New Hampshire in Manchester, a food counter that purported to serve the only healthy meals in the food court; since then, if she didn't stop at one of the mall's proper restaurants she was apt to grab something there. Eastbourne had a mall, the Seacoast Mall, at which she sometimes shopped when she was down there for the Plumley Real Estate awards weekends at the Holiday Inn. Of course she hadn't gone this year, but she would bet that this mall now had a Kitchen Garden counter, too.

She phoned Information and won her bet. But she didn't take the next step, calling the Seacoast Mall and asking if Trulianne Hughes worked there, for fear Trulianne might learn of the inquiry and be spooked. She remembered how Mother used to say, "Softly, softly, catchee monkey." Oh, the hell with caution! She wanted to jump in her car and drive down to the mall and—what?

She walked through the downstairs of Waterlight, the big empty house, to the suite. She could try to convince Trulianne to come live here with Clem.

Pride. She knew about her own pride, and she'd had to contend with Snowy's.

Trulianne wouldn't freeload.

So what other strategy?

At Plumley's, she again pored over the Eastbourne phone book's list of Hugheses, this time seeking the address she'd seen in Leon's computer. There it was, 45 Bungalow Court. The Hugheses who lived here were Everett and Shirley. Trulianne's parents. Clem's other grandparents.

But how did this knowledge help? Could she drive to 45 Bungalow Court and spy on the family? Follow Trulianne to a day-care center, learn Clem's schedule, and kidnap him?

Aloud Bev said, "This way lies madness."

Lorraine Fitch glanced up from her desk with a quizzical expression. Probably Lorraine was thinking that if her archrival had begun talking to herself, chances were improving at winning back the top-producer crown.

Bev repeated silently: This way lies madness.

So she hid in the dailiness of the days, busy, busy. Embarrassed by her snooping, she didn't tell Snowy what she'd found out and she tried to forget what she knew. She concentrated on real estate. On the upkeep of her own estate—the never-ending demands of Waterlight. On the renewal-of-vows ceremony. After badgering from Mimi, she chose green as the main color for the ceremony, an obvious choice because it had always been her color, to match her eyes. Roger e-mailed her his completed draft of the guest list, and it was simplest to okay it: Mimi and Lloyd; Dick and Jessica; Etta and her latest boyfriend (Roger had typed a query, "What's his name?"); Leon and his latest girlfriend ("What's her name?" Roger had typed, and in her reply Bev e-mailed, "They're Steve something and Heather something, and so we don't make a faux pas about these romances,

let's just suggest that Etta and Leon each bring along a guest");
Roger's sisters and brothers and their spouses; Snowy and Tom;
Charl and Dudley; Darl and Bill; Puddles (and Guy, to be polite,
even if Puddles had already refused for him); Snowy's daughter, Ruhamah, and her husband, Dudley Washburn Jr.; Snowy's
roommate, Harriet, and Harriet's boyfriend, Jared; Bev's roommate, Ann (a 1959 bridesmaid), and her husband; Bev's cousin
Elaine (another bridesmaid and daughter of Daddy's sister
Aunt Barbara who had since died) and her husband; Roger's
Dartmouth roommate, Jonathan (his best man), and his wife;
and, if Bev could track her down, the flower girl (for this honor
Mother had rounded up little Carrie, the granddaughter of one
of Mother's cousins who had also died since the wedding). As
an afterthought, Roger had written, "Might as well invite that
boss of yours, to keep on his good side, and tell him to bring a
guest if he'd like."

Geoff? She could have sworn that Roger, who'd met Geoff
at a couple of parties, had never had the slightest suspicion of
their affair. Was he truly thinking of Geoff as just a business
obligation, or did he want to announce to Geoff that he was back
on the scene to stay?

Mimi e-mailed Bev, "Dad sent the grand total of the guest
list. Lloyd and I will do a few extra invitations, just in case. But
right now we're working on a sample for you to okay. What about
presents? Probably you don't want people to bring any? I double-
checked the etiquette, and although mentioning presents is a no-
no on wedding invitations, for anniversary and birthday parties
you can write 'No gifts, please' at the bottom of the invitations.
So is a vows renewal a wedding or an anniversary party?"

Bev e-mailed back, "Let's consider it an anniversary party.
I'll write the note on the invitations." Lists, she thought. Snowy
too was talking about lists, but these were for her trip to Scotland.
Bev knew that she herself should be making lists for the trip to
England, but doing so meant looking ahead to the finality of
having gone through with the ceremony.

Whenever Bev made herself picture the ceremony, the first thing she saw was Clem as ring bearer. She hadn't had a ring bearer in the original ceremony, but now she pictured Clem in a darling white suit lurching sturdily across the lawn, gripping in his little hands a pale green cushion on which perilously reposed her wedding ring and Roger's. The lawn? Yes, she realized, she had got married outdoors on the lawn of Mother and Fred's old Cape, risking rain, and now of course at Waterlight the ceremony must not be in the living room but definitely outdoors, no matter what. With a canopy for shade and to serve along with the porch for a backup, should it dare to rain. The wedding had started in the afternoon at two o'clock; the renewal of vows should have the same timing and the same sort of menu, a buffet of hors d'oeuvres and lots of champagne.

She was pleased to be able to e-mail Mimi these decisions. Mimi e-mailed back, "When you discuss this with Fay at Indulgences, give yourself some leeway in the guest count, in case of last-minute guests. Now, about music. Shall I get in touch with Stacey and Seth, our flute-and-guitar friends? Do you want a special song? And about photography and video, Dad did fine at my wedding, but why not hire a professional, tactfully, the way Dick and Jessica did? After all, Dad will be one of the two stars of the show, so he should be in the limelight, not taking pictures. We have a photographer friend who's a pro, with an assistant videographer."

E-mailing back her meek agreement to all suggestions but saying that she'd have to think about which song would be special, Bev marveled over Mimi's proficiency in these matters, Mimi who had almost decided against a wedding of her own. Then Bev phoned Fay Rollins at Indulgences with her general ideas and the next day stopped there to go over the details, upgrading the menu to substantial buffet-table foods as well as finger foods passed around by Fay's servers, and discussing the endless possibilities of cake. Bev settled on a traditional white cake of the sort that she'd had at her wedding (bought from the late lamented Vachon's

Bakery), three-tiered, buttercream frosting. Atop the 1959 cake had stood a traditional little bride and groom, but Fay said that was passé and suggested flowers or even one of Bev and Roger's wedding photos scanned onto rice paper. Bev did not want those photos on display anywhere at the ceremony for a then-and-now comparison; she insisted on the outdated bride and groom.

She e-mailed the menu to Roger, who wrote back, "Salmon and chicken are fine, but we guys will be hungry for beef, so add prime rib."

February began. Thanks to Snowy's nipping at her heels, Bev remembered to vote for Al Gore in the primary. The following Monday evening, Snowy phoned and said, "Puddles just called me."

"Oh?" Bev was sitting at her desk in her home office, supposedly working but the photos of Clem were propped in front of her. "Oh, I forgot, the cheerleading championships were this weekend?"

"Her squad came in second again, and Puddles is in the slough of despond. I keep telling her it's wonderful, it's second *nationally*, but her hopes were higher."

"Hell and damn."

They had a moment of silent sympathy for Puddles.

Then Bev blurted, "I've found out where Trulianne is working. I snooped in Leon's computer."

"Good for you," said Snowy, ever the best friend. "Where?"

"At the food court at the Seacoast Mall."

"Oh shit, the poor thing."

Bev remembered that one of Snowy's nightmares had been having to support herself by waitressing if the store failed. "Her parents' address was in his computer too. What do I do now? I want to go down and talk to her, but I don't want to scare her off or infuriate her or anything. I'm going crazy, wanting to see Clem. It's like being in love, remember, when we'd plot and scheme about how to bump into a boyfriend accidentally on purpose."

78

"She and Leon are e-mailing each other? That's a good sign. Who's the Heather he's involved with?"

"I haven't really paid attention, but of course he hasn't said much. She lives over in Piperville and works in some office. I think I've got that straight. The girl before was a dental hygienist, Heidi somebody. I think. Am I getting them all mixed up? Heather, Heidi, or maybe a Holly, a Hayley?"

"Is Roger still coming up for his birthday? Are you still going to keep him in the dark?"

"I don't know. I don't know anything!"

The weather would decide whether or not Roger celebrated his sixty-third birthday at Waterlight on the long Presidents' Day weekend. As it turned out, snow was predicted for late Friday afternoon into Saturday, so he arrived at noon that Friday, his birthday. Evidently with retirement on the horizon he no longer felt indispensable at the firm and could start his weekends whenever he liked. Bev hadn't planned to throw him a party, because they'd be having that great big party in June, and anyway, it was a weekday so Etta wouldn't be able to get here until late, but Bev had arranged that Etta would drive home from Amherst on Saturday and Mimi and Lloyd would come over from Leicester, and they'd have a post-birthday dinner. The weather put an end to that plan. Leon didn't get trapped by the storm at Waterlight with Roger; on Friday morning he told Bev, "I'll be away this weekend," and took off in his pickup, presumably to Heather's.

Friday night she served Roger her famous seafood casserole. Then, singing "Happy Birthday to You," she unveiled the coconut cake, his favorite, made not by her but by Indulgences, no need to save it for tomorrow's dinner, and as he blew out the three candles entwined by a decoratively piped 63, she wondered what he wished for. Then she produced the birthday present she'd chosen, a copy of the history of Gunthwaite that the historical society had published for the millennium. Maybe, she thought as he untied the ribbon, this would interest him, even if Snowy's poems didn't. And why *hadn't* he read Snowy's collections? Bev supposed he had a typical aversion to poetry (well, since school days she herself hadn't read any except Snowy's and occasionally some poem by somebody else Snowy suggested), but you'd think curiosity would have goaded him. In high school, he and Snowy had been very alike, good students, ambitious. Was he jealous? Of some thin volumes of poetry?

"Thank you," he said, unwrapping *From Our Past to Our Present: Gunthwaite, NH, 1750–2000*. He put it aside and said, "Tomorrow we'll go over the British guidebooks I've brought."

That evening they watched *Washington Week in Review* and the rerun she'd taped of *Rumpole and the Old, Old Story*. Perhaps, she thought belatedly in the midst of this *Rumpole*, the subject was too close for comfort, the old, old story being infidelity.

But Roger didn't seem perturbed. He said, "When we're in London, we'll visit Rumpole's haunts. The Old Bailey."

Saturday was the nineteenth, the day Daddy had died in 1945. Some years on this day she went to the cemetery, where the urn of Mother's ashes and also the urn of Fred's were now buried beside him, but she'd never made a rite of the visit. It was impossible this year.

Within the blizzard screeching off the lake, the big house creaked and groaned like a windjammer rounding Cape Horn. Roger stirred the fire in the living-room fireplace and rearranged some furniture, swapping the little end table beside his wicker armchair for the drop-leaf table under a window. This, thought Bev, is only temporary. She could change it back after he returned to Ninfield. On the opened drop-leaf table he set his briefcase, the one Bev had given him this Christmas; showing off, she had spent five hundred dollars on the handsome thing. (Guiltily she'd imagined what Snowy would think—but not say—about such a gesture.) He hauled books and legal pads out of it. The British guidebooks; notes he'd taken. He opened a Fodor's guide. "In addition to the Stratford area, I'd like to visit Oxford."

She thought, of course you would. Academic endeavor, how uplifting!

"And Warwick Castle," he said. "It's got everything, even an oubliette."

She knew he was expecting her to ask what an oubliette was, but she remembered from a history class—or maybe a French class, because the word came from *oublier*, French for "forget." Why would he want to see something so awful, a cramped little dungeon where a prisoner was put to be forgotten? She said, "How gruesome, Roger."

"There's a regular dungeon, too," he said with enthusiasm, obviously trying to gross her out, just like a small boy, "and a display of instruments of torture. The rack."

God, males!

Then she recalled Snowy's mention of visiting Warwick Castle on her trip to England with her husband, Alan. Snowy had told about climbing a winding staircase up a tower, and they'd laughed over how Puddles had made them *climb* the Washington Monument during the Girl Scout trip to Washington. It occurred to her that her second honeymoon would be more fun if instead of Roger she went with Snowy and Puddles.

In the afternoon the storm ended, having deposited a foot of snow. Bev and Roger stepped outdoors into the fresh white world. Roger used the snowblower with which Leon usually cleared paths, and Bev tidied up with a shovel, but the driveway remained unplowed, Leon and his pickup (and its plow) at Heather's.

Roger fumed, "He's irresponsible. If we had a house fire right now, the fire engines couldn't get to us."

As always, she started defending Leon. "The roads must be a mess. It will take him a while to drive here."

"I'm going to phone somebody else to do it, some plow service."

"They'll all be busy. Let's just wait."

"Next winter, we'll get someone else. We won't rely on Leon."

She then saw inspiration strike him.

Joyfully he said, "I'll buy myself a plow for the Toyota! *I'll* do the plowing. I'll be retired; I'll have the time, and it'll save money in the long run."

Bev rather doubted that it would, but she was frightened by his referring again to thriftiness in retirement. Good God, senior-citizen specials at Hooper's! During their marriage, until she left him and began earning money in real estate, he had always paid all the bills, and in the early years he had complained about her extravagance but when times became easier he had relaxed into affluence.

During the cocktail hour in front of the fireplace, Roger ferreted around in his briefcase again and extracted a manila folder. Bev was thinking about the meal she was preparing, the pork-tenderloin dinner adjusted for only two, wishing the children were here—all of them, that is, except Leon, to keep peace, but she wished Leon would get here to plow the damn driveway.

She jerked to alertness at the sound of a name.

"Gloria," Roger was saying, laughing. "After all these years. The Internet is incredible!"

"Gloria?" Bev said.

Out of the folder he took what looked like e-mail printouts. "She's organizing the forty-fifth reunion of the Class of '55 and she's tracking everyone down."

Gloria Taylor. Captain of the varsity cheerleading squad, editor of the yearbook, Queen of the Junior Prom. With whom Roger had gone steady their junior year. Bev racked her brain, trying to remember all the intricacies and intrigues of this romantic triangle. Quadrangle? Gloria had broken up with him when she'd fallen in love with an older man, a junior at UNH. Then Bev and Roger had gone steady his senior year until Roger discovered Bev was dating a summer boy on the sly and broke up with her. (Bev hung her head in shame at this memory but couldn't help a jolt of glee at how thrilling the two-timing had been. The summer boy had taught her how to water-ski.) By then, Gloria was no longer pinned to the UNH guy, and she and Roger resumed dating and stayed in touch when he went off to Dartmouth and Gloria to—where? Skidmore? But at a party on New Year's Eve 1955, he and Bev got back together again, dancing to "My One and Only You." Oh, that was it, the special song for the vows ceremony! Instead of the wedding march, she would make her entrance to "Only you can make this world seem right . . ."

Roger was saying, "When Gloria learned I'm returning to Gunthwaite, she asked me to head up an on-the-spot planning committee."

"Where does she live?" Bev asked, thinking that Gloria was two years older and wondering how she'd aged. A phrase from Latin classes came to mind. *Sic transit gloria mundi:* So passes away the glory of the world.

"In Syracuse." Roger consulted an e-mail. "The timing won't interfere with our ceremony. They've settled on June tenth for the reunion. As you predicted, it'll be at Trask's. Gloria says that in the past it was at the country club, the dinner Saturday night and then on Sunday a brunch and golf. She was the class secretary, and she's gone to all the reunions."

I'll bet, thought Bev. She tried to remember who had been president of the Class of 1955 their senior year. Roger had been president their freshman and sophomore years but had declined to run again afterward because he had his hands full: the basketball team, the debate team—

She asked, "Who's the president of your class?"

"What? Oh, Sonny Poor was. Gloria told me he died four years ago, lung cancer. He lived down in Massachusetts."

Sonny Poor. Dead. Bev tried to recall if she had dated him. There had been so many boys and dates.

Roger said, "The vice president is Gary Fuller, but he lives in San Diego and doesn't come back. So, without Sonny, Gloria is running the show. She says that a friend sent her a card that says, 'Old cheerleaders never die; they organize class reunions.'"

Gloria Taylor. Bev decided she wouldn't ask Roger anything else about her, wouldn't display her avid curiosity. But would he fill in blanks? Was Gloria married, divorced, widowed, single? And would he go to the reunion on his own? "June tenth," she said.

Roger said, "Somebody else's reunion must be very dull. You'd probably be bored stiff."

She didn't point out that she knew many members of the Class of 1955 and had dated several, so seeing them would be interesting. Somebody else's reunion could be a lot simpler than one's own. She waited. Was he remembering that in a moment of weakness she had invited him to be her escort to her fortieth and he had begged off? He had claimed he was busy at work; she had suspected a woman.

Finally he asked, "But would you like to go?"

"Yes, thank you," Bev replied primly. She imagined making an entrance with Roger. What to wear? This could be fun!

Then she heard the sound of Leon's pickup grinding its way down the driveway, plowing. She ran to turn on the outside lights.

When he finished the plowing, however, he didn't come in. His headlights went back up the driveway and disappeared.

Sunday morning, Mimi phoned and suggested meeting at the recreation area. Bev and Roger drove over in his SUV. True to her word, Bev had bought cross-country skis after finally getting fed up with loudspeaker music. Her mother used to go snowshoeing a lot, but Bev had seen no point in that and had taken up downhill skiing in sixth grade and junior high, not liking it but liking the boys around and the effect on them of her ski pants. She and Snowy had been vastly relieved to learn in high school that you didn't have to ski to be popular, and they'd promptly given it up. During the ski trip to Telluride with Geoff, Bev had rediscovered glamour. But now, no more downhill, not with this racket! She followed Mimi and Lloyd off on a trail into the woods, copying them, getting the feel of their pace, while Roger swooped down the slopes alone.

After, over cocoa in Waterlight's kitchen, Mimi produced a

84

sample invitation she and Lloyd had made. Bev marveled over this latest example of their talent, a design that managed to be both graceful and amusing. Not for the first time she wondered how her life would have been different if she had, like Mimi, inherited Mother's artistic abilities. If she'd inherited Mother's nimble fingers, skilled with a needle as well as a shuttle, this would at least have affected her workbasket. Bev hated to sew so much that before she could get around to mending her children's clothes, even sewing on a button, they had outgrown them.

To her relief, Roger had no quibbles about the invitation.

Then Mimi asked, "Who is going to preside? Conduct the ceremony?"

Bev and Roger looked at each other. Bev had completely forgotten about this, and obviously he had too. She said, "I'm a notary public," and laughed. "I could!"

Roger asked, "Are you serious?"

"No," Bev said.

Roger pondered. "I suppose whatshisname, the justice of the peace who married us, is dead by now."

Bev heard Snowy's voice in her head, the suggestion Snowy would make if asked. Bev said, "Let's see if Dudley will."

"Dudley?" Roger asked.

"We've already decided to invite Charl and Dudley, the twins and their husbands. He'd be perfect. My classmate, Gunthwaite's mayor."

Roger said, "Hey. Weren't you two in *Our Town* together?"

Flabbergasted by his suddenly remembering this, Bev said, "Yes. Our sophomore year."

"You two got married onstage."

"Well, playing Emily and George we did." Bev remembered the Dramatics Club wedding dress she had worn and how a real kiss-the-bride smooch hadn't been permitted at rehearsals despite Dudley's entertaining attempts to convince Miss Norton, the dramatics teacher, that rehearsing was necessary. He'd told everyone that he was going to make up for this cruel denial the first night, which made Bev worry she'd start laughing, but when the time came his embrace had been perfect, solemn and serious. In the audience, Roger had not been pleased; after the play, he couldn't hide his jealousy, to her delight.

Mimi looked back and forth between them. Lloyd gazed into his cocoa mug.

Bev decided to dig in her heels. "Dudley is a dear old friend. It would be nice to have him preside."

Roger said, "That's what you want? Then fine with me."

Mimi asked, "Who is going to give Mother away?"

"Oh," Bev said. "I hadn't thought of that. Fred gave me away, of course."

Mimi said, "Dad, I loved having you give me away, but admit it, it's archaic. Mother, why don't you give yourself away this time? Now, what about vows? Are you going to write your own vows?"

Again Bev and Roger looked at each other. Yet another thing they'd forgotten.

Roger said, "That would be nice," and Bev knew he was deliberately copying her silly adjective. He added, "It wasn't something people did back when we got married, but it would be nice now."

Bev said desperately to Mimi, "You and Lloyd didn't."

"Not our style," Mimi replied and smiled tenderly at Lloyd, who spooned up a marshmallow.

Oh my God, Bev thought, I'll have to ask Snowy to write my vow!

4

ROGER SPENT A GOOD part of Monday, Presidents' Day, at the desk in the suite's sitting room, phoning classmates who still lived in Gunthwaite, working at his laptop, reading the goddamned guidebooks, making notes on his legal pads. He didn't head back to Ninfield until Tuesday morning; apparently he could also end his weekends whenever he liked. After he left, Bev drove to Plumley Real Estate and tried to concentrate, but then she gave up and did something she rarely did. Instead of waiting for Snowy to be home in the evening, she phoned her at the store.

Ruhamah answered. "Woodcombe General Store," she said, "how may I help you?" Snowy's daughter looked very much like her, but her voice was quite different, rich and throaty.

"Hi, this is Bev. If Snowy isn't awfully busy, could I speak with her for a moment?"

"Sure, Bev. Hang on." A soft tap as Ruhamah set the receiver down.

Ruhamah and D. J. (Dudley Junior) had got married last year and bought the old Thorne farm in Woodcombe, down the road from the house Snowy and Alan used to own. With the farm had come chickens, which Ruhamah kept, selling the eggs at the store. She and D. J. hadn't yet acquired any equivalent of Clover, the horrible cow in Bev's past. Snowy had wondered aloud to Bev about who, if D. J. should win his run for the U.S.

Congress and he and Ruhamah lived part-time in Washington, would take care of the chickens, Pete the farmhand or Snowy the bighearted mother? Actually, Snowy hadn't sounded as if she'd mind the chore, but anyway, D. J. was a Democrat, so the odds in New Hampshire were that he was doomed to lose and Snowy wouldn't have to learn to collect eggs from disgusting and dangerous hens. Bev had never wanted to learn and Mother had never insisted. Dear Mother.

Waiting, listening to customers, Bev pictured the general store with its combination of the practical, the quaint, and the cutting-edge: groceries; a woodstove; a pickle barrel; tables at which customers could drink coffee and eat the sandwiches made by Snowy and Ruhamah (and also by their helper, Rita, a classmate of Snowy and Bev's); a table with a computer and fax for customers' use; on the front porch a deacon's bench on which, in summer, customers read newspapers and ate the ice-cream cones Snowy scooped. How did Snowy get up every morning and confine herself to that space, those duties? One of the best things about selling real estate was being unfettered.

"Hi," Snowy said. "What's wrong?"

"I can't stand it any longer. I've got to go down to the Seacoast Mall. Will you go with me?"

"Of course," Snowy said.

Bev was relieved to hear no hesitation. She knew she ought to go alone and not take up Snowy's time with this obsession, but Snowy's presence would be insurance against any menopausal madness such as kidnapping Clem. Also, because Snowy had lived in Eastbourne she was familiar with the city's geography, whereas Bev really only knew the mall and the Holiday Inn. Bev said, "Is tomorrow okay? It'd have to be a weekday, not your Sunday afternoon off. Trulianne probably tries not to work on weekends. Then again, maybe she works then because her family can be home to take care of Clem." She wailed, "I don't have any idea of her schedule!"

"Let's start with tomorrow."

"Thank you, thank you. Will Rita be working? Do you want Leon to come help out, the way he sometimes does? We just can't tell him where we're going."

"No, that's okay. It's winter, business is slow."

"I may only watch Trulianne, not approach her. I may want to follow her. Does that make me a stalker? Will that upset you after, you know, after that crazy man?"

The media had dubbed him the Old Man Bomber because of his demented plans to blow up New Hampshire's symbol, the rock formation known as the Old Man of the Mountain. He had stalked Snowy before blowing himself up on Mount Pascataquac last fall.

Snowy said, "It's all right, Bev. What time do you want to leave? To get there at lunchtime when she'll probably be working if she's there?"

"Ten-thirty?"

"See you then."

As Bev began phoning people and rearranging tomorrow's appointments, Geoff ambled over to her desk. After she finished a call, he asked, "Have you made plans for your Disney World trip?"

"Not yet. Too busy right now—and by the way, I won't be around tomorrow. A family problem."

The magic word, family, didn't faze him this time. "Everybody okay?" he said. "I saw you with your family at the area Sunday."

"Everybody's fine. Just a little problem to tend to."

"Later, I bumped into Roger in the lift line. Not literally."

"Mmm?" said Bev noncommittally, fussing with papers on her desk.

Geoff said, "He mentioned he was retiring and moving back to Gunthwaite."

"That seems to be the plan." Roger had not said a word to her about this encounter with Geoff. Did this prove that he only thought of Geoff as her boss, so mentioning it to her had slipped his mind? Or, as she had wondered when he suggested inviting Geoff to the ceremony, did he know about Geoff and thus had ulterior motives when announcing to him that the husband would be returning home for good? Had he told Geoff that an invitation to a renewal-of-vows ceremony would be arriving when Mimi and Lloyd had them ready?

Geoff said, "He didn't say anything about being in the market for a condo here, anything like that."

She looked up at Geoff. "No, he isn't a potential customer. He'll be living at Waterlight."

"Ah," said Geoff, and ambled off.

So Roger hadn't spelled out to Geoff that he'd be back in the Waterlight bed. His comments had been offhand. But should she trust this interpretation?

When she got home that afternoon, she found that Leon had returned and was working down cellar on something or other. The house felt back to normal, peaceful, without the constant strain of Roger's presence. To be sure, Leon was maddening at times, but the only thing that really drove her berserk about having him in residence was the god-awful smell of the popcorn he occasionally microwaved for his TV-watching. At her desk upstairs, she took the Disney World envelope out of a drawer and put it in her shoulder bag.

The next morning at ten-thirty, Bev sat on the hall bench pulling on her suede-and-shearling boots. She couldn't help wearing clothes that would be fairly easy to take off to try things on, just in case she did some shopping with her stalking, and she had chosen a white zippered sweater and elastic-waist charcoal slacks. The boots would be troublesome. Boots were always a damn nuisance. So she should only shop for tops, if she shopped at all.

Through a window she saw Snowy's car arrive, a blue Subaru Legacy station wagon that Snowy had bought secondhand at least five years ago. She didn't waste time inviting Snowy in. Grabbing her parka and shoulder bag, she hurried outdoors, across the porch and down the stairs into the surprisingly warm morning. The early sunshine was now obscured by clouds. She'd heard on the radio that the temperature would get up into the high forties today.

Snowy was out of her car and looking up at the sky.

Attempting to avert comments about global warming, Bev remarked, "It's cleared off cloudy, as Mother would say."

But Snowy pointed at some crows cawing in the top of an oak. That apparently was what she was looking at. She said, "Crows always act capable of all those clever antics and supernatural doings in legends and folktales and poems. Yet they're getting wiped out by the West Nile virus. I read that it's as bad as AIDS for the crow populace."

Leave it to Snowy to worry about crows dying from some terrible disease. Bev automatically checked the agitator churning the water at the dock. Then she glanced farther beyond at the bob houses in the bay where ice fishermen were walking around and conferring, circled by the tracks of their pickups and snowmobiles on the snow-covered ice. What a mystery, people and their hobbies. Of course it had once been a vital necessity, part of the survival struggle, to chop a hole in the ice and drop a line in and hope a fish would bite before you froze to death. But now? The activity seemed especially harebrained and mortal below the density of the stark blue mountains.

Bev asked Snowy, "All set?"

Snowy looked from the crows back to earth. "Thanks for the chance to play hooky. Are we off?"

They were. In Bev's Outback they got on Route 11 and Bev drove east along the south shore of Lake Winnipesaukee, telling Snowy the so-called highlights of the long weekend, about marinating the pork tenderloin in honey and soy sauce, about

91

cross-country skiing. Snowy talked about snowshoeing with Tom up some mountain.

Bev said, "And we got several decisions made. Do you think Dudley would do the honors at the ceremony?"

If Snowy wanted to giggle over the mention of the renewal of vows, she controlled herself and said enthusiastically, "Oh Bev, I'm sure he'd love to."

"Okay, I'll phone him tomorrow. Would you believe that Roger remembered how Dudley and I got married in *Our Town?*"

"I bet the main part he remembered was the big clinch."

They laughed, and Bev asked, "Does Tom move furniture?"

"What?"

"Roger switched tables in the living room. I switched them back last evening."

"Well, *I* moved into Tom's place. I guess I must've been the one to move things around, not Tom. I moved most of my stuff in, and he had to build more bookcases."

Bev flicked directionals and swung onto the Spaulding Turnpike. She did not want to sound like Lynne Starling. "Roger has always had a different system from mine whenever he puts things in the dishwasher. I'm used to that, it doesn't exasperate me anymore."

"Sometimes I can't stand it and rearrange Tom's system into *my* logical system."

Bev said, "Monday, Roger went into my office to use my pencil sharpener. He came out and asked why my filing system goes backward. It doesn't! It's perfectly sensible for my purposes, adapted from what I learned at Katie Gibbs. But he snooped, and he criticized."

"Shit," Snowy said.

Bev had assumed he'd at least been only surface snooping. He hadn't opened the folder deep in her desk and seen the photos of Clem. If he had, he'd have asked who the child was, wouldn't he? He could see exactly who the father was! But just in case he snooped again, yesterday she had taken the photos to the Gunthwaite Savings Bank and put them in her safe-deposit box. She had decided that if he went exploring in Waterlight's attic and found the booster seat, she would tell him it had been left by the previous owners. She said to Snowy, "And then he got talking about turning one of the other bedrooms into his office. I asked why he needed an office if he was retired, and he said he might do some consulting and he'll still be on the Lambert and Lambert letterhead, and anyway, a guy needed a den. He has a home office, a den, at home. In Ninfield. And during my—er—absence, he added a hideous recliner and one of those huge enormous TV screens. I know he'll transfer them to his Waterlight den."

"I took over Tom's spare room for my office."

"Oh. Yes."

"Eek, is Waterlight suddenly seeming *small?*"

Bev perceived she had to tell Snowy her hopes, even though it broke her rule about trying not to mention real estate in Snowy's presence. "I'm thinking of an office of my own. A business office. Not in Waterlight. I'm going to take the broker's exam in May, oh dread dread dread, and if I pass, I'll be my own boss."

"Bev! This is wonderful!"

Snowy again sounded genuinely enthusiastic. Bev said superstitiously, "*If* I pass," and in lieu of wood to knock on, knocked on her head.

"You'll pass."

"If I do, being my own boss will be terrifying. I haven't told Roger or anybody. Not Geoff until it's a fait accompli. If."

"You'd rent office space somewhere?"

"Yes. At first I thought of the suite in Waterlight, but I can't work out of the house with Roger in it all day."

"Also," Snowy said, "I find that with a home office I'm tempted to go throw in a load of laundry instead of tending strictly to business."

"There's that. And when Roger kept talking about his den, I realized he'd decided on the suite for himself. He's already started using the desk there."

"Um, does this mean separate bedrooms?"

Bev made her femme-fatale face. "Roger? You must be joshing. No, that bedroom would be more like a pad where he can loll and watch basketball games, tennis matches. Not a bad idea, I'm deciding."

"Hmm."

Snowy brooded, and Bev drove, trying to recapture the excitement of the moment on New Year's Eve when she had said yes to Roger's renewal-of-vows proposal. Unable to, she tried to remember the thrill of dating big-deal Roger in high school. Maybe she ought to take a look in that old "Roger Scrapbook" to refresh her memory. Which reminded her: "Oh, guess what! Gloria Taylor got in touch with Roger. Plans are afoot for the forty-fifth reunion of the Class of '55."

"Who? Gloria Taylor? Oh my God, you mean—Gloria Taylor!"

Bev knew that Snowy had been in awe of Gloria's accomplishments. Snowy had pretended to loathe her out of loyalty to Bev, but even this devotion to her best friend hadn't kept Snowy from buying a white leather jacket like Gloria's with money earned at Sweetland, the long-gone Main Street restaurant where Snowy and Bev had waitressed summers. Bev realized that although unlike Snowy she'd forgotten many high-school details, she still remembered that their paycheck their first summer, the summer after their sophomore year, was twenty-three dollars, supplemented by tips of a nickel or dime. The white leather jacket had cost Snowy thirty dollars. Bev said, "She's living in Syracuse. That's the only information Roger deigned to impart."

"Syracuse. She went to Skidmore, didn't she? Upstate New York must appeal."

"Roger learned from Gloria that Sonny Poor died four years ago."

"Oh hell. Sonny. That's too bad and too young. Where was he living? I guess Charl never heard or she'd have told us. She dated him some—didn't she go to a junior prom with him? And Rita dated him once or twice."

"Did they? Did I ever date him?"

"Not that I recall. But, Bev, you dated so many . . ."

"Yes, hard to keep track; so many boys, so little time. He lived in Massachusetts. Well, with the class president deceased, Gloria is in charge of their reunions now. She and Roger have been e-mailing, and evidently she gathered that he's going to be in Gunthwaite enough to do some sub-organizing for her, an on-the-spot planning committee. The reunion is June tenth, and he invited me." Bev deleted his trying to wiggle out of it. "So now I have to get something to wear to that as well as figure out what to do about a dress for the renewal of vows. Should I wear my wedding dress or buy something new? I suppose I could wear something old to the reunion, even what I wore to *our* reunion, but where's the fun in that?"

Snowy didn't reply, apparently lost in memories of Gloria.

So Bev turned to her and quickly made her Gloria face, remembering how to all these years later. In high school Snowy had noticed that whenever Gloria went past a mirror in the girls' gym office or locker room, she checked her dark hair that fell in carefully arranged curls to her shoulders (how Bev had gloated, reveling in her own naturally curly hair, imagining Gloria's nightly torture of sleeping in pin curls), and then into the mirror Gloria would make a face, but instead of clowning around as Bev did, Gloria always seriously made a movie-star face, opening her big blue eyes wide and pouting her Hazel Bishop Kiss-Proof mouth, and then she maintained the expression as she left the room until distractions made it fade. Snowy had pointed all this out to Bev, who had practiced in her bedroom mirror until she'd got the routine exactly right. Hilarious!

Snowy burst out laughing. "Do you suppose she still does that?"

"Would you like to bet?"

"I guess not."

Now the traffic was growing complicated. Bev concentrated on lanes and exit signs.

"Up ahead," Snowy said.

"Yes." Bev took the mall exit and drove into the free-for-all of streets that had been put in without design as more and more stores were built onto and around the original Seacoast Mall. An Old Navy had gone up since she was last here. How appropriate for a seacoast mall!

Unlike the drivers of other cars, she didn't prowl looking for a space close to the mall's main entrance. Snowy preferred a hike, and she herself could use more than the treadmill miles. Besides, it wasn't cold out. She parked, and they trekked across the messily plowed pavement.

Bev said, "I still don't have any plan."

"Play it by ear."

"Maybe she won't be working today. Maybe I'll just go shopping. Do you need to get anything? For your trip?"

"Well, not really. As you know, I've been shopping for it out of the L. L. Bean travel catalogue."

"Oh, that's right," Bev said. She should be doing the same for the second-honeymoon trip, but whenever she'd perused travel-clothing catalogues for other trips she had recoiled in horror from polyester, no matter how improved Snowy said it was. Bev had seen the improvement with her own eyes when Snowy wore and washed a wrinkle-free shirt on their trip to Hilton Head, but she still couldn't bring herself to buy any, no matter how much she hated to have Snowy braver about clothing than she was.

She quickened her pace. As they reached the main entrance, outside of which banished smokers stood looking brazen, furtive, or embarrassed, she rushed through the fug of cigarette smoke more hastily than she usually did in such a Coventry, and the automatic doors opened to usher her and Snowy into the mall.

Snowy laughed. "I always remember our first automatic doors, the ones at the new supermarket near the high school, remember, our freshman year? Puddles was so fascinated she kept going in and out until a clerk told her to cease and desist."

"Uh-huh," Bev said, intent on the food court ahead, inhaling the smell of hot fat and oregano, egg rolls and pizza, scanning the lunchtime crowd and the food counters. These places were always grubby, uncivilized, ghastly. You couldn't enjoy even a guilty-pleasure fast-food treat at a little plastic table wobbling on a cement floor, surrounded by people and shopping bags at a million other such tables. It was worse than eating lunch in the Gunthwaite High School cafeteria! Usually she went to the Mexican restaurant down the corridor to the right or the Ruby Tuesday to the left; they might not be the height of gourmet dining but at least you were in a regular restaurant, being served.

THE KITCHEN GARDEN
Fresh & Healthful Nourishment

The sign stopped Bev in her tracks midway across the court. She stared up at it, then slowly lowered her gaze to the counter below. Two women in crisp white caps and jackets were working there. One of them was Trulianne, small, compact, moving competently, her hair in a ponytail. Bev watched her ladle soup into a Styrofoam bowl, arrange a crusty whole-wheat roll on a paper plate, and place them on a tray for a grandmotherly woman clutching a Macy's bag, who then carried her lunch into the thicket of tables, hunting for an empty one. Grandmotherly. I'm a grandmother, Bev thought. I am Clement Hughes's Gaga, and I have rights. She straightened her back and swept up to the counter.

"Trulianne!" she exclaimed. "Such a surprise to see you! We're down here to shop what's left of the Presidents' Day sales—you remember Snowy, don't you?"

"Yes." Entirely self-possessed, Trulianne stepped to the computer cash register. "What can I get you?"

"That soup looked good," said Bev, without the faintest idea what kind it had been. "I'll have a bowl of that." She glanced at Snowy, who was studying the menu on the wall as if food were really an important part of this mission. "Snowy?"

"Portobello mushrooms and roasted red peppers on focaccia," Snowy decided, opening her shoulder bag. "And an iced tea."

Bev whipped out her jade Cole Haan wallet. "My treat. These Kitchen Garden places are great," she gushed to Trulianne while Trulianne rang up the order and the other woman tossed mushrooms and red peppers onto the grill. "I've been to the Kitchen Garden in the Manchester mall and it's divine to take a break from shopping and be revived by a lovely *healthy* lunch." Trulianne handed her the change from her twenty-dollar bill, and Bev dropped all the bills and coins into the tips jar, then wished she hadn't made such a lavish gesture, which Trulianne might think a bribe. And then as Trulianne, impassive and unresponsive, ladled soup and the other woman began assembling Snowy's sandwich, Bev hurtled wildly on, "How *are* you? How is Clem? He must have grown so much since I saw him almost two whole months ago. I suppose he's at a day care while you're working?"

"He's fine, Mrs. Lambert."

"Bev," reminded Bev, "please call me Bev." There were now people waiting in line behind her and Snowy. Onto a tray Trulianne swiftly set the soup, a roll, the sandwich, and the iced tea. The Kitchen Garden's fare might be comparatively healthy but it was still fast food, too fast. Bev pleaded, "I would love to see him. If not in Eastbourne, couldn't you come to Waterlight when you have time?"

Trulianne pushed the tray toward her. "It's Leon's space. I don't invade his and he doesn't invade mine."

Bev said, "But—"

Snowy grabbed a straw and a bunch of napkins and picked

up the tray. She said gently to Bev, "Let's go. People are waiting to order. Let's go, Bev. We're in the way."

Bev wanted to scream and scream.

But she tried to get a grip on herself and followed as Snowy wove a path amongst tables, past seated women opening shopping bags and comparing bargains, their coats flopped over chairs, boots drooling snow.

"Aha!" Snowy snared a table on which someone had spilled coffee, and she shoved the tray into Bev's arms while she wiped it with some of the napkins. "Sit," Snowy said, taking the tray back.

Bev obeyed. "Trulianne is lying. 'Space'! If they're e-mailing each other, they're invading each other's cyberspace. And Leon has her real address, her phone number, he knows her Eastbourne space."

Snowy set the Styrofoam bowl in front of Bev. "Potato-leek. Yum." She sat down, slid off her parka, and tucked into her sandwich.

Bev had no appetite whatsoever. Hunched in her parka, she strained for glimpses of Trulianne through the crowd. "I am not going to cry. I am not. What do you suppose she earns working here? Minimum wage? No benefits? I am not going to cry. Trulianne is so *stubborn!* I'm sure she's a Taurus."

"Like Tom." Snowy sipped iced tea.

"Do you know where Bungalow Court is? Her parents live at 45 Bungalow Court. If you don't, where can we get a city map? At the newsdealer place here, over there beside the Dunkin' Donuts?"

"I know where Bungalow Court is. Not far from where Alan grew up."

Bev was jerked back to an awareness of Snowy's connection to Eastbourne. "Oh God, I'm sorry, will that upset you?"

"No. I should have thought to ask you before, the street's name. If you're worried about Clem's surroundings, you don't have to be. Unless something has happened since I was last in the neighborhood, Bungalow Court is safe, a little down-at-the-heels but respectable."

Alan's relatives, Bev remembered, had moved to Florida sometime after New England's Ice Storm of '98. Snowy's mother-in-law, sister-in-law, and sister-in-law's husband had exchanged blizzards for hurricanes. So it had only been a year or two. Too soon for the neighborhood to have changed, gone further down? "I just want to see the house. I won't do anything crazy, bang on the door and demand to see my grandson."

"Okay." Snowy finished her sandwich and sucked up a last discreet gurgle of iced tea.

"He's probably at day care anyway." Bev opened her shoulder bag, in which were the photocopied day-care centers and the Disney World envelope. She took out the envelope. "Would you like my soup?"

"In my heyday, yes. But alas—"

"Then let's go." Bev jumped up, hurried to the counter where the lunch-hour rush had slowed so she didn't have to trample anyone, and she thrust the Disney World envelope at Trulianne, who was startled enough to take it, like an out-and-out bribe. Bev said, "For you and Clem. Please give Clem my love," and made her exit from the food court.

So Bev didn't do any shopping after all. They visited the restroom and returned to the car. She put on her sunglasses, although the day had remained cloudy and not the kind of cloudy that did demand her Christian Dior shades.

Snowy shot her an amused glance .

Bev said, "Beverly Lambert, Private Eye. I realize the car isn't disguised."

100

Snowy delved into her shoulder bag and handed Bev a little box of Tic Tacs. "Makeshift toothbrush."

"Thanks." Bev took one, handed the box back, and asked, "Where do we go from here?"

Snowy popped a Tic Tac into her own mouth and directed her away from the mall into the city's streets.

As she drove, Bev remembered visiting Snowy in Eastbourne back when Snowy and Alan were living first in Alan's apartment over a downtown store and then in the apartment in the Ruhamah Reed House. Even in the latter, set in the center of the historic Old Eastbourne section, and despite the antique furniture that Snowy had begun buying, there was a certain air that would have been called bohemian back then. The Bennington Potters dishes. And Snowy and Alan had put off having a child for ten years, so they had seemed younger, free. These decades later, Snowy was still unencumbered, comparatively. Snowy wasn't chasing around after a grandson.

Snowy asked, "What did you give Trulianne in that envelope?"

"The trip to Disney World she refused earlier. Maybe now she's had to take this awful job, she'll figure she and Clem deserve a treat."

"Um, if she just recently started working there, can she take a vacation?"

"She seems resourceful. She could concoct some excuse to have to be gone five days."

"Turn left here."

Suddenly Bev's real-estate instincts kicked in. On trips to the awards weekends, she had observed how Eastbourne had changed since those Snowy years, how the old seafaring town with its cannery (where Snowy's father-in-law had worked) had been cleaned up, the revitalization having started with that preservation of the waterfront historic district. Now the downtown was packed with self-consciously old-timey or chichi shops and many restaurants you heard about or read reviews of, and in droves came the tourists to play and yuppies to raise families and affluent senior citizens to retire. Why had she forgotten this? Why had she pictured Clem in a hovel and seen herself rescuing him from the jaws of poverty, plague, pestilence? Granted, not all of Eastbourne's housing could be prime real estate, but New Hampshire's seacoast was so short that every inch of it was potentially worth considerable, wasn't it? The property taxes must be considerable too.

"Another left," Snowy said.

They were now leaving the downtown for a residential area of everyday houses that looked spruced up by new and energetic owners.

Snowy gestured at a comfortable white house. "Alan's parents'. Alan and I pointed it out when you and Roger visited us here."

Bev had forgotten. Although she would never say anything against vinyl siding to a customer, to Snowy she could remark, "The new owners put on vinyl siding," and make the French Canadian scolding noise they'd learned from friends in their youth. "Vaa!"

"No, Alan's father did the awful deed. It's a wonder Alan ever entered the house again. Now a right, and the first right after that is Bungalow Court."

Bev made the turns into a warren of narrower streets. The houses were smaller, squashed together in a picturesque fashion. After the second turn, onto a short dead-end street, Snowy began counting the house numbers, but Bev didn't need to. She saw ahead, on the right, snow melting off a low roof shingled in a variety of colors and guessed that Trulianne's father had got a deal on leftovers. The house was dingy white, built maybe in the 1920s, just barely two-storied, with a crooked little front porch—Bev's eyes zeroed in on, between a snow shovel and a bucket of sand, a red plastic sled.

"That's the house," Snowy said.

Bev had already slowed the Outback to a crawl. There was no garage. No cars were parked out front.

Snowy said, "Looks like everybody's at work."

Did Snowy sound relieved? Bev couldn't remember ever feeling so frustrated, not even when Roger used to come down from Dartmouth to see her at Katie Gibbs and they couldn't find anywhere to go parking in the Heap because they were in a city. She let the car idle and made herself think real estate. This section of Eastbourne hadn't yet been grabbed up, but it would be. The Hugheses were hanging onto their only asset, this house, but she was positive the taxes must be killing them. Could she make a dazzling offer and buy the place? What would that accomplish, besides reaping her some profit in a couple of years or so? How would it better Clem's life and prospects? The Hugheses would have to use the money to buy a house in a town with lower taxes, or rent something. She *was* insane. Trulianne would never agree to let her buy her parents' house. Talk about invading spaces!

She said, "I can't think straight. I don't know what to do. I brought a list of the day-care centers in Eastbourne, but we can't drive around to each one and lurk."

"We certainly can't."

Bev put her boot down on the gas pedal. "I know, I'm an idiot, an utter simpleton." She drove to the end of the street and defiantly turned around in a driveway posted with a sign saying No Turning and started back. "Well, at least I've seen where Clem lives, at least I've accomplished that. Thank you for humoring me—"

"Look!" Snowy said.

Bev blinked. Ahead, a car had pulled up in front of the Hugheses' house. It was one of the new Volkswagens, and her heart raced at the sight of this saucy yellow buttercup of a car. Had Trulianne bought a new VW? How? Bev braked and stopped across the street two houses away.

Snowy snatched a map of New Hampshire out of her door's pocket and unfolded it, evidently pretending to be a lost tourist although she was blind as a bat without her reading glasses.

Bev watched the Volkswagen's door open. The short woman who got out matched the car. Snowy used to be cute, and even at sixty she might still seem so to some people, and her hair was miraculously still more blonde than gray (miraculously thanks to her hairdresser's highlights), but this woman was still *really* cute and her short bobbed hair was unabashedly yellow. She looked chubby, not matronly, in her gold wool jacket trimmed with black fur (faux, Bev hoped). Black slacks; high-heeled black boots.

This had to be Shirley Hughes. Gram.

And probably Trulianne had bought the old VW from her mother when this new one was acquired. Probably her father had a pickup truck that Clem loved to ride in.

Gram opened the Volkswagen's rear door, bent in, and began doing something. Bev recognized her motions. She was extricating a child from a child's car seat. Bev held her breath, willed herself not to leap out of the car. Gram straightened up, holding Clem in his blue snowsuit. Ferocious jealousy possessed Bev's soul.

Gram now noticed the Outback and called, "Need directions?"

From behind the map, Snowy whispered, "Do we?"

In a panic, Bev told Snowy, "No! You answer her, get her attention off me!"

Snowy pushed the button to open her window and called back, "Thank you, but I see where we went wrong," and Bev accelerated out of Bungalow Court.

That evening when in her bedroom Bev was sprawled on the wicker settee staring blankly at the TV news, the phone on the bedside table rang. Turning down the TV's volume, Bev dragged herself up to look at the caller ID. "Hi, Puddles."

"I've just been talking to Snowy," Puddles said, "and she told me to consult you as a fashion expert. My cheerleaders want a new look, new uniforms, and I think a change might boost their morale after the loss this year—"

Bev interrupted, "You came in second nationally! That isn't a loss!"

"You know precisely what I mean, Beverly Colby Lambert. But it's an expensive proposition, and the girls have to pay for the uniforms themselves, so I'm not sure. Snowy says that it strikes her that the uniforms today are too 'busy,' the designs are too cluttered and distracting. Back in our day, our uniforms were pretty plain."

Bev remembered very clearly the Gunthwaite cheerleaders' uniforms, a costume she had never worn. Short green jumpers and white blouses, with green wool jackets for football season. The only insignia was the white GHS on the backs of those jackets. In the years since, she had paid no particular attention to cheerleading—neither Mimi nor Etta had given a damn about it, lucky them—but occasionally she glimpsed cheerleaders in the background of games on TV, wearing a dizzying array of contrasting-colored insignia, bodices, gores, gussets. "Snowy is right. The same basic fashion rule should apply to cheerleading uniforms: Simpler is better, less is more."

"My girls think the exact opposite. After I started coaching five years ago when that squad's uniform was fairly mild, titsy orange jerseys and orange skirts with white inserts, the girls wanted and got halter tops with the school's letters a mile high and so-called fly-away skirts with glitter trim, they look like orange sherbet cones with sprinkles, exploding, but now this squad doesn't think even that grabs enough attention. Well, I'll give 'less is more' a try. Oh, about your ceremony in June. On a Saturday? I'm hoping that if I can organize my schedule at the clinic I can come a few days early, on Wednesday, to soak up New

England. And who knows, I might run into an old boyfriend. Like, say, Norm Noyes, so I could find out if you and Snowy are right about his being faithful to my memory and never marrying and if he's still carrying a torch all these years."

That had been obvious at their fortieth reunion, which Puddles hadn't attended but Norm had, asking wistful questions about Puddles, who in high school had airily dismissed his dogged devotion, considering him a drip. Puddles had only dated him whenever nobody else asked her out, so there wasn't exactly a romance to rekindle. Was there? Bev nervously thought of Guy, age seventy and, according to Puddles, interested only in golf nowadays. Puddles had once had an affair, probably out of sheer boredom. Oh, Bev chided herself, I mustn't judge, for *I* haven't been faithful to those vows I'm supposedly going to renew!

Puddles was saying, "Do you believe it's been twelve years since I came up and you and Snowy and I had a reunion in Maine?"

"Twelve years? Impossible. Puddles, it goes without saying that you'll stay here, at Waterlight."

"From your description and photos, I know you have room, so I'll accept with pleasure. Thanks for the fashion advice and for letting me chew the fat. Bye!"

Puddles hadn't mentioned the trip to Eastbourne; Snowy had remembered that Clem was a secret.

The phone rang again. Caller ID told her it was Roger. She almost let the machine take it, then sighed. "Hello, Roger."

"I thought I might drive up this weekend."

So soon? He'd just left yesterday!

He was continuing, "The weather isn't looking too swell, I won't be skiing, but I'll bring some of my stuff and start organizing my den."

What could she say? "Are you planning on arriving Friday or Saturday?"

"Saturday."

Thank God for two days of peace and quiet before he got here. He said, "See you then. Miss you. Bye."

Bev turned the volume of the TV back up. During most of the drive home to Gunthwaite, she had speculated aloud, trying to figure out the routine of the Hughes household, saying to Snowy things like, "Trulianne told me her mother was a hotel clerk. Do you suppose that means she works a late afternoon shift, so she takes care of Clem during the day? Or maybe today was her day off. I suppose she'd been shopping, but I didn't see any shopping bags. I only had eyes for Clem. I suppose the bags would be in the trunk. Are the trunks in the new VWs in the front, as the old ones were? Maybe she works a morning shift and picked him up after work. Maybe she works a night shift. A hotel. How many hotels are there in Eastbourne, a zillion? Hey, I never thought, maybe she works at the Holiday Inn, where we have the awards weekends. No, wouldn't Trulianne have said, 'My mom's a clerk at the Holiday Inn,' wouldn't that be more likely? Oh, Snowy, wasn't he adorable!" And on and on. She couldn't stop herself. Snowy had been very patient.

When Bev had finally run down, after a spell of silence Snowy asked about Etta's latest boyfriend.

Bev had tried to do justice to the subject of Steve, the very eligible young veterinarian, but as she talked she thought again that if she told Roger about Clem, maybe he could come up with some legal angle, some actual rights she did have as a grandmother.

She now was wondering this again. Yet always she felt drowned in dread at the prospect of Roger's reaction to what he'd regard as the ultimate disgrace of Leon's purposeless life.

So she didn't tell him when he came up for the weekend, his SUV packed to the brim with cartons. She did report on her phone conversation with Dudley, who had said he would be delighted to perform the ceremony and of course agreed to use the "husband and wife" form instead of the "man and wife" used at the original ceremony; Snowy was the first woman Bev knew who had rewritten "man" to "husband" for her wedding ceremony. Roger didn't seem to be listening.

He rearranged furniture in the suite, and in the living room he swapped the end table for the drop-leaf table without comment. When he left Sunday afternoon, she didn't bother changing anything back.

The following weekend, the first in March, he arrived unannounced on Saturday with more of his belongings and did more phoning to local classmates. He stayed on through Monday morning to visit the high school with a couple of them, explaining that "Gloria thought it might give us some ideas for helping to plan the reunion."

On both weekends, Leon was elsewhere, presumably at Heather's in Piperville.

That Monday evening, Bev e-mailed Snowy: "Roger seems to be moving in here ahead of schedule. I didn't think he would until June. But thus, if he's sort of living here, I guess he feels he isn't visiting so he doesn't have to let me know when he's coming up. No more common courtesy. He took my spare key without even asking. At the same time, he and Gloria are carrying on a hot and heavy e-mail correspondence and who knows what else!" Bev gazed at the screen and then couldn't help adding another exclamation point for good measure.

What *was* going on between Roger and Gloria? Just plain planning and organizing? Or billets-doux in cyberspace? More than that? Because of his trips to Gunthwaite, he didn't have time to drive up to Syracuse to see Gloria, did he? But Gloria might have time to drive down to Ninfield. Bev pictured Gloria in Roger's bed. As usual, the idea of Roger with another woman was voyeuristically titillating, and that could be fun; however, when the other woman in the image was Gloria Taylor looking the way Bev had last seen her decades ago, young and perfect, the arousal was spoiled by the old jealousy.

The phone rang. Frankie, who said, "Isn't it time you gave yourself a getaway?"

"Yes," Bev said before she could think.

"Great!" said Frankie, sounding overjoyed. "When, when?"

Gratified by his reaction, Bev consulted her desk calendar. March was busy with appointments and a real-estate course about property disclosure, and there was also Snowy's birthday. Bev told him, "I'm not free until toward the end of the month. We'll meet in Phoenix and drive to Sedona? I can manage two days there." And nights, she thought, suddenly sizzling with anticipation and guilt at the images of the lovemaking ahead, a change from Roger. Lovemaking. But it wasn't love, was it? Was it even with Roger? What about romance? Once she had remarked to Snowy, "I'm good at romance. I'm no good at the long haul," and Snowy had said, "I was thinking that the romance *was* the long haul." Oh hell and damn. She said to Frankie, "How about we meet Thursday, March thirtieth, stay in Sedona Friday and Saturday, and I'll fly home Sunday, April second. Tomorrow I'll look into flights to and from Phoenix."

Frankie said, "I'll fly too. The drive takes too long, eight hours, and it's at least eleven hours or so with stops, not that I'd want to stop with you as my destination."

Bev basked, smiling to herself. "Where do we stay?"

"I'll check things out and e-mail you."

She said primly, "Separate rooms, if you please," thinking about appearances, alibis, separate bathrooms. At his condo, Frankie's guest room and his spare bathroom were hers (and were they also used by those other girlfriends she wondered about?).

Undismayed, he said, "Connecting rooms."

"Dutch," she said.

After their good-byes, suddenly she saw in her mind's eye the scene in *Smokey and the Bandit* in which Sally Field's character, having bolted from her wedding ceremony in her wedding dress, flags down Burt Reynolds's car and makes a break for freedom. In Eastbourne she had remarked to Snowy that Trulianne could concoct an excuse to skip work and go to Disney World. Now she herself had a similar challenge. After much pondering during the week, she decided on her excuses. She told Geoff that the family problem she'd mentioned earlier had turned more serious and she had to go tend to an ailing cousin who'd retired to a condo in Sedona. When Roger arrived unannounced Saturday, she mentioned that she would be attending a national real-estate convention in Sedona. The skiing was over at the recreation area, so Roger and Geoff wouldn't be bumping into each other again there. In the unlikely event that Roger and Geoff should encounter each other elsewhere and compare stories, one would think the other had got the information mixed up. Or so she hoped.

Geoff asked her, "Sedona? Do you know what your cousin paid for a condo there?"

Roger asked her, "Isn't Sedona full of New Age crap?"

What to tell Snowy? The truth?

Bev used the real-estate convention story when Mimi delivered the invitations one evening. Mimi accepted it without comment and stayed to help her address the invitations at the dining-room table. Looking at Mimi writing diligently away, working on this family celebration, Bev fretted. Even though Mimi wasn't interested in children, she would love to know that she had a nephew. Etta, too. They would get a kick out of being aunts; they would want to see him. Bev had no real qualms about her Sedona lies, but she felt sick with the secret of Clem.

Back in their school days, Bev and Snowy and Puddles had exchanged birthday presents, but in the ensuing years when they'd almost lost touch, being too busy with their families, they had just sent birthday cards and that had remained the custom after they'd renewed the friendship. Last year Snowy and Bev

110

hadn't even done that, because they weren't speaking to each other, and Snowy hadn't gone to the big sixtieth birthday party that Mimi had thrown for Bev.

This year, Bev spent precious time searching for the right card—funny? pretty? sentimental?—and found it at All Booked Up, the bookstore in the Abnaki Mall: a black-and-white snapshot, taken from the back, of two little girls in 1950s cotton dresses with big-bow sashes, each with an arm around the other's waist. The message inside said, "Friends Forever. Happy Birthday!" She had plumped for sentimental.

Snowy would be sixty-one, no longer just on the brink of heading for seventy but solidly in her sixties and on her way. Bev remembered an illustration in her childhood copy of *Anne of Green Gables,* Anne at a stream, with a quotation from Longfellow:

> Standing with reluctant feet,
> Where the brook and river meet.

Baby boomers approaching their sixtieth birthdays might be trying to sell everybody on the notion that at age sixty nowadays you were younger than springtime, but how to sugarcoat the age of seventy? That was *old.* And next month Bev herself would turn sixty-one. When she was a maiden, her feet had not been reluctant to advance to womanhood, but here on this brink of true old-womanhood, they were dragging.

She phoned Snowy and asked, "What are you and Tom doing on your birthday?" This year it fell on a Sunday, so Snowy would have the afternoon off.

"I asked for a present of time. Ruhamah is giving me the morning off, Tom will do all the chores, I'll work in my office all day, and we'll go out to supper at Peggy Ann's Place."

So Bev didn't suggest going to the outlet stores in North Conway that Snowy liked. She took a breath and said, "I'm giving myself an early birthday present, a trip to Sedona.

Frankie and I will meet in Phoenix and drive up. Needless to say, I've told Roger I'm attending a real-estate convention in Sedona."

There was a pause. Bev pictured Snowy raising an eyebrow. Snowy said neutrally, "Oh?"

In a sudden flash, Bev wondered if the reason that Snowy had misgivings about Bev's behavior was sheer envy. Snowy too had dated Frankie in junior high and high school. Frankie had been the captain of the football team their senior year, and now he was a sexy cowboy (well, a real-estate developer sporting modified Wild West outfits). Bev said, "It'll be a—final fling. In a gorgeous setting. I don't know why, but I've been intrigued by Sedona ever since I read an article about it at Frankie's, in one of his Southwest magazines. I thought I'd have a psychic reading done."

After another pause, Snowy laughed. "Ah, Bev."

Heartened, Bev said, "It's where a lot of those old Westerns we used to watch were made. It'll be fun to see the actual places. Remember how we used to play cowgirls? I used to pretend to be rescued by the hero in those red rock canyons."

Snowy said, "Happy trails! Have fun!"

When Bev left Waterlight that Thursday morning to drive to Logan Airport in Boston, the temperature was thirty-five degrees, and she wore a black fleece jacket over her black jersey and long copper-and-sage paisley skirt (she'd learned that for her, skirts were more comfortable than pants on planes). When she and Frankie drove away from the Phoenix Airport in his rented Toyota Avalon, the late afternoon was warm, she had shed the jacket, and there were palm trees and orange trees.

She leaned back, sighing contentedly. "Bliss."

Frankie said, "So it is."

She rolled her head sideways to look at him. He was wearing a brown suede jacket, beige turtleneck, and designer jeans. She recognized on his feet the most expensive Western boots in his collection, which was more like a menagerie; he owned regular calf-leather boots and also snakeskin and goatskin and lizard and kangaroo, and these were ostrich. Back when she'd first seen the entire collection, she had been revolted—it was as bad as wearing real fur!—but then she began to find it funny. And the boots certainly were beautiful. And Frankie was handsome.

She said, "I always forget how very different the Southwest is."

He said, "Isn't it time you swapped New England for the Southwest?"

In the past, he had lightly made this suggestion. Now his tone was earnest. Oh my God, was this a marriage proposal? At the airport he'd welcomed her as if he would never let her go again, pressing her against him in a long kiss that must have struck onlookers as unseemly for senior citizens. The times he'd met her in New Mexico, he'd waited until they were in his car and had some privacy.

Again she saw Sally Field making a run for it in *Smokey and the Bandit*. Had she herself dashed out of the frying pan into the fire?

She decided to pretend to fall asleep.

After a few moments, he whispered, "Bev?"

She breathed evenly.

He then tended to his driving. From beneath her eyelashes she peeked at the scenery while they headed north. Mountains erupted upward, covered with bushes instead of trees. On hillsides, cacti stuck up, phallic symbols. Suddenly she didn't want to go through with the night ahead, even though she had bought three new Victoria's Secret frothy nightgowns in honor of this final fling.

At a sign for the Sunset Point Rest Area, he turned off. He whispered, "Bev? Bev, there's a sunset."

She opened her eyes wide, and so there was. She stretched and sat up straight. "How perfect."

"It sure is."

And thus they began necking in a parked car, like kids. Frankie hadn't had a driver's license when they went out in eighth grade. She couldn't remember what kind of car he had in high school. Frankie. Roger.

The evening darkening, they drove on, into the lights of the Village of Oak Creek, then darkness, then the lights of Sedona. She tried to sense New Age spirits but found herself wondering whether or not Roger would take advantage of her absence to arrive with a moving van packed with Ninfield furniture and rearrange all of Waterlight.

Frankie had driven through Sedona before but had never stayed here. So he'd done research on the Internet, consulted friends, and e-mailed her the choices; they had decided upon a suite with a sitting room, kitchenette, and two bedrooms and bathrooms, in the highly recommended Manzanita Lodge. They had also decided that because they'd be tired from their flights and the drive, they would just have supper in the suite instead of going out to dinner. Now Bev roused herself and squinted at signs, but it was Frankie who spotted the market that a friend had suggested.

The weather felt colder up here. Frankie helped her put on her jacket, and together they went in. This was not ordinary grocery shopping. As they chose cheese and pâté and olives and a baguette, she thought how romantic such shopping was, yet when Frankie strode on ahead gathering up more goodies, she remembered newlywed shopping with Roger in Boston at a Charles Street grocery store.

She was *not* being unfaithful! She and Roger hadn't lived together for almost thirteen years! They'd had affairs! Roger could be in bed with Gloria Taylor right now!

114

Laden, she and Frankie got back into the car and drove on.

In the artful lighting of its grounds, Manzanita Lodge looked romantic and Western. A bellman took them to their suite, whose rooms were done up in colors that made her think of deserts and canyons, shades of sand, pastel pink, deep red, with turquoise accents. She directed her luggage to the frillier of the two bedrooms and took her vanity case into its bathroom, where she avoided looking herself directly in the eye in the mirror as she brushed her teeth and freshened her makeup. When she emerged, the bellman was gone. A fire had been lit in the fire-place in front of the sofa. Frankie took her in his arms and kissed her madly.

"Wait," she gasped. "Wait."

"Sorry."

She hurried to the kitchenette to organize the groceries. Frankie followed, found a corkscrew in a drawer, and opened a bottle of pinot noir. Then he set it down, reached for her, and was kissing her again.

How could she tell him, darling Frankie, that it was over? She should never have flown out here. She should have ended things by e-mail. Filled with guilt, she kissed him back passionately.

His voice hoarse, he said, "Let's have supper later."

Bev looked at the sofa's buffalo throw and pictured it flung down in front of the fireplace. That would be romantic and fun. "Let me take a shower first."

The next morning Bev opened the curtains of her bedroom and caught her breath. Red mountains. They were clay-pot red, with battlements and turrets like castles, and they flowed on into the background where the far mountains were snowcapped.

When she came out of her bathroom after her shower, during which she thought of how she had wept in confusion during the shower she'd taken last night before the session on the buffalo throw, the mountains were still there. And so they were when, after breakfasting on coffee, bread, and prickly-pear jelly, she and Frankie went outdoors, Frankie carrying his camera and the suite's complimentary map of Sedona. Her camera was in her shoulder bag. During her visits to see him in Santa Fe, she had only photographed the scenery, without him in it, and she had asked him not to snap her, for the sake of discretion. He had looked unhappy but had obeyed—at least as far as she was aware. He didn't have a mysterious digital camera; like her, he used a real-estate Polaroid, so they made rueful jokes about being old fogeys, behind the times.

The manzanita bushes around the lodge were very delicate, with little white blossoms and a generic flowery scent that made her think of stepping into a florist's shop. What flowers should she choose for the vows ceremony? At the wedding there had been, outdoors, Mother's gardens, while indoors stood vases filled from those gardens, peonies, roses, sweet william, as well as florist bouquets of white irises and—

In the rented Toyota, she and Frankie set off sightseeing. At first it was sort of a busman's holiday. They drove through or past condo developments and golf resorts, discussing potentials and prices, Bev making mental notes for Geoff about her fictitious cousin's condo. Cherry trees and virburnum were flowering. Occasionally Frankie would stop the car and they would climb out and gaze upward at the red mountains and eventually remember their cameras. Some of the mountains looked less like castles built out of rock and more like the dribble castles she used to make at the beach, though of course these here would be made of red sand. Then there were mountains like red spires, red spindles, red sentries.

At such a stop at noontime, before they got out of the car Frankie said in a low voice, "Look over to your right."

116

In a vacant lot, a coyote stood watching them before loping off.

Bev shivered. "I saw one once in the field behind Snowy's store. This one seems larger and blonder."

"It's Western. Everything's bigger and better out here."

"The Wild West," she said, wondering how many hours of her childhood had been spent watching Westerns, pretending to be here. Numberless!

"Time for lunch?"

"Fine."

Frankie drove to the main strip, which immediately reminded Bev of North Conway, a frenzy of shopping below beautiful scenery. In North Conway, Snowy always had an attack of conscience, waffling on about how the combination of attractions was understandable but bewildering, deplorable yet seductive, and wondering if all the shoppers forgot to look up at Mount Washington. Bev probably would have without her reminder, and now she tore her eyes away from the stores and virtuously looked up at red mountains.

Frankie pointed to a sign: Jeep Tours, Horseback Tours. "How about taking a Jeep tour after lunch?"

Bev demanded, "Frankie, do you remember my stepfather's horrible Jeep?" Fred had driven his beloved Jeep to work daily, and Bev had had to accompany him in it, humiliated, as far as Snowy's house, from which she and Snowy would walk to school. Bev had known she was destined for limousines, not Jeeps.

Frankie said, "That was a swell little CJ3. Well, if not a Jeep tour, then how about horseback? Didn't you say you used to ride?"

In Santa Fe, he had once suggested a ranch weekend, and she had declined.

She said, "I rode only occasionally, years and years ago with Etta. I'd probably fall off nowadays. Why don't you take a Jeep tour and I'll go shopping." She had no qualms about suggesting this. He was used to her going off shopping when she visited him, and although she knew he thought it a waste of their time together, he didn't object and, thank God, he didn't tag along. No need for a husband bench for Frankie.

"Okay," he said equably. He pulled into the tours place, got out and read the posted Jeep Tours schedule, and went in to sign up.

She would have the afternoon to herself.

At a restaurant recommended by one of his friends, they sat in a glassed-in sunporch looking up at red rocks. He always liked to reminisce with her; he hadn't really had a chance yet on this trip, so over her salmon quesadilla and his prime-rib burrito and the iced tea that came in a big wine bottle, they talked of dear old Gunthwaite Junior High and High School. He didn't miss New Hampshire, she was sure; what he missed was youth.

It wasn't *absolutely* necessary to tell him face-to-face, here in Sedona, that she was renewing her vows to Roger. That wouldn't officially happen until June. She could wait and tell him by phone or e-mail. She, a poultry farmer's daughter, could chicken out.

They drove back to the Jeep Tours. After waving good-bye to him from the car, Bev cruised slowly along the strip, suddenly embarrassed at the idea of entering one of the many New Age shops. Crystals! Angels! Instead, she stopped and browsed in a clothing boutique. Ah, who could resist an A-line silk denim skirt? But after buying that, as she drove on she told herself sternly that clothes weren't why she had come to Sedona. So she steered into the parking lot of the next New Age shop she saw. A sign advertised everything from aromatherapy to tarot cards, aura photography to spiritual travels. Channeling and psychic readings, just what she wanted. She got out of the car and locked it. Outside the shop stood a bargain table of books and trinkets, with a sign that warned: Theft Is Bad Karma.

Indoors, she blinked at the clear glitter of glass. New Age music; incense. In the airy atmosphere she found herself tiptoeing past dangling wind chimes and feathery dream catchers, aroma lamps, china angels, and shelves of crystals and baskets of little brocade pouches to put your crystals in. She came to a poster that announced that Aurora gave psychic readings upstairs, sixty dollars for half an hour.

Collecting her courage, she went over to a salesclerk who stood behind a counter of tempting jewelry. "The, um, the psychic reading?"

"Sure thing. Let me check." The woman went up the stairs.

Bev was buying crystal earrings from another woman when the first returned and said, "Aurora has an opening now, if that would be convenient for you."

"Um, fine."

"Just go up those stairs."

Bev's knees trembled as she climbed.

But the woman who greeted her at the top looked sane and pleasant, a few years older than Mimi, maybe forty, brunette and attractive. "How do you do? I am Aurora."

"I'm, um, Beverly."

Aurora led the way into a darkened room with a shawl-draped table, at which she seated herself, gesturing at Bev to sit opposite. Bev did so and discovered that under the shawl it was an ordinary teetery card table. She relaxed a bit. There was no crystal ball on the table, but there were a computer, a tape recorder, and a credit-card machine.

Aurora asked, "Would you like a tape of the reading? It's five dollars extra."

"A tape? Oh. Yes, please. Should I pay now? Do you take Visa?"

"Yes," Aurora said, tapping the credit-card box. "All major credit cards."

While Bev signed the slip, Aurora set up the tape recorder.

"Now," Aurora said, "when were you born?"

"April eighteenth, nineteen-thirty-nine."

"Aries. A fire sign. Impulsive, romantic, intense, proud, intelligent, dynamic, generous, demanding. At what time of day were you born?"

119

A few evenings ago, Bev had checked the time in the pink baby book that Mother had kept. "Five-thirty A.M."

Aurora typed the information into the computer, and out of the printer came an astrology chart. "Ah, your planets are in conjunction," she informed Bev, picking up a yellow highlighter and proceeding to explain how this was good as she highlighted the printout.

Bev couldn't follow it at all. Too vague! Bev wanted to know precisely whether or not to renew her vows to Roger. Should she ask straight out? Before she could decide, Aurora rose and began walking around her, pinging a tuning fork. Bev was overcome with the urge to giggle. Thank heavens Snowy wasn't here!

Aurora sat back down. "Now close your eyes and imagine yourself filling with a white substance. Relax. You are relaxing."

Eyes closed, Bev heard Aurora begin to chant something unintelligible. Oh, don't laugh, don't laugh!

Aurora said, "You may be worrying as you venture into a new aspect of your career, but you should not worry. The new aspect is auspicious. Go ahead with confidence."

So, Bev thought, instead of advice about Roger, I'm getting advice about becoming a broker! In desperation she opened her eyes and asked outright, "What about men?"

"There will always be men in your life if you desire them."

A tactful answer to an older woman.

Aurora added, "Because you were born under the sign of Aries, you take risks with your love life."

Too true, Bev thought. She asked, "Do you do channeling?"

"Yes, if Spirit allows."

Bev looked around the dark room. She knew in her head that Mother and Daddy were dead and would never speak again. But in her heart? Her heart wanted to believe in boundless possibilities. Not here, though, at this shawl-covered table.

She would just have to continue talking to her parents in her heart.

Aurora said, "Would you like to schedule a channeling appointment?"

"No. No, I think not, thank you. But—what about grandchildren? I have a grandson, only it's—difficult. I can't see him, visit him, have him visit me."

Aurora looked curious and sympathetic. She said, "His energy is with you."

What the hell did that mean? But Aurora was popping the tape out of the recorder, and the session was over.

Before leaving the shop, Bev stopped and bought a pendant that said: Miracles Happen—Ask the Angels.

Then she explored other shops, choosing presents, for Mimi a book about Navajo blanket-and-rug weaving, for Etta a trinket box atop which reared a copper mustang, for Leon a T-shirt with a petroglyph design, and for Dick and Jessica and the Ninfield house a set of Kokopelli bookends. That Kokopelli was a fertility deity was a bonus, a subliminal hint. For Snowy she chose a souvenir sack of pancake mix made from Hopi blue corn. You couldn't go wrong with a gift of food for Snowy. She hesitated over a leather belt for Roger, but the ornate silver buckle would remind her of Frankie's belts, of Frankie's undoing his belts . . . She almost decided to get Roger nothing. After all, she was supposedly at a real-estate convention, concentrating on her career. But then she spotted a mesquite desk set of pen, pencil, and letter opener, and she bought it for his Waterlight den.

At the tours place, Frankie was patiently waiting. He raved

about the sights he'd seen, wanted to see more, and began trying to persuade her to take a horseback tour tomorrow, their last day here, just a short ride into one of the canyons. He showed her the brochure. She read: Strong Wranglers, Gentle Horses.

The major guilt about the renewal of vows and the minor guilt about having left Frankie to go shopping during their two short days in Sedona made her say, "Okay, okay. I hope it's like riding a bicycle and I haven't forgotten."

He immediately signed them up.

That evening in an extremely nice restaurant, after the shrimp scampi with jalapenos (her) and mesquite lamb (him), over the Dessert Sampler for Two he finally said, "Bev. You know what I've been trying to ask. Will you marry me?"

It was her cue to announce the renewal of vows. It was her cue to tell him, and she did, kind of. "I'm already married, Frankie."

"Not very," he pointed out.

She should explain that the situation had changed. Instead she said, "It's unconventional but it suits me." Then she listened to what she'd said.

So did Frankie. He sat for a spell, not eating, not sipping his coffee. Finally he asked, "If I moved back to New Hampshire, would you change your mind?"

"You love the Southwest. You've loved it since you first set foot here."

"I love *you.*"

"Oh, Frankie, you love our memories. Remember Blue Island and the Girl Scout jamboree?"

Undeflected, he implored, "Just think about it. Please."

She was reminded of the way she had pleaded with Trulianne. "I can't," she said.

"Why not?"

This was her cue again. But she said, "You'd hate it, New Hampshire, and you'd hate me because I was the reason you left New Mexico."

"I love you. Please, think about us together, either in New Hampshire or New Mexico."

She didn't reply, but she felt so sorry for him that she let him spend the entire night in her bed.

The next morning she awoke wondering why she had been dreaming about her mother's friend Emma Gardner. She couldn't remember the dream itself, just Emma's face. Frankie was already up and had started coffee. She put on her bathrobe and opened the curtains to check on the red mountains. Emma and Mother had met through the crafts league. Emma had been a potter. What had she dreamed about Emma, and why?

After her shower, she dressed in jeans, shirt, and sweater, wishing she hadn't let Frankie talk her into this ride and hoping she wouldn't ruin her childhood Western fantasies by falling ignominiously off a gentle horse. She was sixty years old! No matter how much calcium she consumed, her bones were inexorably aging. She must concentrate on simply staying in the saddle, not on what kind of figure she cut seated there.

But when they drove away from Manzanita Lodge, her mind kept returning to Emma Gardner.

Frankie said, "I'd better top up," and pulled into a gas station.

And sitting in the car at the gas pumps, looking at the service bay, Bev suddenly remembered Mother laughing over the phone years and years ago, Mother phoning her in that young-marrieds ranch house in Connecticut and saying, "Emma is the most resourceful woman I know. She's been lonesome; she missed her son ever since he moved to Massachusetts and became too busy with his work and his hobby to come home often enough to suit her. Emma can't do anything about his work, but she can about his hobby, which is running in marathons. Emma has set about organizing a series of Gunthwaite marathons. He's coming home this weekend for the first and no doubt will run in them all, year after year."

Bev reached into her shirt and pulled up the pendant. Miracles Happen—Ask the Angels.

The angels had given her the answer.

She would buy Trulianne a garage.

5

"I'VE LANDED," BEV TOLD Snowy over her cell phone that rainy Sunday night, having waited to call until after she'd negotiated the Boston traffic's gleaming wet congestion and reached New Hampshire on I-93. "I'm back from the Wild West, and guess what? I rode a horse in a red rock canyon!"

Snowy asked, "Are you talking and driving?"

God, Snowy the worrier! Snowy would just have to lump it. Bev said, "Talking to you will keep me awake while I drive. The horseback ride was wonderful. Thank heavens the pace was leisurely."

Snowy harped, "It's raining. You can't pull over and talk?"

"*That* would be dangerous," Bev said repressively. "For the ride, I was worried they'd make me wear a helmet, which no heroine ever wore in any Western I ever saw, but Frankie bought me a Stetson on our way to the place, and that was fine with them. I looked the part as much as I could at age sixty in the twenty-first century. And even if the pace was slow and the guide unglamorous, I could pretend that the cowboy hero and I were stopping a stampede over a cliff, et cetera. The canyon felt so familiar I'm sure I've seen it in umpteen movies. Oh, at one restaurant Frankie and I went to, there were some movie stars' autographed photos—and one signed by Zachary Scott's stand-in!"

Snowy sighed. "You had fun?"

"Yes," Bev said. "Mostly. But Frankie asked me to marry him."

Silence, as Snowy digested this.

Bev said, "I suppose at my age a proposal is a feather in my cap—in my Stetson."

"First a renewal-of-vows proposal and now a marriage proposal. Feathers!"

It was Bev's turn to fall silent. Her car's headlights showed only the highway ahead. She could be driving anywhere. On the flight home, she had remembered how, during flights back to Ninfield after staying with dying Mother in Florida, she wanted to get off the plane somewhere in between and just disappear, so she wouldn't have to return to the wife-and-mother role in a household that Roger hadn't been able to control with her away, appliances and children rebelling. Finally she said, "I reminded Frankie that I'm already married, but he was persistent. He even suggested he'd move to New Hampshire."

"You didn't tell him about the vows renewal?"

"I kept losing my nerve and putting off telling him, and then after the proposal it would have been like kicking a man when he's down."

"So how did you leave things with him?"

"He's hoping I'll change my mind."

"Will you?"

"I *do* like the Southwest. But New Hampshire is home. And it's where Clem is. And the children are here—well, Massachusetts and Connecticut, too. Dumping Frankie face-to-face was just impossible; I'll have to write him a Dear John letter." Bev changed the subject. "Snowy, I had a psychic reading done, and it was hilarious!" She sped onward, regaling Snowy with the story, embellishing it but leaving out the desire for a channeling session. Snowy was giggling satisfyingly. Bev also left out the angels when she concluded, "However, the psychic experience inspired me with a great idea for another type of proposal. I'm going to find a garage for sale in the Gunthwaite area and entice Trulianne with this proposition: I'll buy it if she'll run it.

I'll be checking the real-estate listings, of course, but if you or Tom hear of any such garage, let me know."

Snowy said slowly, sounding stunned, "You're going to bank-roll Trulianne? You're going into the garage business? "

"When you think about it, there have been a lot of cars in our lives. It's not as if I know nothing about cars. Anyway, I don't have to fix the damn things. That'll be Trulianne's department. The point is, if I play this right I'll have a child's car seat in the back of this car!" Punchy, Bev laughed and laughed.

When she reached Waterlight at ten o'clock, she saw that Leon had turned on the outside lights for her. She didn't see Roger's SUV. Indoors, she found Leon coming into the hall to welcome her home.

He asked, "Have a good time?" and took her suitcase and vanity case.

She kissed him, her baby boy. Then, pulling off her jacket, tossing it on the hall bench, she said, "The scenery was gorgeous, and some of the meetings were very interesting. Is everything all right here?"

"Everything's fine."

As he started up the stairs with her luggage, she asked casually, "Did your father happen to come up this weekend?"

"Yeah."

"Oh?"

"Well, I guess so. I wasn't here. But when I came back this afternoon, I could tell." Leon continued up the stairs.

Although Bev felt drained now by the exhaustion she'd staved off during the drive home, she walked to the suite instead of going directly to the kitchen. In its sitting room were more boxes of books and Staples cartons of papers. In the bedroom, to which on earlier trips he'd brought other things from his Ninfield den, books, the mahogany coffee table, the Boston rocker, stereo equipment, racks of CDs and tapes, he had added boxes overflowing with magazines—even, she saw as she bent closer, old

*TV Guide*s, for God's sake. Was he doing any weeding out at all before he moved here?

He hadn't yet brought the hideous recliner and monster TV. No doubt he was saving the best for last.

Wearily, she went down the hall to the kitchen. Leon came in as she was making herself a comfort sandwich, marshmallow fluff and raspberry jam, which she and Snowy had invented when they were children.

"Look," Leon said. He opened the cupboard under the sink. On the back of the door was a little rack where she always hung her Playtex rubber gloves. Now they were firmly locked onto the rack by a clothespin.

Bev stared at the clothespin. The arrangement seemed vaguely familiar. She said, "I assume you didn't do that?"

"Nope."

"Well, I suppose my gloves do slip off occasionally. I suppose it can be annoying to you and your father."

Leon repeated, "Annoying." He gave a laugh and headed for the door. "I'm to bed. Good night, Mother."

Bev said absently, "Good night, darling." She was remembering that Amanda, her old friend and Roger's ex-mistress, used the clothespin trick with her dishwashing gloves.

Had Roger completely forgotten where he'd seen this bit of ingenuity? If not, had he thought that Bev would have forgotten? But then again, he didn't know that she knew about Amanda, thanks to Gretchen, did he? So it wouldn't matter if she connected the clothespin to Amanda.

Bev removed the clothespin, threw it in the wastebasket, took a bottle of chardonnay out of the fridge, and poured some into a wineglass. Carrying the glass and her sandwich plate, she went upstairs. She should eat, drink, and collapse into bed, but she walked past her bedroom to her office, where at the computer she searched the listings of businesses for sale. A small marina. Could Trulianne repair boat engines? A gas station-cum-convenience store. No, too complicated. Auto lube and repair, too expensive at $400,000. An auto repair shop for $275,000. Hmm.

Then she came upon: "Small engine sales and service business, with detached home. Business established in 1964. Yearly cash flow: $29,000. Yearly gross income: $244,000. Choice location in the heart of the Lakes Region, high traffic count, excellent visibility, paved parking lot. Products include well-known brand names such as Troy-Bilt. Service includes repairs and maintenance. House: 4 bedrooms, 2 ½ baths, family room with fireplace. Asking price, business premises and house: $249,000. Gile & LaBrecque Realty."

A business *and* a home! She had been intending to check apartments for rent, but the convenience of a house with the business would be perfect for Trulianne. She would phone Nick LaBrecque tomorrow. If Trulianne could fix automobile engines, surely she could fix small engines, couldn't she? She would have taken a course in small engines at the Eastbourne technical college, wouldn't she? But would she be any good at sales?

Misgivings assailed Bev. Second thoughts. She clicked off the computer. Was Trulianne capable of running a business?

As well as being stubborn, Trulianne did seem levelheaded (if you ignored her decision to conceive a child to raise alone).

But would men bring in chain saws and snowblowers to be repaired by a woman? Would they buy them from a woman? Women, however, also bought some of these things. Since her return to Gunthwaite, Leon made such purchases for her, but in previous years, because Roger wasn't interested, Bev herself had bought the household lawn mower, grass trimmer, leaf blower, hedge trimmer, and probably other items she'd forgotten. Eek, Leon, what if he went into this place and encountered Trulianne? Okay, well, so what if he did? But then she remembered that he'd got their latest leaf blower at Home Depot (competition!), and when the lawn mower had needed fixing he'd taken it to a place in Leicester that Mimi and Lloyd had recommended (more competition!).

Roger. The goddamned clothespin. To Frankie, these words had popped out about her marriage to Roger: "It's unconventional but it suits me." Why was she changing a situation that suited her and agreeing to be properly married again?

In bed at last, Bev suddenly remembered Roger's sweatshirt, one of those gray sweatshirts everyone had worn in high school, which he had worn on their second date when he'd picked her up in the Heap on a Friday night after working late at his uncle's grocery store. They had gone to Hooper's Dairy Bar and then had gone parking on the Cat Path, Gunthwaite's lovers' lane. The softness of that sweatshirt over his smooth muscles—it had been the most erotic sensation she had ever experienced at her ripe old age of fifteen.

She mustn't forget this ever again. This was what was important, their history together and their hot-and-bothered love, not the petty annoyances and irritating adjustments.

Trying to ignore jet lag, the next morning after her shower she went into her office in her bathrobe. As she phoned Nick LaBrecque, she pictured him at his desk at Gile & LaBrecque Realty, a rehabbed mill house on State Avenue. He was a bantam rooster of a man, pushing sixty and full of joie de vivre. Before he took up real estate, Nick had been a truck driver, and he still prided himself on knowing where all the restrooms in New Hampshire were. The first time Bev had ever dealt with him about some property, he had advised, "When in doubt, beautiful lady, go to a hospital. They've got plenty of bathrooms. I call it my emergency room!" And he had roared with laughter.

Characteristically, he was at work early and answered the phone himself. "Good morning! Nick LaBrecque here!"

"Hi, Nick," she said. "Bev Lambert. I've been reviewing your listings, and I'd like to see that small engine place. Could we meet there today?"

He said, "Your wish is my command, beautiful lady. What time?"

"Later this morning? Say, eleven?"

"If we could go to lunch together afterward."

Although Nick was very heavily married, he very heavily flirted whenever their paths crossed. It was tiresome, but she'd learned to turn this sort of thing to her own advantage. "Perhaps," she flirted back, and for her own amusement she made her coy face.

"I'll take that as a yes!" he said.

"Where is the place?"

"Doloff's Small Engine Sales and Service is on the Gunthwaite end of North Road, near Little Harbor. I'll bet you've driven past a million times."

North Road, Bev thought. That was indeed a main thoroughfare and one she traveled often. She certainly should know this place—but with Leon in charge of the equipment, she hadn't needed to notice small engine places. She should at least have noticed a for-sale sign, so probably the owner hadn't wanted one put up. Such a sign would be bad for business. She said, "I'll see you there. Thank you, Nick."

After they hung up, she gazed out the window beside her desk and realized that the lake was now unpopulated. Since she left for Sedona, people had removed their bob houses, which had to be off the ice by the first of April. She always both missed the entertaining winter activity on the stage of her bay and relished having the bay to herself for this respite before the summer people arrived. The ice looked treacherous, honeycombed. Sometimes the procrastinators left their bob houses out there until the last minute. What suspense!

She went back to her bedroom, into her closet, and deliberated. If she was going to be crawling around inspecting a garage

131

of some sort she ought to wear her most ancient jeans, but to keep Nick happy she would doll herself up a bit more.

At ten-thirty, wearing a magenta sweater and matching silk scarf with black jeans under her yellow slicker, she left Waterlight and drove to North Road. Rain still fell, and she thought of Southwest sunshine. She passed a strip mall containing a Laundromat, a diner, a dollar store; then along the road were 1950s ranch houses and small pre-World-War-II summer cottages and an occasional much older farmhouse in a field.

Then, beyond some woods, on the left she saw an unassuming weather-blackened sign: Doloff's Small Engine Sales & Service. No realtor's sign.

She pulled into the paved parking lot. Nick's car wasn't here yet; she sat in hers and looked through the rain at the property. On one side squatted a prefab building, its pallid metal walls growing stripes of rust. Ahead was a structure that had plainly started life as a very modest one-story cottage, white with blue trim. Over the front door an old handmade sign of birch-stick lettering on a blue board announced its summer-vacation name: Bide-a-Wee. A second story with ungainly dormers had been built above, and ells and porches and sheds had been added hither and thither, so the original cottage seemed to be a small creature peeking shyly out of a forest.

It dawned on her that in this haphazard house there was room for an apartment *and* a real-estate office. Her real-estate office. The house could be converted into these two purposes and serve other purposes, such as saving money and seeing Clem often.

For a wistful moment she thought of how she'd daydreamed of starting her real-estate business in the elegant house on Pleasant Street that Arlene's in-laws were leaving. She still hadn't sold it. She could still try to buy it. But for much less than the $350,000 they were asking she could buy Trulianne a business and a place to live, as well as buy herself a real-estate office—and now that she'd seen this place, she was sure she could get the price down further.

The house on Pleasant Street was the right setting for Beverly Lambert, Realtor. A rambling helter-skelter house beside a repair shop was not.

What if she flunked the broker's exam?

If she flunked and had to stay at Plumley Real Estate, she would still have moved Trulianne and Clem to Gunthwaite.

Out of her shoulder bag she lifted her Polaroid. She opened her window and photographed the repair shop and the house.

When Nick arrived in his Mercedes five minutes later, she was ready to start negotiating, but she went through all the motions and the flirting. She listened attentively as Nick explained that the owner of the business, who with his wife was spending this winter in Florida, had turned sixty-five and wanted to retire. She acted fascinated while Nick showed her all around the repair shop, as cold as a metal igloo and smelling of ingrained cigarette smoke. The house itself was kept heated, but just barely, and Mr. Doloff smoked here too, so it also stank, but she soldiered on. As they roamed the chilly rooms she asked incisive questions; she explored the cellar that had been dug under the cottage when it was winterized. And she agreed to go to lunch.

Nick said, "While we're at this end of town, how about the Schoolhouse Cafe?"

"Lovely," she said.

She followed his Mercedes up North Road past another stretch of woods, through which on the right several private driveways curved out of sight to old summer cottages and new McMansions on the lake. At Little Harbor, across from some public docks and a saucer of beach were an RV campground and an ice-cream stand, both closed now, and a minimart and the gray-shingled cafe. Once upon a time the Schoolhouse Cafe had been a one-room schoolhouse. Sold long before anybody thought about preservation, it had been transformed almost beyond recognition, though Bev always fancied she could perceive vestiges of the separate doors for girls and boys. Inside, the overhead music was from the more recent past—the Mamas and the Papas singing "Monday, Monday"—but the decor was a mixture of old slates, school bells, and such, plus old farm implements. Bev usually imagined a potbellied stove whose stovepipe ran across the room, keeping the children from freezing, and whenever she sat down in a booth she imagined them seated at primitive desks in their homespun clothes, but today she imagined bringing Trulianne and Clem here.

After the waitress had taken Bev's order for a baby spinach salad and Nick's for a Reuben on rye, Nick placed a folder of papers on the table and said, "Well, beautiful lady, can I ask what you've got in mind about Doloff's?"

She had decided that when the moment came, she would be straightforward. There was too much riding on this to play wheeler-dealer. Or was she wrong, was so much riding on this that she should use all the tricks she'd learned? She reached for the folder. "May I?"

"Be my guest."

She took her glasses out of her shoulder bag. Sipping the iced tea the waitress brought, she read the material, skimming and studying while Nick hummed softly to the music, Beatles, John Denver, Gladys Knight and the Pips. She settled on being as candid as possible at this stage of the game. So over their meal she explained to Nick that she was interested in buying the place herself for an investment and that a mechanic friend would be running the business and living in the house. "But of course she'll have to see it before a decision is made."

"*She?*" said Nick.

Bev twinkled at him, while fearing that his reaction was all too typical. "And what," she asked lightly, "is wrong with a woman mechanic?"

"Not a thing!" he replied hastily.

When Bev drove away from the cafe, she was agonizing over the next step: how to get Trulianne here. Phone her? Go to see her at the Kitchen Garden or Bungalow Court? Invite her to

Waterlight without telling her about the place and then, should a miracle happen and Trulianne accept the invitation, take her on a sightseeing ride that just happened to stop at Doloff's Small Engine Sales and Service?

En route to Plumley's to catch up on work, she pulled into the Abnaki Mall to drop off some dry cleaning. As she was walking past Indulgences, she glanced in and saw the white signs on the wall listing the wares in gold lettering. A specialty, a tradition taken over from the old Vachon's Bakery, was tourtière—Canadian meat pie, pork pie. It was pronounced tootkay. Roger's mother used to make the family version, as did Mémère, his grandmother, but the recipe had never been written down until the last years of his mother's life, when Roger had asked Bev to get it and also Mémère's recipe for salmon pie. So Bev had sat in the Montreal kitchen taking notes while his mother cooked. And Bev had made the meat pie and salmon pie when she wanted to give Roger a treat. How long had it been since she'd made either one? Fifteen years? But the recipes were still in her recipe file box.

Bev didn't go on to Plumley's. She went to the supermarket and bought ground pork and ground beef.

Roger. If Trulianne and Clem came to live in Gunthwaite, he would *have* to be told.

It was raining again the next afternoon as Bev drove to Eastbourne. A wicker pie basket rode on the backseat. Attached by a little-boy-blue ribbon to the handle was a recipe card on which she had written:

135

Mémère's Tourtière à la Bev

Prepare pastry for a 9" two-crust pie.

In a Dutch oven, brown:
> ½ lb. ground pork
> ½ lb. ground beef

Add:
> ½ c. water
> salt and pepper

Bring to a boil and simmer 1 hour, adding more water if necessary.

Chop 1 onion.
Peel and slice 1 large potato.
Add to meat mixture and cook until onion and potato are done.
Drain mixture.
Mash with a potato masher.

Add:
> 1 t. cinnamon
> 1 t. ground cloves
> 1 t. nutmeg

Fill piecrust and cover with second crust.

Bake at 350° about 45 minutes.

Was the rain letting up some? She saw a field of robins. Although spring was officially here, some local weather forecasters liked to warn that April was a winter month in New Hampshire. So the robins' return seemed like a harbinger.

She had aimed for a grandmotherly look to her clothes today but knew she hadn't quite succeeded in a loon sweatshirt and navy blue pants beneath her slicker, low-cut L. L. Bean boots on her feet. Well, she couldn't have worn an apron, could she? Her white hair was certainly grandmotherly. She had decided against asking Snowy to accompany her this time. Snowy was too busy, with Ruhamah's birthday tomorrow and the departure for Scotland Friday, and besides, Snowy's Eastbourne know-how was no longer needed. Also, although Bev might still want Snowy's moral support, for once Bev didn't want an audience. If this trip amounted to nothing or if it was a disaster . . .

She parked at the Seacoast Mall. Carrying the basket, she went inside and scouted the food court. Trulianne wasn't at the Kitchen Garden; two other women were working there. Bev couldn't tell if either was the one who'd worked with Trulianne last time. In case Trulianne was off on a break, she said to the nearest woman, "Is Trulianne working today?"

"She isn't working here, period."

Bev stared at the woman.

The woman said, "Are you a friend of hers?"

"Yes."

"You didn't know she'd gotten canned?"

"No."

"It's too bad but she kind of asked for it." The woman looked past Bev at an arriving customer. "Can I help you?"

The customer said to Bev, "Excuse me."

Bev moved aside, stood there, then walked out of the mall. She had an awful feeling she knew why Trulianne had been fired.

Then, as she drove to Bungalow Court, she realized that Trulianne was now more vulnerable and might more easily be persuaded. Trulianne couldn't find a mechanic job and she couldn't even keep a food-court job.

But if Trulianne had lost the Kitchen Garden job because of taking the Disney World trip, she would blame and hate Bev, the serpent who had tempted her.

In front of the Hughes bungalow a car was parked, the old VW Bev had last seen at Waterlight. She parked behind it and sat, scared. She touched her pendant. Miracles happen, she told herself; ask the angels.

Then she inhaled a deep breath, exhaled, reached for her shoulder bag, got out of her car, and, much as she'd seen Trulianne's mother do here, she leaned into the backseat. Carrying the pie basket, she crossed the sidewalk and went up the front walk to the crooked little porch. The red sled was gone. For a second she panicked—maybe Clem no longer lived here!—but then she reasoned that it was April, robins had returned, sledding had ended. She lifted the wrought-iron door knocker, which was shaped like a whale, and tapped it twice.

While she waited, she saw herself from far away, a supplicant on this front porch. What paths through the years had led her to this spot?

She tapped the knocker again, louder, and waited again, wondering if she was being observed from one of the windows.

The door opened and Trulianne stood there in jersey and jeans. She didn't seem devastated by the loss of the Kitchen Garden job. She seemed her usual self, small and sturdy—and stubborn.

"Hi," Bev said inadequately. When Trulianne didn't reply, she continued, "May I come in?" and stepped forward, barging right into the living room, which was densely furnished in what looked like Ethan Allen, much polished, the upholstery on the sofa and armchairs well-worn but sprucely vacuumed. The walls were beaverboard painted cream; in the acoustical-tile ceiling were recessed lights; under her feet lay yellow ocher wall-to-wall carpeting. The sight of an open blue toy box heaped with

Clem's possessions emphasized the importance and uncertainty of her mission and unnerved her again. In a dry sink in front of a window, houseplants were thriving. Bev touched the leaf of a prayer plant and remembered how, one of the days before Mother committed suicide, Mother had told her not to bother adopting any of the houseplants except the orchid on a shelf on the front porch of Mother's Florida bungalow. After Mother's death, during all the turmoil of putting the bungalow up for sale, selling Mother's car, and hiring movers to transport the best furniture and other treasures to Ninfield, Bev forgot that request. But as she was leaving for the last time, weeping as she carried her suitcase out the door, the orchid leapt into her arms. It had actually seemed to hurl itself off the shelf. She had dropped the suitcase and caught it. The phenomenon had been too eerie—and personal—to tell anybody about, even Snowy. Should she have confided in Aurora in Sedona?

Clem was Mother's great-grandson. Roger's Mémère's great-great-grandson. Bev held up the basket and announced, "I've brought a part of my grandson's heritage."

This startled Trulianne into speech. "A pie basket?"

"Its contents. Tourtière, made from Clem's great-great-grandmother's recipe." Bev waggled the recipe card. "I've brought the recipe for you. Is that the kitchen?" She headed for the doorway.

Trulianne followed.

Parts of the kitchen had obviously been renovated over the years, most recently by vinyl flooring. But the Hugheses had had the sense to keep the original cupboards and cabinets, which were made of narrow beaded vertical boards. Painted canary yellow. Gram certainly did love yellow. However, the refrigerator and stove were from the avocado era and the dishwasher from the almond. On the fridge, magnets held riotous finger paintings. Oh, how Bev coveted those! The wall clock was a sunny smiley face. An old pedestal table filled the center of the room, its leaf in, seven chairs elbow-to-elbow around it, one containing a booster seat. A sideboard had been "antiqued" during that particular refinishing craze, maybe in the 1960s. Bev remembered antiquing a bookcase, painting it pale green and then wiping off the paint with a cloth, and she pictured Gram doing the same here, only in this antique yellow. The cafe curtains at the windows were a mattress-ticking fabric that reminded her of a dress she'd had in high school, except these of course were yellow. Red geraniums bloomed on windowsills, so Gram was like Puddles's mother and could keep geraniums going year-round. One of the windows was over the sink; Mother always said there had to be a window over a kitchen sink or else you'd go mad doing dishes. The view out this window and the window of the back door beside it showed a small backyard in which stood a little bright-hued plastic gym set. Bev imagined Clem playing on it, crawling through the tunnel under the slide. With all her heart she wanted a gym set.

She put the basket on the counter. A door to the left stood open, and she saw the infamous one bathroom, which was also the laundry room. On the wall beside the toilet a little rack cozily held a copy of *Reader's Digest*. A buff-colored cat slept on the dryer. The maw of the dryer and the stack of clothes on the washing machine were evidence that Bev had interrupted Trulianne folding laundry. Bev asked, "Is Clem napping?"

Continuing to look mulish, Trulianne said, "Yes."

Don't let on, Bev told herself, don't let on you know she's been fired. Bev plunked her shoulder bag down on the counter, took off her slicker, and hung it on one of the pegs near the back door. From the shoulder bag she extracted her glasses case and a folder. She sat down at the table and began to spread out papers and photographs "I'd like to invest in this business, but I need someone to run it. It's a small engine repair shop that also sells some equipment. Here are pictures of it. They were taken in the rain so they don't do it justice. Here are the figures, the inventory, and such." She sensed Trulianne moving toward her. Softly, softly, catchee monkey. "And here are pictures of the house that comes with the shop." She added cunningly, "Two bathrooms and a half bath."

Trulianne stood at the table. Very slowly she picked up the photos and examined them. Then she sank into the chair next to Bev and began to read the paperwork. Bev watched the cat rise and stretch, stretch, stretch, the way she knew she herself should before and after the treadmill but seldom did.

Now Trulianne was again holding a photo of the house. "Does the sign really say Bide-a-Wee?"

"The house was originally a summer cottage."

"The address on the papers. The place is in Gunthwaite?"

Bev tried a diversionary tactic. "Can you repair these kinds of engines?"

"Yes. It's in Gunthwaite?"

Well, Bev had known there was no way to get around this. "It is, in a very good location—"

Trulianne put the photo down.

Bev rushed on, "—at the north end of town on a main road that goes past the lake. Why don't you come up and see it? You and Clem could come back with me this afternoon and spend the night at Waterlight, or you could drive up tomorrow, if your schedule allows. See what you think of the place. If it doesn't suit you, then that's that." Not for long, Bev thought; I'll keep hunting.

The cat undulated down off the dryer and strolled into the kitchen.

Bev said, "Hello there. What's your name?"

Trulianne snatched the cat onto her lap. "Her name is Goldie. Mrs. Lambert, I've told you over and over. Leon and I had a deal. No strings. Separate spaces."

Bev tried to sound reasonable, tried not to plead or wheedle. "Gunthwaite is a city, and the odds are you wouldn't run into each other. Even if you did, you could still stay separate, keep yourselves to yourselves."

Trulianne ignored that and said bluntly, "Besides, an engine

141

repair shop? You wouldn't be thinking of buying a business like this if you weren't trying to get me and Clem to Gunthwaite."

It didn't take much acting effort for Bev to make tears pour down her face.

"Oh shit." Trulianne jumped up, and the cat, forgotten, leapt for the back door. "Oh shit, oh shit, oh shit."

Bev sat and sobbed. This was what had happened when she first met Trulianne, but those tears had sprung unbidden.

Trulianne ran to the back door. Was she bolting, leaving Bev alone with Clem? No. Trulianne let the cat out and stood there looking into the yard, her shoulders squared, strong. Yet her voice was shaky as she said, "Mrs. Lambert—Bev—I appreciate what you're doing. It's unbelievable, what you're doing. And I know you love Clem and want to spoil him rotten the way grandmothers are supposed to. But look at it from my point of view. It's, like, charity. I was brought up to be self-reliant. I know that sounds stupid, here I am living back at home. But."

Bev stood up, went to the counter, and rooted in her shoulder bag for a Kleenex. She had hoped to avoid until later the subject of her office in the Bide-a-Wee house and her close proximity. "Trulianne, you'd be helping *me* out. I'm going to be needing an office of my own, a real-estate office"—knock on wood, Bev thought, drying her eyes, careful not to smear mascara—"so I've been trying to figure out how to swing it. Part of the house can be my office, and the rest would be your home. Yours and Clem's. With this arrangement, when you're on your feet financially you'll be paying me rent for the house and repair shop and helping me offset my costs."

Trulianne turned and regarded her. "You'd have an office there?"

"That's the idea. For *your* office, there's an area in the repair shop."

After a moment, Trulianne observed cautiously, "Sounds like family. Us working out of the same place."

"Well . . ."

From upstairs came a little shout: "Mom!"

Trulianne shouted back, "Okay, sweetie, just a sec!" She touched the pie basket, the recipe card. "I made your meat loaf. Everybody loved it."

Bev smiled tremulously. The meat-loaf recipe *had* established a relationship, as she had hoped. More hopes rose.

But Trulianne said, "I told my mom I found the recipe online."

Hopes dashed, Bev clutched the Kleenex.

Then Trulianne said, "I'll drive up with Clem tomorrow and see what I think. I'm not promising anything."

If, Bev thought, I had been a cheerleader, I could do a cartwheel right now. Well, no. Neither Snowy nor Puddles could manage that anymore. Bev breathed, "Thank you, Trulianne," and tried to let this triumph be enough, but she looked at the ceiling with the best yearning-grandmother face she could manage.

Trulianne volunteered an update. "He's talking more. His favorite word is 'no.'"

"Ah, the 'terrible twos.' Or don't they call it that nowadays?"

Trulianne hesitated and then asked, "Want to help me get him up?"

That evening at Waterlight, in her office Bev finally found a chance to look at the day's mail she'd brought in from the mailbox. The reply cards had begun arriving before her Sedona trip, including acceptances from Roger's sisters and brothers, Snowy and Tom, Ruhamah and D. J., Charl and Dudley, Darl and Bill, and Puddles. On her reply card Puddles had written in, "I'll wear my maid-of-honor dress. I saved it all these years because

143

it's just my color, ha ha!" In 1959, planning her wedding, Bev had originally decided on blue for the maid-of-honor's dress, to match Snowy's eyes, and planned other sweet pastels for the bridesmaids and flower girl. But Snowy had declined the honor, citing a couple of reasons: (1) Bennington's classes went on to the end of June, leaving Snowy no free time to come to Gunthwaite for fittings and the rehearsal and other preliminaries; (2) Snowy claimed she couldn't afford the dress, a dubious reason because Snowy's parents would of course have bought it for her, but Snowy stuck to the flimsy excuse and wouldn't let Bev pay either. So Bev had asked Puddles to be maid of honor instead of a bridesmaid and switched the color scheme to sophisticated lime green for her and also for the two remaining bridesmaids and even the flower girl. Puddles had complained that Bev had chosen a shade to make them look at death's door, so Bev herself would look more radiant.

Bev had found a role for Snowy at the wedding, overseeing the guest book at the reception. Although Bev had feared she might wear something bohemian, Snowy was demure in a blue sheath and wide-brimmed straw hat trimmed with cornflowers, with blue ribbons hanging down the back. Yet despite the conventional outfit, Snowy had appeared footloose and fancy-free to Bev, now Mrs. Roger Lambert, hitched, the knot tied, the little woman, the old ball and chain.

Here were two more reply envelopes, and also a regular note-card envelope addressed in her roommate's handwriting, with Ann's Lake Forest return address. Bev picked up the silver letter opener that had belonged to Mother and slit Ann's envelope. Probably Ann thought the reply card too formal and thus was replying in a more personal way.

At Katharine Gibbs, Ann's ambition had been to be the private secretary to a globe-trotting employer, but her first job had taken her to Chicago, where she had fallen for the son of the owner of a Ford dealership, and after their marriage she'd settled down to suburban life, caring for him and their two sons. Eventually her husband had inherited and expanded the business. By now he was semiretired, and Ann's Christmas and birthday cards to Bev recounted tours and cruises. At last, Ann was globe-trotting! Bev pulled out the note card, a reproduction of a Monet garden painting. Ann had actually been to Giverny two years ago, had seen the real garden at Giverny with her own eyes.

Inside, Ann wrote, "This vows renewal is a wonderful idea. Thank you so much for inviting us. But I'm afraid we won't be able to attend the great event. I didn't want to mention health problems on my Christmas card. Not the season for such news. It's breast cancer. My left breast. Remember when we were so worried about the size of our breasts? I've had a lumpectomy. Now radiation. The prognosis is hopeful, my hopes are high. But I've got to save all my energy for this battle, so we can't make the trip to New Hampshire, much as I would love to. Why did I waste travel time on faraway trips while always figuring you and I would get together 'one of these days'? Isn't it funny how busy we think we are, when we're really wasting time until there's not much left. I'll be at your ceremony in spirit, toasting you and Roger. Love, Ann."

Even if Bev hadn't cried herself out at Trulianne's, she couldn't have now. The shock was beyond tears. She sat immobile, her mind blank.

After a while, thoughts crept in. She reminded herself about Miranda, her housecleaner, who was doing so well. And Irene, who'd worked at Snowy's store, who after a mastectomy had hit the open road in an RV with her sister to see America.

But Frankie's wife, Janet, had died.

Bev reached for the phone to call Puddles, nurse practitioner. Puddles would know the latest details about the treatment of breast cancer. But on *Today* and *Good Morning America* and other shows there were always segments that kept you informed—kept you abreast. She was appalled by a jolt of laughter over her pun. No, it wasn't heartlessness, it was near hysteria.

Should she phone Ann? Ann had chosen to write, not phone. That would be safer, more controlled. Not an e-mail. They had never exchanged e-addresses; Bev didn't know if Ann used a computer. She must write a real letter back, and she should do it tonight. What in the world could she say?

She hadn't been able to write Frankie yet, e-mail or otherwise.

Postponing both letters, she opened the reply envelopes and considered phoning Snowy. She hadn't yet asked Snowy to write her vow. She wished she could ask her to write Ann and Frankie too. That was out of the question. Could she tell Snowy about Ann without breaking down? But Snowy shouldn't be upset by any bad news before her trip. Don't call her now, Bev told herself, and don't mention it during the bon-voyage call on Thursday. Bon voyage. Snowy was getting into an airplane and flying from Boston to Glasgow. What if there was a plane crash? Snowy might die. Ann might be dying. All of us, Bev thought, we are all staring death in the face, one way or another. We are all at death's door.

The cards were two more acceptances, one from Roger's roommate—and eek, the other from Geoff! Bev had thought Geoff would invent a convenient excuse. At the office, he hadn't mentioned receiving the invitation, so she'd decided he was just plain ignoring her vows renewal. But here he was accepting, as a single, not bringing a guest.

Out of the blue came a daring idea: How about inviting Trulianne and her parents? And Clem.

She remembered the sight of Clem upstairs in Trulianne's bedroom, standing up jouncing and laughing in a toddler bed with side rails beside Trulianne's girlhood bed. He had looked directly at Bev and recited with dramatic emphasis, "If you were a bee and a bull sat on *you*, what would *you* do?"

Trulianne said, "We were reading about Ferdinand before his nap."

But Trulianne didn't need to explain to Bev, mother of four, who promptly made her angry bee face, buzzing and stinging, and then became Ferdinand snorting and bellowing. When Clem's giggles subsided, Bev asked him, "Remember Gaga?"

"No. No? Gaga!" And he lifted his arms to her.

As she hugged the memory the way she'd hugged him, there returned the worry that had accompanied her on her drive back from Eastbourne. Had Trulianne been lying about coming up to Gunthwaite tomorrow? Had she just said that to get rid of Bev? Trulianne had refused to meet at Waterlight, so Bev had written out the directions to North Road and the repair shop. Would Trulianne not show up at the appointed time, eleven o'clock?

She picked up Ann's Monet note card and held it.

In the repair shop, carrying Clem, Trulianne sniffed disgustedly at the cigarette smoke and pulled up the collar of his little blue fleece jacket around his interested face.

Bev said hastily, "I'm sorry, I should have warned you. The house also smells. I'll get professionals to take care of this problem. I've done it many times with places I'm selling."

Trulianne didn't answer. She inspected the repair shop without any comment except murmurs to Clem. Bev hadn't yet dared ask to hold him; she was too happy, too delirious with relief that Trulianne had shown up, to risk annoying her.

Finally Trulianne said, "The owner's been letting things go."

Bev apologized, "Retirement was overtaking him."

"Okay. The house?"

They went back outdoors into the sunny morning. Under his jacket Clem wore a striped rugby jersey and denim overalls with a dinosaur on the bib, and Trulianne was wearing a lined denim

147

jacket over a sweater and denim jeans. Bev hoped it was a good sign that she herself had been inspired to wear denim, the silk denim skirt from Sedona, with a carved leather vest from Santa Fe and an old white shirt. Unbuttoning her black car coat as they crossed the parking lot to the house's front walk, she said, "Warmer outside than in. The heat is on low in the house, so it won't be quite so cold there. But would you like a blanket for Clem? I've got one in the car."

Trulianne asked Clem, "Are you warm enough?"

He beamed. "No."

Trulianne laughed. Oh, a *good* sign! Bev didn't pursue the blanket idea but said, "If he needs a bathroom, the water is on in the house." She unlocked the front door. "The place has been enlarged over the years without much rhyme or reason. This hall was added on with this ell." The hall was partly blocked by what must be a lawn ornament brought indoors at the last minute when the Doloffs left for Florida, a wooden burro sporting a sombrero and hooked up to a cart of red plastic flowers.

"Donkey!" cried Clem, reaching.

Trulianne said, "It's not a toy, sweetie." Clem looked suddenly mutinous, but Trulianne wiggled distracting fingers in his face and promised, "You can play with your trucks soon."

"Soon?"

"Soon."

Bev said, "The original part of the house starts here on the right." As they stepped into the low-ceilinged living room, she explained, "I'm thinking of having my office in these downstairs rooms at the front. The living room, the dining room, and the side porch off the dining room. And the half bath under the stairs out in the hall. The rest will be yours." Tentatively, Bev stroked Clem's curls and asked Trulianne, "May I hold him?"

"God, this cigarette stench, let's make it quick." But Trulianne transferred him to Bev before she began prowling fast.

148

Bev followed, Clem held close, remembering how she'd grown up in a house full of cigarette smoke, as had Snowy and most of the kids she knew. The good old days.

The Doloffs went in for tiny floral patterns on wallpaper and upholstery and lots of framed photos of their five children and numerous grandchildren. The kitchen beyond the dining room was probably double the size it had been in its cottage days, with an old pantry whose shelves were frilly with shelving paper, and off it were both a full bathroom and a laundry room. Also a back porch. As Bev and Clem hurried after Trulianne into the ell for the "family room with fireplace" and a sewing room and a bedroom, Bev sensed Trulianne spreading her wings; when they climbed the stairs to the three other bedrooms and the upstairs bathroom, she thought that Trulianne might flap with joy.

Of course not. "It's humongous," Trulianne said. "It must cost a fortune to heat."

"The rooms that aren't used can be closed off in the winter. I'm sure the Doloffs have been doing that since their children left home." How crafty, a reminder of Trulianne's home where the children had returned or, in the case of one brother, had never left. "And who knows, in time I may need more room. We can adjust as we go—"

"Go potty," Clem said.

Trulianne scooped him out of Bev's arms and headed for the bathroom. "Meet you outdoors."

Bev went downstairs, but instead of escaping from the cigarette smell she stepped back into the living room. A well-prepared real-estate agent, she always kept in her shoulder bag a tape measure, just as in her car she kept a measuring wheel for checking property lines, and now she whipped out the tape measure, a notepad, a pen, and measured the windows for curtains. She would place her desk kitty-corner near the door where she could see out the front windows. If she should have salespeople working for her, their desks would be toward the farther wall. In the dining room, she measured the windows and imagined filing cabinets, fax and copying machines and such, along with a conference table not from an office-supply store but some marvelous discovery unearthed at an antique shop. To her amazement, she realized she was also imagining Lorraine Fitch here. Lorraine, her archrival! Why would Lorraine leave Plumley's to work for Bev Lambert? Why, for that matter, hadn't Lorraine become a broker and started her own business?

Probably, Bev thought, because Lorraine knew it was a crazy thing to do. Utterly idiotic. Fear spurted up, choking her. She was committed now, and it was giving her acid reflux!

But she'd be off the hook if Trulianne decided not to accept the offer. She could drop the whole idea of luring Trulianne to Gunthwaite. She could forget her broker hopes.

Bev thrust the tape measure and notes into her shoulder bag, rushed outdoors, and gulped the fresh air, looking around at this tacky place.

Trulianne came out carrying Clem. She set him down but held him firmly by the hand. "The traffic."

"I'd put up a fence, and you'd teach him." Bev ventured, "How about lunch? I'll show you Little Harbor nearby. There's a nice cafe that used to be a one-room schoolhouse."

As Trulianne hesitated, Clem reminded her, "Trucks."

"Okay," Trulianne said to Clem and to Bev.

So, after Bev drove up North Road, Trulianne following in the old VW, it was as she'd daydreamed when she was at the cafe with Nick: She sat in a booth with Trulianne and Clem opposite, Clem on a booster seat supplied by the waitress and playing with his miniature dump truck.

Bev said, "Aren't little boys funny! Trucks. It was the same with Leon and Dick." Oops, a gaffe, mentioning Leon. She hastened on, "My friend Puddles—that's her nickname because her maiden name is Pond, she's Jean Pond Cram—" Oh God, was this another gaffe, mentioning maiden and married names? "Puddles calls it the vroom-vroom gene." Was this yet another gaffe, one that implied Trulianne was masculine if she was interested in vehicles? Blushing, embarrassed, Bev remembered Snowy's wisecrack about lesbians. Mercifully, at this moment the waitress brought Clem's milk, Trulianne's Pepsi, and Bev's iced tea. Squeezing her lemon wedge, onward Bev plunged, "Names are so fascinating. Yours, for instance. It's lovely. Where did it come from?"

"My mother had the hots for a singer named Guy Mitchell."

Bev stared at her, perplexed.

Trulianne seemed to enjoy the reaction. She didn't explain further, and there was silence, except for Clem's vrooming, the chat of customers in neighboring booths, and the overhead music, which at the moment was Petula Clark singing "Downtown." And then Bev was downtown in her memory, putting a precious dime out of her allowance into a jukebox at Hooper's or Sweetland to play a Guy Mitchell song. In junior high, early 1950s? She'd have to ask Snowy. They had both loved Guy Mitchell, and when one of his songs came on the Gunthwaite radio station or a Boston station, they would turn up the volume, songs like— She went blank.

The waitress brought a tray of Clem's grilled cheese, Trulianne's roast-beef wrap, and Bev's Greek salad.

Bev cried, "'My Truly, Truly Fair'!"

The waitress gaped at her as if she'd lost her marbles.

Trulianne said, "You got it."

Bev said to the waitress, "Thank you, everything looks delicious," and to Trulianne she said, "I loved that song! But I'd forgotten all about it. Your mother, did she actually *know* Guy Mitchell?"

"No, she was just a fan. Her middle name is Anne, so she changed things around to that. See, Clem, your grilled cheese is all nice and gooey."

He crowed, "Nice and gooey!"

Bev asked, "What are your parents' names?", even though she already knew, from the Eastbourne phone book.

"Mom is Shirley, Dad's Everett. Your pie was delicious, Mrs.

Lambert. We all enjoyed it. I told them who you were and how you'd come down to see Clem. I didn't tell them about today."

Clem said, "Gooey and Huey and Dewey and Louie. Gooey and Goofy. Mickey!"

"Guess what," Trulianne said wryly. "We went to Disney World."

Bev fussed with her salad. "I hope you both had fun."

"It was incredible. I ought to have written to thank you. Well, better late than never. Thank you. Clem, thank your Gaga for the trip to Disney World."

"No," said Clem. "Thank you."

"You're very welcome," Bev said, treasuring the "your Gaga."

Trulianne said, "I told my mom and dad that a friend had won the trip and couldn't use it. I told the Kitchen Garden there was a family emergency and I had to take some days off. They were cool."

So Trulianne was exercising tact. She wasn't going to let Bev know that someone at the Kitchen Garden had found out about the trip. She wouldn't let Bev feel to blame. Bev did still feel guilty as hell, but gratitude and respect were mixed in.

With a paper napkin, Trulianne tidied Clem's face. Concentrating on the chore, she went on, "And thank you for finding this place for him and me. If you really want to do it, I'll give it my best shot."

Trulianne was saying yes. Bev was not off the hook She had to forge ahead and buy the Doloff home and business. Christine, her accountant, would think she'd gone stark raving mad. She remembered how Aurora had talked about a new aspect of her career, advising, "Go ahead with confidence." Bev had assumed she meant the broker career. But had Aurora been foreseeing investment in a small engine repair shop? Not likely. Perhaps, however, she should listen to that tape Aurora had made of the psychic reading, seeking nuances.

Bev said, "I really want to do it."

"What about Leon? Will you tell him about our plans?"

Our! They were in this together, not as mother-in-law and daughter-in-law, not yet anyway, but connected. "Let's wait awhile, don't you think?"

Trulianne nodded emphatically, and Clem copied her.

Bev said, "This afternoon I'll see the broker who listed the place and get things moving as fast as possible. Could I have your e-mail address and your phone number? What do you think the new name of the shop should be? And what would you and Clem like for dessert?"

"I don't know about the shop's name, but can we keep the Bide-a-Wee sign on the house? Reminds me of cottages at home."

"Dessert," said Clem.

Snowy said, "Doloff's! Tom goes there now and then. I didn't realize it's for sale. You've *bought* it?"

Into her phone in her Waterlight office, Bev said, "It will soon become the Lakes Region Small Engine Sales and Service." This was her bon-voyage call to Snowy on the following evening, Thursday. During the negotiations yesterday afternoon and today, she had got the price down from $249,000 to $225,000 but she still felt terrified—and clandestine. She had asked Nick to be discreet about her purchase, saying she considered her investment a private matter; she fervently hoped Geoff wouldn't learn of it. However, she also felt exhilarated. Her desk was layered with sheets of paper full of her scribbles, floor-plan sketches, color-scheme notes, and on top was the latest Pottery Barn catalogue, open to office furniture. It would be tempting fate to order anything before she took the exam. But she had decided to rent that office space to somebody if she flunked and couldn't use it herself, and for that the two rooms, half bath, and side porch would have to be cleaned up and painted, same as if she were using them, and thus it was okay to choose paint colors. Probably the exteriors of both the house and the shop should be painted too. She said, "Please ask Tom to keep patronizing the shop. And if, knock on wood, I pass the broker's exam, I'll have my office in the downstairs front of the house."

"Really? On the same premises as Trulianne and Clem?"

Bev laughed uncertainly. "Am I not clever?"

"Trulianne didn't have any objections?"

"I guess I made her an offer she couldn't refuse."

"But Bev, what if Leon goes in there to buy a new weed whacker or something?"

"He never patronized it when it was Doloff's. And so what if he and Trulianne do meet?" Time to change the subject. "Is your packing done?"

"We're fighting about the hiking boots. Tom claims it'd be simpler to wear them on the plane so they won't take up room in our luggage. I refuse to sit for hours over the Atlantic in hiking boots. Those seats are uncomfortable enough without that."

Bev said, "You could take them off once you're seated and fly in your socks."

"I know." Snowy sighed. "We've been around that. But the floor space is so cramped."

"Are you excited?"

"I'm past that now. Now it's details and checking our tickets every other minute. Bev, will Trulianne be living in Gunthwaite without Roger knowing anything about her and Clem?"

"I'm going one step at a time here. Sort of. Crossing each bridge as I come to it." So many bridges! "Do you remember Guy Mitchell?"

"The singer?"

"When were we listening to his songs?"

154

As usual, Snowy was quick to catch on. "'My Truly, Truly Fair'! Is that where Trulianne's name comes from?"

"Her mother was a fan. Were we in junior high?"

"Let me think." Snowy hummed the tune. "Yes, junior high. Remember 'The Roving Kind' and 'My Heart Cries for You'? Then some others in later years—'Singing the Blues,' remember?"

"I'd've been going out with Frankie then, in junior high."

"Frankie and lots of others. Remember how we'd go to the movies in gangs of girls and boys in those years and then pair off? Remember all the pajama parties?"

"And the arrival of Puddles in eighth grade. That certainly was a milestone. Well," Bev said. "Bon voyage. Tell Tom I want a photo of you eating haggis. Thank you again for the birthday card." Snowy had sent it early, because she'd be away, and like Bev she had chosen a sentimental one, hers with birds and flowers. God, they *were* getting old. "I'll miss you, Snowy. Two whole weeks! I hope you have a glorious time."

"In about two months, you'll be emoting in Stratford!"

After they hung up, Bev thought: Two months. It was all approaching too fast, and between now and June lay the broker's exam. She put her face in her hands. What have I done? Lakes Region Small Engine Sales and Service! What have I got myself into? And what do I tell Roger?

She picked up the phone again, tapped Mimi's number, and said, "Hi, darling. Could I come see you tomorrow about placing an order for five sets of curtains?"

"Wow," Mimi said. "You're redoing Waterlight for the vows renewal? You'll want them done by June?"

"Would that be possible?"

"Yes, if you've got any clout with the weaver, which I do believe you have."

"Thank you, Mimi. I'll stop by in the morning."

"See you then. Bye."

Bev looked at the jotted measurements. The curtains would

155

be too short for Waterlight's living-room windows. They wouldn't fit the dining-room windows either. But they were close enough for her bedroom and office, so she'd pretend that's what she was redoing.

Out of the bottom drawer she took the plastic case containing the psychic-reading tape. Then she laughed and put it back.

6

"I'LL FOLLOW SNOWY'S EXAMPLE," Bev e-mailed Roger, her teeth gritted as she typed, "and give myself a birthday present of time. A quiet day."

On April 17, the eve of her birthday, she was replying with restraint to his e-mail she'd just discovered, in which he said he wouldn't be coming up tomorrow—Tuesday—for the occasion after all. He would be up this weekend instead, arriving Friday afternoon, and some of those members of the Class of 1955 who still lived in Gunthwaite would join him at Waterlight Saturday afternoon for a reunion-planning meeting.

Her reply was restrained, yes, but her thoughts were steaming, scalding, scathing. How considerate he was! He hadn't phoned her to tell her about changing the birthday plans and inviting all these classmates to Waterlight. What if she hadn't checked her e-mail? But he knew that she, a businessperson, checked it often. And oh, he'd added at the end, his present would be delivered tomorrow. Whoopee.

She tried to calm down. Wouldn't she really prefer a birthday all to herself?

"So don't worry," she concluded, even though he certainly didn't seem to be worrying. "I'll have fun enjoying my quiet day. Love, Bev."

After she sent the message, she looked again at the other message she'd found tonight, a ribald e-card from Puddles.

Sending a cyberspace birthday card was a first for the triumvirate. Then she took off her glasses and went down to the kitchen, where she moved a steak from the freezer section of the refrigerator to a shelf below to thaw for tomorrow, in lieu of going out to dinner with Roger as planned. She opened the sink door. During his one visit since her return from Sedona, the clothespin had not reappeared. Maybe the Amanda connection had occurred to him.

Next morning, she didn't give herself a present of a reprieve from the treadmill, and striding away the miles, reading a mystery by Cynthia Harrod-Eagles that Snowy had recommended, she thought how she was going nowhere while everybody else seemed to be moving. Roger would arrive Friday with more of his belongings. Dick and Jessica were beginning to move theirs into the Ninfield house. Now that the sale of the repair shop had gone through, the Doloffs were packing up the contents of the house for their permanent move to Florida. At the end of the month Trulianne and Clem would be moving into that house. Everybody making changes.

What if she moved to Santa Fe?

Spring fever. Snowy, who right now was God knew where in the Hebrides taking ferries from island to island, wrote in her poetry about the itchiness of spring—Snowy and probably a zillion other poets. Were you born with an itchy foot if you were born in springtime? Bev looked out the window at the cloudy evanescence of the light over the gray lake. Some treetops were rosy with new buds.

After her shower, she dressed in old jeans and a green French terry sweatshirt, thinking about islands. A black-and-white photograph on the bedroom bookcase, snapped by Mother, showed Daddy in dungarees and a work shirt standing outside their farmhouse, staring down with comical incredulity at swaddled baby Bev he was carefully holding.

Iwo Jima, 650 miles south of Tokyo, was a volcanic island shaped like a pork chop. It measured approximately eight square miles. Its name meant Sulphur Island. One of the many books Bev had read said that the lowering of the landing boats for the assault looked like all the cats in the world having kittens. Seizing the island was supposed to be easy. American planes and ships had already been bombing it for seventy-two days. But nobody apparently knew how thoroughly the Japanese had fortified it with underground tunnels and concealed gun emplacements and pillboxes. Nobody knew (except the Japanese) how treacherous the beach's volcanic ash would be for traction, nor that the beach ended in a fifteen-foot terrace. As the assault began, there was hardly any enemy fire; instead, there was a traffic jam of bogged-down vehicles, equipment, men. Daddy had been in the third wave. Then the Japanese opened up with artillery and mortar fire. He had been killed on this beach. February 19, 1945.

Almost seven thousand men had died by the time the island was finally taken on March 26.

Propped around her bedroom were the birthday cards she'd received, including one from Ann thanking her for the letter she had managed to write, an outpouring she hadn't dared reread before she mailed it for fear she'd said all the wrong things. Hidden in her underwear drawer was the birthday card from Frankie, to whom she still hadn't written that Dear John letter.

She went downstairs to the living room. Having expected Roger to be here today, she had put the presents sent by Mimi and Lloyd, Dick and Jessica, and Etta on one of the coffee tables, to open with him. Well, maybe she'd wait until later today to open them. In the kitchen she found on the table a vase holding a spray of forsythia, Leon's traditional present along with getting the wicker porch swing out of the cellar where it had been stored for the winter and hanging it on the back porch. This year the forsythia's springtime yellow reminded her of Trulianne's mother. Gram. Shirley. Shirley and Everett. Out the sink window, across the porch (where the swing had indeed returned, another sign of spring), she could see the backyard's forsythia bushes, a riot of yellow. The reborn grass was studded with crocuses, purple, white, yellow, while the green shoots of daffodils were popping up. She and Leon had planted the crocus and daffodil bulbs her first autumn at Waterlight. He was at work in the backyard right now, raking out the bed of daylilies near the boathouse.

She looked in the fridge at orange juice, Egg Beaters, bagels. She opened a cupboard, looked at the various cereals she bought for Leon, and remembered Clem eating Cheerios here. She must find out Clem's exact day of birth. Visions of the birthday party she'd throw for him when he turned three made her think of her own early birthdays when she had realized she was the star of the show, her name spelled out in candy letters on the cake Mother made using the plentiful eggs from Daddy's chickens. After Daddy's death, Mother had bought birthday cakes at Vachon's Bakery.

There was no birthday cake in this kitchen, because she'd intended to have instead some sinful dessert at dinner tonight with Roger.

She grabbed the vase, and over the sink she drew out the forsythia branches and shook off water droplets. With the forsythia she ran to the hall closet for a jacket and ran on outdoors to the garage. She put the forsythia in the back of the car. As she drove into town, she played a Patsy Cline CD, although probably it wasn't the smartest choice, these wonderful lovelorn crying-in-your-beer songs. How she envied Snowy her lifelong love of Tom, interrupted of course by marriage to Alan but always there, enduring. How simple that must be compared with her own checkered love life. Had Roger and Gloria fallen in love again via e-mail? Were they meeting in Ninfield or Syracuse or both? Was that why Roger wasn't here today?

She pulled into the Abnaki Mall. In Indulgences she chatted with Fay Rollins about the vows-renewal catering. Then she bought a chocolate cake, a chocolate croissant, and a container of black coffee. Carrying them to her car, she took a shortcut on side streets over to South Main Street in order to drive past the Gunthwaite hospital, where sixty-one years ago, after Bev's early-morning arrival, Mother must have been feeling relieved, exhausted, overwhelmed, and scared to death at the prospect of taking care of this suddenly very real baby, all emotions Bev remembered far too well from the birth of her first child.

Back when she was born in 1939, they kept mothers and babies in the hospital for two or more weeks. So mothers got a vacation, time to recuperate—and lots of time in which to fret. Daddy hadn't brought Mother and baby Bev home until May eleventh, and by then, Mother said, the hospital stay had made her stir-crazy, desperate to return to the farm and show Bev springtime and introduce her to the chickens and Clover. Of course during those introductions Bev had burst into wails.

Other side streets led Bev to Mudgett Street, to the section of town into which Lake Winnipesaukee poked a long bay like a fjord. On Bayview Drive, she passed a fishing-tackle store, the Twilite Motel, and a gift shop in front of which sat an unoccupied husband bench. The land rose to a groomed expanse of lawn with gravestones looking down at the bay. An arched wrought-iron sign over the granite gateposts read: Birchwood Cemetery.

In the parking area she turned off the CD, reached into her shoulder bag and turned off her cell phone, pressed her window button to let in the spring air, and had her breakfast picnic of croissant and coffee there in the car. The new grass was pushing thickly up through the old thatch. Groves of white birches matched the marble that a few gravestones had been cut from. Most were gray granite, some pink.

You could drive on the wide macadam lanes that crisscrossed the cemetery, and in February, if the nineteenth was very cold, she did drive. Usually, she walked. So after she'd wiped her mouth on an Indulgences napkin and washed her hands with Purell, she climbed out and retrieved the forsythia. Today, walking past gravestones and the more self-important obelisks, she kept an eye out for angels but saw only one, in bas-relief.

161

She glanced over to the right at the site of Snowy's parents' plot, but she didn't often visit it and she didn't today. She continued straight ahead on her route past other families' graves with their vases of dead flowers or plastic flowers looking just as dead. In one plot, though, crisp little pansies had been set out. She read names. Women were mostly identified as "Wife of" or "His Wife." Beside some gravestones, small flags from the American Legion fluttered, and soon she could see one at the far side of the cemetery, at the plot Mother had chosen close above the drop to the bay. Her pace quickened, and her heartbeat.

The three gray granite stones set flat in the ground read: Richard William Colby. Julia Cushman Colby Miller. Frederick John Miller. And their dates. On Daddy's stone: U.S. Marine Corps.

Bev asked herself the questions she always asked, questions that Mother had never been able to answer satisfactorily. Why had he enlisted? Patriotism? The hankering for adventure that she'd inherited, along with his red hair? Why the Marines? More dramatic—another trait she'd inherited?

Mother usually said, "It was something he felt he had to do. He was a very brave man." Only years later, when she and Bev were talking about Snowy's husband's suicide and Snowy's grief, did Mother admit, "I was furious at your father when he told me he'd decided to enlist. I couldn't convince him not to. I was furious and hurt and heartbroken, that he could leave you and me like that, and of course I was terrified for him." After a silence, Mother said, "Then he left us forever. I tried to be stoic. Mourning, I told myself, was a form of self-pity. But of course I never stopped missing him and loving him, all my life."

During her childhood after his death, Bev would look at recruiting ads for women's branches of the services and think of following in his footsteps, trying to decide which uniform would be most flattering. Dressed in it, she would die as heroically as a woman could back then. And all the while she was growing up, somewhere in the recesses of her mind she had assumed that like her father she would die young, tragically. But now here she was, sixty-one years old.

Mother had added, "When Fred died, I made no attempt at stoicism and gave myself up to grief."

Bev smiled affectionately at Fred's stone, remembering the awful Jeep. She remembered, too, her first mixed emotions at Fred's appearance in their lives and hearing Mother laugh again. Flat feet had kept Fred out of the War, had kept him alive.

She knelt and fanned out the forsythia spray in front of the three stones. Then she walked back to her car. Birthday or no birthday, she should study today for the broker's exam next month. But she stopped at the Dilly-Dilly Deli for supplies for a celebratory lunch to sustain her.

As she drove down Waterlight's driveway, she saw parked out front a van lettered Blue Skies Satellites. What the hell? She jumped out. Nobody was in the van. Something to do with Leon? The moment she thought this, Leon came around the end of the house.

She said, "Hi, darling. I took your lovely forsythia to the cemetery. Thank you for it and the swing. What's going on here?"

Leon rubbed his stubbly chin. "Dad swore me to secrecy. I had to promise to stick around today for these guys. It's your birthday present from him."

"My present?" Bev read aloud the van's sign. "Blue Skies Satellites?"

"A satellite dish."

Bev stared at Leon. "You mean—a satellite dish? But we already have cable and we don't watch anywhere near half of what's on that!"

"Surprise, surprise." Leon gave a laugh. "Guess Dad wants a satellite. Oops, I mean he thinks it's what you've been wanting for your birthday."

Bev turned back to the car so Leon wouldn't see her fury,

163

though of course he knew. Her hands were shaking with rage as she lifted out the Indulgences cake box.

Leon said, "Let me take that." He took the deli bag too.

What to do but follow him indoors? On the hall table she noticed a package, a book mailer, and picked it up.

Leon said, "The UPS guy came. A busy morning. I'm worn to a frazzle."

He was joking, using her phrase, to cheer her up. She smiled at him, her composure now under control. Sort of. She said, "Thanks for coping." She couldn't read the book mailer's return address without her glasses, so she carried it onward to the kitchen, where Leon set the box and bag down on the counter. She said, "It's birthday cake. I thought we'd have steak for dinner, if you're going to be here, and for lunch I'll make sandwiches." She lifted out her deli purchases. "There's crabmeat salad, chicken salad, ham, Swiss cheese. Which would you like?"

He said valiantly, "We could go out to dinner."

She put them in the fridge. "No, that's fine." In her shoulder bag she found her glasses. The return address on the book mailer was Wingfield Press. Snowy's publisher. "Oh my goodness!" she said. "This must be Snowy's new book!" In the past, though, Snowy had always sent Bev the new collections herself or had given them to her in person. But with this one she was off in Scotland, so she must have asked to have it sent.

"Crabmeat," Leon said, and he left the kitchen.

Was it her fault that he had no interest in poetry? She hadn't read *A Child's Garden of Verses* to him or Dick as much in their formative years as she had to Mimi and Etta. Bev tugged the tab that ripped the mailer open and carefully extracted the book. Another slim volume. Then she saw the title: *Site Fidelity*. A couple of years ago when Snowy had first been worried that Bev might move to Santa Fe, Snowy had used those two words, explaining it was an ornithologist's term. And Bev had replied that this should be the title of her next collection, a suggestion she'd completely forgotten until now. She started opening the book the way Mother had taught her to open a new book, pressing it flat in sections to ease the binding, but she didn't get past the first pages, the dedication page:

To Beverly Colby Lambert

On Saturday afternoon Snowy phoned and began describing a harrowing drive home from Logan last night in rain that became wet snow.

Bev was hiding out in her office from the Class of '55's planning meeting down in the dining room. Before her on her desk lay the Pottery Barn catalogue, open as usual to office furniture. Beside this were catalogues of travel clothes; she was trying to adjust at last to the idea of polyester, twenty-first-century variety. She interrupted, "Snowy, I can't wait to thank you, though I don't know how to thank you; I'm speechless. The book came. Right on my birthday."

"Oh," Snowy said, sounding shy. "So the timing worked out. When I realized that Kara—my editor—would be having my copies shipped to me while Tom and I were away, I asked her to hold them but have one sent to you."

"It's wonderful. The poems are wonderful, too. I'm—well, thrilled and honored and everything and, obviously, still speechless."

"In Scotland," Snowy said, rapidly switching subjects, "remember after my trip with Ruhamah I told you about seeing lots of redheads? On this trip I saw even more. On one little ferry almost everybody was redheaded, including a baby with a curl like a Kewpie doll!"

Bev laughed, remembering how she used to tie a pink bow in baby Etta's red curls, defying the rule that redheads couldn't wear pink. "Tell all about the trip! Did you have fun?"

"Yes, but I'd better wait to tell all until I reread my journal and untangle the memories. And until the photos are developed so I can bore you with those. Meanwhile, you tell all about what's been going on with you."

"For starters, guess who's downstairs."

"Who?"

"Wally Smith."

"Who?" said Snowy like an owl. "Holy shit, Wally Smith?"

"Wally and a half-dozen other members of the great Class of 1955. They and Roger are all sitting around my dining-room table with notepads and laptops planning the reunion, which won't just consist of dinner at Trask's that Saturday night. On Sunday there'll be a brunch and golf for the people who can stick around longer. Roger has only asked me to the dinner."

"Does Roger play golf?"

"Enough to be sociable. He's not a golf nut like Puddles's husband; it's tennis he loves. Maybe he'll spend his retirement on Waterlight's tennis court. Anyway, he and Wally and the others are downstairs planning like mad. I served beer, chips, iced tea, cookies, and fled."

"I used to sit near Wally in study halls. Alphabetically, I came after the Smiths. Poor Wally. Remember how he always got his girls on the rebound?"

"I'd forgotten all about him. But he's been living in Gunthwaite ever since graduation. He told me he worked at Trask's until it folded and since then he's worked for some construction company."

"Who else is there?"

"Nobody I remember. Snowy, another guess. Guess what Roger gave me for my birthday."

"Is this X-rated?"

"He gave me a satellite dish. Just what I always wanted. Now I can watch soccer games in Zanzibar." Then Bev remembered that Snowy and Tom still actually had an antenna on their roof. No cable company would bother with little Woodcombe. They

166

could have bought a satellite dish, but they stuck with an antenna, an *antique,* for heaven's sake.

Snowy asked, "He didn't consult you about this?"

"No indeed." Bev eyed the Pottery Barn catalogue. She still hadn't dared to order anything; she was still daydreaming over the pages. "Other news: Trulianne is going to be moving into the house next weekend. I gather that her brothers will be helping with moving whatever she's got. I don't think it's much. I bought the Doloffs' appliances and some odds and ends they didn't want, for her to use. She'll reopen the repair shop that Monday, May first, to get spring business as soon as possible. Tell everybody! There'll be an ad in the *Gunthwaite Herald.* I'm going to try to stay out from underfoot after she moves in, but I doubt if I'll manage to."

"And it's all still a deep dark secret from Roger?"

"Yes."

Snowy was silent and then asked, "Have you decided what you're going to wear to the reunion?"

"No. Or what I'm going to wear to the vows ceremony." Bev took a breath. "Snowy, speaking of vows, Roger decided that we're going to write our own. I haven't the foggiest! Could you help?" She waited for noises of Snowy smothering giggles.

But after a moment Snowy said, sounding thoughtful, "I guess writing your own doesn't mean you can't use a quote or read or recite a poem. When David—Tom's son—got married, he read Robert Frost's poem about cleaning the pasture spring, which can be considered a great love poem. But even though you lived on a farm that poem wouldn't really suit you—" She broke off.

They were suddenly on treacherous ground, the farm that Bev had almost turned into a development. Bev said quickly, "A poem is a brilliant idea! Roger can't object because I won't show him what I'm going to say; I'll tell him we should keep the vows secret, save them for the ceremony. But shouldn't the poem be written by a woman? Maybe one of your poems?"

Snowy said awkwardly, "Um, wouldn't that be too much me? You know what I mean, mine and not yours. Better find one elsewhere."

Bev did see what she meant. "How about Edna St. Vincent Millay? I'll look in Mother's anthologies."

"If you need it, I'll lend you my volume of Edna's collected poems."

"Thank you, I'll let you know if I do. And Snowy, thank you again, so much, for the dedication. You didn't have a chance to sign the book. Will you do that next time we get together?"

"Of course. I'm glad you like the book, Bev."

Now Snowy was sounding tired, jet-lagged. Bev said, "You get some rest. Did Tom take a photo of you eating haggis?"

"As a matter of fact, he did. I made the mistake of relaying your request to him, figuring he'd treat it as a joke and forget about it. Imagine my embarrassment when he started snapping in a restaurant. I liked haggis better this trip than last."

"That you liked it at all is remarkable, but you would."

"An acquired taste. It comes with turnips, called 'neeps,' and believe me, it needs them."

Bev made her famous retching noise, and they said good-bye laughing. She left her office. Standing on the balcony above the living room, she could hear more laughter, this coming from the dining room. In her bedroom, she went into the closet and pulled out the wedding-dress box she had stored at the back. She carried it to the settee and in one motion yanked up the lid, fast, like yanking off a Band-Aid. But then gingerly she lifted out the veil and the dress and carried them to the bed, where she slowly unfolded and smoothed out the dress's layers.

It was still beautiful all these years later. Timeless. And well preserved, creased but not yellowed. She had called the bodice Audrey-Hepburn style, sleeveless with a bateau neckline, and its intricate lace was a welcome disguise for flat-chestedness. It tapered into the skirt's billows of satin and tulle.

She held up the veil. Because she had decided to show off

her red hair—auburn—she'd chosen a very sheer tulle fingertip veil instead of anything more mysterious.

Who had caught her bouquet? Cousin Elaine? As part of the theme of having her hair the only color, the bouquet had been white roses. God, if she chose white roses for the vows ceremony, they would *match* her hair!

Gazing again at the dress, she saw that although it had seemed so grown-up to her then, it was a young woman's dress, a girl's, a maiden's. She had been only twenty years old. Twenty and full of what hopes and dreams in 1959? She had settled for domesticity. Fixing up their newlywed apartment. Roger's career. The surprise of actually producing children. Creating a family.

She would have to buy a new dress.

Bev did manage to stay away from Bide-a-Wee on the following Saturday. She had appointments to show customers several houses; afterward, she could have driven on to North Road, but she went back to Plumley's to do paperwork, feeling virtuous. Last night Roger had arrived, the SUV again loaded to the gunwales; today he and the rest of the planning committee were touring the Gunthwaite Conference and Convention Center, née Trask's. When she got home, Roger was back from the tour and insisted on playing tennis, finding fault with Waterlight's court and, as he always had, with her game.

Sunday afternoon, the minute Roger left for Ninfield she lost all control and drove to North Road. She had bought the repair shop's new sign at the sign-painting business owned by Dudley, now run by two of his children, Johnny and Arlene; she'd chosen a blue the color of the lake on a summer day (feminine) and for the lettering a bold black (masculine): Lakes Region Small Engine Sales & Service.

In front of Bide-a-Wee sat Shirley Hughes's new yellow VW. Bev almost did a U-turn, but curiosity overcame discretion and she braked to a stop beside it. She looked down at herself and decided she was presentable enough for this momentous meeting while informal enough to roll up sleeves and help: jeans and a dark green Liz Claiborne corduroy shirt. She and Shirley must be about the same age, and they were both mothers of four. What else, she wondered with trepidation, could they find they had in common, besides Trulianne and Leon and Clem?

As she stepped out of her car into the sunny brisk day and adjusted her shoulder bag, a gray-haired man came out of the repair shop. He was tall, lanky, wearing work pants, a New England Patriots sweatshirt, a Boston Red Sox cap, and a guarded expression.

"Hello," Bev said, holding out her hand. "I'm Beverly Lambert. You must be Everett, Trulianne's father?"

He said cautiously, "Ah," but he shook her hand with his large calloused one.

The strong silent type. Easy to see where Trulianne got her taciturnity. Bev said, "I stopped by to ask if Trulianne needs anything." How much had Trulianne explained to her parents about the arrangement? And just how many Lambert family details had Trulianne gone into when she explained the arrival of the tourtière in their kitchen?

"Well," he said.

"I'll pop in and say hi." Bev suited action to words and headed for Bide-a-Wee. He didn't tackle her or try to stop her any other way. As she knocked on the front door, she glanced back and saw him returning to the repair shop. She knocked again, then opened the door (*her* front door so it was okay) and called, "Hello? Trulianne? It's Bev!"

No answer. She went into the hall and opened the door to the living room, her office. She'd been here earlier this week after

170

the Doloffs had officially moved out, and as she had made some more redecorating decisions she had been struck again by how a house echoes when people are gone. In the real-estate business, she had walked through so many echoing houses. But now, though this room and the dining room were still empty of furniture, the house seemed full again. She realized she smelled Toll House cookies; she heard a woman's voice and Clem's giggle.

To stick to the boundaries of territories, she didn't open the closed door into the kitchen from the dining room but went back into the hall and walked down it to the other kitchen door, which was open. "Hello? Bev here." She peeped in.

On the linoleum floor had been placed a braided rug that was coming unstitched. Clem, squatting there with his trucks, said, "Gaga!"

Cute little Shirley, pleasingly plump, was looking and acting like a true Gram. Over a tunic sweater and capri pants she wore a yellow apron crocheted with daisies, and she was taking a sheet of cookies out of the oven. "For heaven's sake," she exclaimed, "at long last! I was asking Trulianne if I'd get to meet you!"

From her mother Trulianne had inherited that slight overbite that supposedly bewitched men.

"How do you do," Bev said, and as she wondered if she should shake hands with Shirley as well as with Everett, Shirley set the cookie sheet on the stove and reached up to give her a pot-holder hug.

"At last," Shirley said. "Let's have some tea. I sent groceries with Trulianne and the boys yesterday and I brought more today, including the makings for these cookies, Clem's favorite, so he'll feel at home quicker." She lifted a kettle off the stove, filled it at the sink, and set it back on a burner. "Trulianne is out in the repair shop with her dad."

Which Dad hadn't bothered to mention. "Thank you, I'd love some tea." Bev hung her shoulder bag over a kitchen chair. Out the back door's window, across the back porch, she saw in the backyard bordered by woods the little gym set, brought from

171

Eastbourne. So she wouldn't have a chance to buy one for here, but maybe someday for Waterlight? She knelt down beside Clem, who smiled his Leon smile and pushed a pickup truck toward her. She said to him, "Vroom vroom," and to Shirley, "This is amazing, Trulianne getting settled in so fast."

With a spatula Shirley transferred the cookies to cooling racks. "Well, as I told her, the ideal situation is to have leeway to fix up a place before you move in, but if you can't do that, get everything done fast so you're not living out of boxes. In our early apartments, Everett—my husband—and I were moving in the front door while the previous occupants were moving out the back." She went into the pantry and opened cupboards, taking down two mugs decorated with seagulls, Clem's blue plastic glass, a box of Celestial Seasonings tea, and a box of Lipton. "Trulianne only likes these perfumey teas, so I made sure she had some real kind here too. Which do you prefer?"

"Real, please." Bev pushed the truck back to Clem.

Shirley, who apparently was a talker to make up for Everett, emerged from the pantry and continued, lifting a half gallon of milk out of the refrigerator, "Not that Trulianne has that much furniture to arrange. Her things from her apartment, she stored them in our cellar when she moved back home. Home," Shirley repeated, her tone fading to forlorn. "She's never lived this far away before."

It sounded as though Trulianne had moved to China.

"But," Shirley went on, pouring milk into the blue glass, "this is a wonderful opportunity. I can't tell you how glad her dad and I are that you ran across this place. We were so upset to see all her education going to waste after she was laid off. When Trulianne makes up her mind to do something, she does it, like becoming an auto mechanic and becoming a single mother."

Their eyes met, and Bev knew they were both thinking of Leon.

The kettle whistled. Clem imitated the racket with a shriek, then laughed.

172

"But," Shirley said, turning off the burner, lifting the kettle, "when Trulianne made those plans of hers she was too young to have learned that things don't always go as planned. Mostly they don't. The garage owner was good about some maternity leave, and she went back to work as soon as she could, sooner than I thought she should, but when the crunch came she got laid off first and there she was with no job and Clem, and—"

Bev interrupted, "I hadn't any idea he existed until January first of this year."

Kettle in hand, Shirley whirled around to gape at her.

Bev stroked Clem's hair. "Needless to say, it's easier for the mother of a son, like me, to be kept in the dark about a baby."

"Bev," Shirley said. "What you missed. I am so sorry. Everett and I, we just assumed you and your husband didn't want to be involved."

Tears welled in Bev's eyes, unbidden.

Shirley said, pouring boiling water into the mugs, "Trulianne brought Leon over to our house once when they were dating. He is a nice young man. So good-looking and such good manners. And then when they weren't dating but the baby was on the way, I happened to be at her apartment a couple of times when he drove down to see how she was doing. Trulianne ordered me not to call him when she went into the hospital, but I did, and he got there just in time to be with her and me when Clem was born. She had too much on her mind right then to get mad at either of us. Maybe, maybe one of these days they'll get back together. Especially if they're in the same town."

Bev faltered, "I hope so too," overwhelmed by the image of Leon in the delivery room, becoming a father. She tried to comprehend how he could have gone through all this without telling anybody, particularly his mother.

"What you missed," Shirley repeated.

To have held Clem, newborn. Bev drew him close.

Shirley said, "I didn't know you didn't know." After a moment she cleared her throat and went on, "Well, come sit down and we'll make up for lost time. Do you have milk or lemon in your tea?"

"Just plain, thank you." Bev got to her feet, creaking like a grandmother, and hoisted Clem into the booster seat on one of the kitchen chairs. The fake-maple dining set must have been bought in some discount furniture store. Bev imagined Trulianne furniture-shopping with her first paychecks from that garage that had eventually fired her, and she nearly wept with more sadness. Then suddenly her purchase of the repair shop and Bide-a-Wee no longer made her feel guilty or Machiavellian, manipulative, scheming. She felt proud of what she'd done. Shirley was right. This was Trulianne's opportunity, a second chance.

"To begin with," Shirley said, setting a plate of cookies on the table, sitting down on the other side of Clem, "tell me all about yourself."

Oh God. Attempting to steer the talk away from any revelations about her unconventional marriage, Bev replied, "Tell me all about *you*. Are you an Eastbourne native? My best friend lived there years ago. It's a beautiful city."

"Everett and I were both born and brought up there." Shirley gave Clem a cookie and asked him, "What do you say?"

"Thank you." He smiled sunnily at his grandmothers.

Bev and Shirley smiled back at him. But alas, Bev realized, Shirley wasn't deflected by this or by Bev's ploy, for she returned to the difficult subject. "Are you and your husband Gunthwaite natives? I asked Trulianne and she thought so but wasn't sure. Trulianne is a genius with engines but she isn't much of a people person."

What *had* Trulianne said to Shirley about Leon's parents? What on earth did Trulianne know about Roger, from Leon, if anything? "Yes," Bev said, "we both are Gunthwaite natives." She paused to pick and choose phrasing for the most favorable slant. "Roger's work—he's a lawyer—took us to Connecticut, and it kept him there when I came back here several years ago to go

174

into real estate. I wanted to take advantage of the Winnipesaukee possibilities. Now he is retiring and moving back." Then Bev lost her mind. She went mad. She went gaga. She heard herself utter irretrievable words. "In fact, we're renewing our marriage vows in June on our forty-first anniversary. I'll send you and your husband an invitation. I hope you can come. I'll send one to Trulianne and Clem too."

"Renewing your vows!" said Shirley. "Isn't that romantic!"

Bev never knew what to do about May ninth, the anniversary of Alan's suicide in 1987, but ever since Snowy and Tom started living together Bev hadn't felt it necessary to call her for a quiet talk, and this year she almost forgot about it entirely because of the upcoming broker's exam, but when Snowy phoned on the evening of the eighth to say she could bring the Scotland photos over tomorrow evening, Bev checked her calendar to make sure she was free and the date jogged her memory.

The ninth was a warm day and stayed warm, so that evening they sat at the big wicker table on the back porch with decaf coffee (loon mugs, of course) and Indulgences lemon squares. Snowy gave Bev a souvenir of Scotland, a crystal thistle paperweight, and after Bev had admired it and thanked her, trying not to jinx things by imagining it on her desk in her broker's office instead of just in her office upstairs or at Plumley's, Snowy said, "Feel free to skim," and pushed toward her an album whose covers were plaid. Typically but maddeningly, Snowy had already got the photos organized and labeled. As Bev began looking at green scenery dotted with sheep, Snowy inscribed *Site Fidelity*, put down her pen, and then whenever Bev glanced up from the album to comment or ask a question, she found Snowy gazing out at the lake and knew

175

she must be thinking of Woodcombe Lake in which Alan had drowned. Were cheery travel questions and oohs and aahs a help or a hindrance? Bev exclaimed, "You took a photo of a bathtub?"

Snowy laughed. "Oh, at the inn on South Uist. Well, have you ever seen such a lengthy bathtub? Tom claimed it needed a lifeguard."

Back to water dangers and drowning. Bev hastily turned a page, but Snowy was smiling, in some reverie, and Bev remembered that Tom had spent a high-school summer as a lifeguard at the Gunthwaite public beach. In the Scottish tub, he and Snowy must have had great fun splashing together. Such frolicking, and they hadn't even been on their first honeymoon, much less their second!

Snowy sipped her coffee. "We had the best breakfast there. The usual fare, but done beautifully—porridge, eggs, oatmeal-bread toast, and kippers."

"Speaking of food, where are you and the haggis?"

"I moved those photos out of sequence to the end, to leave you laughing." Snowy gestured at the boathouse with her mug. "Will Leon launch the boats soon?"

"He already has, ahead of schedule. Roger got thinking out loud to me about the boats during his latest visit, about putting them in when he next came up. He was assuming he'd do it himself this year, with Leon helping. So I just happened to mention this to Leon, and he immediately rounded up that buddy of his who helps him with things that one person can't handle, and they got the boats in."

"The old fait-accompli strategy."

"I can't imagine what this house will be like with both Roger and Leon under this roof permanently, and I suspect that won't occur. Leon will move in with Heather. But if he and Trulianne could get back together, there's plenty of room at Bide-a-Wee . . ." Bev came to the last photos, Snowy at a table in a restaurant that had tartan wallpaper, no less! "You actually do look as if you're enjoying the haggis."

176

"Note that on Tom's plate there's grilled salmon. I called him a coward."

Bev sat back. "All these photos are a delight. They're *real*. Roger has bought a digital camera, but I'll bring my Polaroid for some real ones for you. I can't believe, though, that I'm actually going to be in England." She closed the album and asked hesitantly, "How are you doing today?"

Snowy said, "I'm okay, Bev," yet in her tone Bev heard Mother saying, "I never stopped missing him and loving him, all my life." Then Snowy finished her coffee and asked, "The cram course was last weekend?"

"Yes, two days in a conference room at the Gunthwaite Ramada. The exam is this Saturday, in Concord." Bev made her oh-horrors face.

"I won't phone you the night before and disrupt your concentration to wish you luck." Snowy got to her feet and gathered up the album. "I'll wish you luck now, Bev."

"We don't have to wait nowadays for the exam results. We find out right after the exam. If I pass, I'll go shopping afterward to celebrate, on a mission to find a reunion outfit and a vows dress. And if I flunk, I'll do the same, for therapy."

After Snowy left, Bev opened *Site Fidelity* to see what Snowy had written. Snowy always kept her inscriptions simple, and this one was the same as the inscriptions in her other collections:

To Bev—
Love,
Snowy

The night before the exam, Bev sat at her Waterlight desk, still cramming. In high school, Snowy had teased her about going into a coma in the days before a Dramatics Club play. Well, maybe, and if so it was a successful technique. She had never come up with a successful one for studying. Why could she memorize lines but not information? When the phone rang, without checking caller ID she let the machine answer it. She would ignore the caller even if it was Snowy phoning after all to wish her luck tomorrow. But as she read the next sample question before her, she heard Puddles announcing to the machine, "It's official, my grandson is now a teenager!" and she just had to grab up the phone, say "Hi," and listen to Puddles talk about the thirteenth birthday of Little Guy, who was no longer known by the "Little" nickname except in the family, all the while longing to tell Puddles about her own wonderful grandson.

Then Puddles said, "I've worked out my schedule and bought my plane ticket. I'll be arriving at the Manchester airport Wednesday, the twenty-first of June. Can't wait to see Waterlight at last. Can't wait to see New England again."

Bev said automatically, "I can't wait to see you," thinking that Puddles's plane ticket made the vows ceremony even more imminent, with no escape.

Puddles said, "Choosing cheerleading uniforms is complicated. The sales rep is a former cheerleader, and she sure as shit is more of a diplomat than I'll ever be."

Suddenly Bev howled with laughter, which she certainly hadn't expected to on the night before the exam. "*You*, dearest Puddles, diplomatic on *any* occasion?"

Puddles emitted a grudging laugh. "No need to get hysterical. As I predicted, the girls don't understand the 'less is more' principle. They still want hot uniforms. But the rep is supposed to go along with what the coach—me—wants while also giving the girls what they want, seeing as how the girls are the ones spending all this money on new uniforms. Compromise lies ahead, I know, but I hate compromise!"

Bev laughed again. And after she and Puddles said good-bye, she closed her books, shut off her computer, and went into her bedroom.

Remembering how Roger had hidden the certificate for her Connecticut real-estate exam, she wondered what her life would have been like if she'd flunked it. Roger wouldn't have hidden the certificate, there wouldn't have been his presentation of it at Mimi's wedding reception so she wouldn't have got furious with him and stayed on in Gunthwaite afterward; she would have returned to Ninfield with Roger. If back then you were given the results immediately instead of having them mailed to you, the same thing would have happened whether she'd passed or flunked. But if she'd flunked, would she have had the courage, the stamina, the sheer persistence to try taking the exam a second time? Did she now?

To put herself to sleep tonight, she used Snowy's trick of listening to an audio book on a pillow speaker, which always reminded her of Mother reading her to sleep with Raggedy Ann books and Pooh books, Peter Pan, all the others. Snowy got audio books from the library, but Bev bought them and from the accumulation on a bookshelf she chose *A Midsummer-Night's Dream,* acted by professionals. She had acted in it as an amateur, the only Shakespearean play in which she'd performed. (Reading plays aloud in English classes, or emoting at prize-speaking contests as Juliet and Portia and Lady Macbeth, these didn't count). It had been performed by the Ninfield Players, a daring departure from their usual Broadway fare. She had played Hippolyta, queen of the Amazons, betrothed to Theseus. Lying in her white king-size bed, she spoke her opening lines along with the tape, lines about her upcoming wedding:

> Four days will quickly steep themselves in night;
> Four nights will quickly dream away the time;
> And then the moon, like to a silver bow
> New-bent in heaven, shall behold the night
> Of our solemnities.

The next morning in her closet she took down the clothes she'd planned to wear today. She had ordered coordinating outfits for her second honeymoon, along with two travel-friendly nightgowns and a robe, and she'd decided to start testing out this overseas-trip trousseau today, give it an exam. She dressed in the sage green polyester-Lycra pants and white rayon shirt, went down to the kitchen and managed to chew half a bagel with some swallows of coffee, went back upstairs and flossed and brushed her teeth again, applied lipstick, and put on the sage green drip-dry basket-weave blazer, and then she drove to Concord listening to a National Public Radio Saturday morning news program, trying not to think about real estate. Let it all simmer in her subconscious.

The exam was held in the H&R Block office in a shopping plaza. She parked and for the millionth time checked her shoulder bag to make sure she'd remembered her calculator. You were allowed to use one during the exam, thank heavens. Oh, why had she *ever* wanted to go into real estate enough to put herself through these agonies? Answer: Because when she'd tried to assess what she could do, she realized she had been learning about houses all her married life, that's why. But she had learned to cook well too. Why hadn't she done something like Fay and opened a bakery? You didn't have to take exams to do that, did you?

She walked into H&R Block. How could she walk, when she couldn't breathe? In a carrel, she was instructed to get acquainted with the computer, but fear nearly blinded her, blackness pulsing in her brain. And then the broker's exam began.

The time limit was three-and-a-half hours. She used them all. When she finished, she felt keyed up with hope—it hadn't been *that* bad—and worn out with worry—you were told to guess when you didn't know the answer, and how many times had she guessed wrong? She stood up, stiff, and then went swiftly to the testing supervisor to learn the results, the prisoner running to the guillotine to get it over with.

180

That evening she phoned Snowy and said, "I've found my vows dress."

"Oh?" Snowy said, sounding cautious. "Um, for which reason did you go shopping?"

Bev screamed, "I passed!" and finally she knew it was true. What relief, what jubilation, and shared with Snowy, a real-estate subject though it was!

Snowy exclaimed, "Oh Bev, congratulations!"

"I hit the malls in Concord and Manchester. I didn't find anything for Roger's reunion, I guess I'll wear what I wore to our fortieth, but I did find *the* dress."

"Where? Describe it!"

"In Talbots. It's sort of a suit, silk, with a long straight skirt and a lace shell under the jacket, classic but pretty. When I saw it, I decided I want to be a bit tailored for this occasion. The color is called 'iceberg green,' and Puddles may think I'm wearing it to atone for those lime green dresses I forced on her and the bridesmaids, but it's actually very flattering."

"Sounds lovely. Have you told Roger about the exam, about passing?"

"No. Not yet. Just you."

"What happens next? Tell Geoff and resign?"

"And order office furniture."

"Oh, congratulations, Bev!"

After she and Snowy hung up, Bev phoned Mimi and said, "I've found my outfit for the ceremony. Could you sometime come and see it and then make a ring bearer's cushion in the same shade of green? I know the cushions are usually white, but I'd like green."

"A ring bearer?" Mimi said. "Have I missed something, or have you just thought of this? And a flower girl? You've got some kids in mind?"

"Only a ring bearer." Bev savored her insanity. What was she staging? She had sent the invitation to Shirley and Everett, and Shirley had immediately returned the reply card marked yes.

But Trulianne? Whenever Bev had stopped at Bide-a-Wee to contemplate the office, timing her visits for Trulianne's lunch break and finding some excuse to lean into the kitchen to say hi to Clem, Trulianne hadn't said anything about the invitation Bev had sent her and Bev couldn't summon up the nerve to bring up the subject. However, Trulianne still hadn't returned the reply card with a no. Bev asked Mimi, "Can you do the cushion, a silky fabric but not too smooth so the rings won't roll off?"

"Sure," Mimi said. "You're using your old wedding rings, not getting new ones?"

Bev paused. Here was another decision to be made that hadn't occurred to her or Roger. She decided, "Yes. They'll be the 'something old.' Aside from us ourselves, of course."

Mimi said, "That's so sweet."

In the following days, Bev wondered if this was how manic-depressives felt, these swooping swings from joy to terror, from energy to exhaustion. She marshaled her forces. Through Jared, Harriet's carpenter boyfriend, she located people who would work at such short notice on the renovation of her new office: carpenters, a floor guy, and the painters who would do her office area and the exteriors of Bide-a-Wee and the repair shop. At her favorite antique store she found armchairs, a wing chair, and, to use as a conference table, a big dining-room table with eight ladder-back upholstered-seat chairs. At her favorite furniture store, after much soul-searching and with much trepidation, she chose the fabric for the new upholstery for all those chairs and for the sofa she ordered here; she also bought white wicker chairs for the office's side porch. At the oriental rugs gallery she decided on Hamadan rugs, beautiful but practical, known as "rugs of iron" and able to withstand a business's foot traffic. At Bill's Office Equipment owned by Bill LeHoullier, Darl's husband, she bought computers, printers, a scanner, a fax-copier, and was given her usual old-school-chum discount by bookkeeper Darl. From the Pottery Barn she at last ordered office furniture. She went to Dudley's sign-painting business, and from Johnny and Arlene she ordered a sign, white with black lettering: Beverly Lambert, Realtor. She wouldn't have it put up until she was officially open for business, after her return from England. At Gunthwaite Gardens she bought houseplants for indoors and, for outdoors, tubs and windowboxes that she would plant when the weather had warmed up enough by the end of the month. And at a bridal shop she ordered a ring bearer's suit in Clem's size. After the exhilaration of each of these accomplishments came the fears.

She did all this while still working at Plumley's. She kept putting off telling Geoff. Secretly, she was cleaning out her desk.

Finally one afternoon at Plumley's she walked over to his desk and said, "How about a drink after work?"

He looked at her quizzically. "I can't have missed some sale you're celebrating."

"No." She didn't elaborate and walked back to her desk, feeling his eyes watching.

At five o'clock he was at her desk, asking, "Where would you like to go?"

She replied, "The Gunthwaite Inn."

They drove in their separate cars down the Miracle Mile and out Main Street. Set behind a splendid four-foot-high white picket fence, beyond flower beds packed with daffodils and tulips, its dogwoods blooming, the big white colonial had been an inn ever since Bev could remember. In her youth, when dining out wasn't so common as now, it had been the place people went for a treat or special occasions. Fred used to take Mother to the Gunthwaite Inn on her birthday. Puddles had chosen the inn for her wedding reception. And when Bev had decided not to return to Ninfield with Roger, she had stayed here until she found a house to rent. That is, Geoff had found the house.

The inn had kept up with the times and survived, but still the bar was in a back room and dark with heavy curtains to cloak sin. Bev always felt that she should be wearing a flapper's dress, entering a speakeasy.

And now here she and Geoff were, seated at a dim table, out in public in Gunthwaite together as a couple for the first and last time. Looking at his endearing widow's peak and the poignant leather patches on the elbows of his old tweed sport coat (a perfect touch), she wanted to tell him that he was the cat's pajamas. Instead, after she ordered a glass of chardonnay and he ordered a single-malt scotch, she said, "Remember thirteen years ago when I came into your office to ask about houses for rent, hoping against hope I might be able to find one near a riding stable, for Etta?"

"Vividly," he said. "Didn't I offer you a job on the spot?"

"We got talking shop. I told you I had my Connecticut license. You said if I'd get my New Hampshire license, I could come to work at Plumley's."

They shared a silence full of reminiscence. The waitress brought their drinks.

Geoff lifted his glass. Bev thought of how in the olden days, before the advent of single malts in New Hampshire state liquor stores, Mother and Fred's occasional nightcap had been ordinary blended scotch. Geoff asked, "Should we be toasting your renewal of vows?"

"That was Roger's idea, inviting my boss. Please don't feel obliged to attend."

"Boss? You're an independent contractor."

"But you taught me everything I know." She let him digest any double entendre he wanted to discern in this sentence and then said, "What I'd like us to toast is my passing the broker's exam."

He set down his glass and stared at her.

184

"Yes," she said quietly. "The baby bird is leaving the nest. It's time."

He stood up and walked out of the bar.

After she paid and went outdoors, she stopped and examined the inn's fancy fence. No matter what it might cost, this was what she would have built at Bide-a-Wee for Clem's safety.

She didn't go back to Plumley's the next day. She drove to the office of Beverly Lambert, Realtor, and began working with the painters, that day and the following days. The painters had already removed all the awful wallpaper and primed everything; now while they continued work on the living room and dining room, she did the same in the front hall and the half bath under the stairs, sanding and washing woodwork, painting the ceiling and woodwork white and the walls a soft green, almost a soothing aquamarine, which reminded her of the phase in high school when she'd doted on Revlon Aquamarine Lotion, whose scent had been heavenly.

Now that she was here all day, she could observe the small engine business more closely than she had when she was running in and out organizing the renovations. She saw customers arriving with equipment to be repaired and other customers arriving to buy. Her unofficial estimate was that over half were women, and her guess was that these were new customers who had never frequented Mr. Doloff's uninviting premises. She hadn't dared mention in the newspaper ads that a woman now ran the shop, so the news must be spreading via good old word of mouth.

When the carpenters started putting up the tall picket fence, Trulianne stuck her head in the office and said, "Wow, that fence is going to be perfect!" and Bev felt as though a compliment greater than all the applause of all her curtain calls had been bestowed on her.

Trulianne kept Clem out in the shop during the mornings, in a play area she'd devised. With the weather getting warmer, instead of lunch in their kitchen she and Clem often ate on the back porch where Trulianne had set out the porch furniture Bev had bought from the Doloffs, old plastic-webbed chairs and a metal table. Bev had also bought, for Clem's amusement, the Doloffs' damn wooden burro, but instead of the front lawn Bev pastured it on the back. The backyard's trees were teeming with twittering birds. Trulianne put up a pole and hung a tube bird feeder.

Bev ate her own lunch circumspectly on the side porch, in one of the drop-cloth-draped new wicker armchairs, but one day, after too many instances of witnessing Trulianne dashing out to greet a noontime customer, Clem on her hip clutching a sandwich, and seeing Trulianne every afternoon dashing in from the shop to check on him while he napped, Bev took her sandwich to the back porch and asked, "May I join you?"

To her vast relief, Trulianne answered calmly, "Sure."

Clem said, "Is yours olive loaf? I want olive loaf. Peanut butter, no!"

Trulianne rolled her eyes.

Bev said, "Mine is even better than olive loaf. It's turkey. With your mother's permission, I'll swap you a half." Then to Trulianne she said, "If a customer comes during your lunch break, I could look after Clem. And I could keep tabs on him later, while he naps."

Trulianne stayed silent, absorbing the proposal, before replying, "That would help a lot. Thanks. Yes, Clem, you can swap."

After this a routine developed, lunch together on the back porch, Bev and Trulianne talking more to Clem than to each other, naming the birds on the bird feeder, chickadee, nuthatch, goldfinch, pointing out chipmunks and squirrels. When Trulianne had to tend to a customer, Bev took Clem exploring in the backyard or played on the gym set. During his naps, she periodically left off painting to go upstairs to his bedroom, where the wallpaper was still Doloff floral and the furnishings were basic, bed, bureau, bookcase, toy box, and as she made sure he was sleeping happily, she gave the room a makeover in her mind (white walls and Dartmouth green woodwork, Pottery Barn quilt and rugs with trucks or fire engines or tractors). She knew Trulianne wouldn't permit redecorating, but she did go to Gunthwaite Gardens and buy a birdbath for the backyard; she returned to her favorite furniture store and bought wicker furniture for Trulianne's porch, including an adorable child's chair, easily justifying the purchase of these items to Trulianne because they were safer than sagging plastic and rusty metal.

Bev thought: This part of my life is bliss.

Snowy phoned her at Waterlight and said, "Tom drove past your new place today and reports that it's all freshly painted, the house and the shop. And he says to say he's sorry that he hasn't yet needed any small engine sales or service. How are things going?"

Wary of talking about real estate, about renovating her office, Bev exclaimed, "Trulianne is attracting new customers and lots of them are women!"

"That's terrific. And the ceremony plans?"

"Ceremony? What ceremony?"

Snowy laughed, but Bev heard worry in that laughter.

Mimi brought to Waterlight the curtains she'd woven in the muted jade color Bev had chosen, and she also brought a pale green raw-silk cushion, stabbed with two pearl hat pins. She said, "These pins will hold the rings in place. Want me to help you hang the curtains upstairs?"

"Thank you, darling, but I'm going to wait a bit. They are lovely, and so is the cushion. Exactly what I had in mind."

Mimi then produced a checklist of final things to be done and proceeded to grill Bev with questions about overlooked details, such as favors. "How about CDs of loon calls? I could wrap them in the same green silk and tie them with darker green ribbons."

"That's a brilliant idea, darling."

Even Leon was getting involved, asking what Bev would want from the gardens. Bev was thus forced finally to make a list of Waterlight flowers and florist flowers and reach a decision about her bouquet. Smaller than her wedding bouquet, but white roses. And a white rose for Roger's boutonniere, same as at the wedding.

Whenever Roger drove up for a weekend, she spent the time at Waterlight, because she knew that if she went to her real-estate office and worked, she would return smelling of paint even though she left her paint clothes in the half bath, and how would she explain that? There were more meetings here of the reunion committee and this kept him busy, especially the assembling of mock yearbooks made up of the classmates' autobiographies that Gloria had accumulated via e-mail. Bev did household chores and worked in her upstairs office or in Waterlight's gardens. If she was outdoors and there was no meeting, sooner or later he appeared at her side, he who had never paid attention to her gardening work at Ninfield except to admire the results, here he would be in the rock garden asking why the plants were so stunted or there he would be amongst the roses (which *had* survived the winter) asking why they weren't blooming yet. So she would give up and suggest taking out the *Loon,* the *Grebe,* or the *Heron,* the canoes and sailboat named by the previous owners, or her Chris-Craft. She'd named it the *Waterlight,* and Dudley's daughter Arlene had lettered the name in gold leaf on the stern.

Of the three, Roger preferred the *Waterlight.* "The canoes and sailboat are quiet," he said, "but they're more like work. They remind me of a pal of my father's who, before working at Trask's, worked on one of the old paddle wheelers on the lake. He shoveled a ton of coal on the trip across the lake and a ton back. Out on the lake, I just want to relax. Besides, this old Chris-Craft is a beauty."

She had to laugh and agree. In the Chris-Craft she felt she'd returned to the Fabulous Fifties, waterskiing with a summer boy and wearing her favorite bathing suit that was called Pharaoh's Darling, patterned in browns and golds.

Before Memorial Day weekend and the onslaught of summer people who would strip all the garden centers of plants, Bev drove to Gunthwaite Gardens for her supply. During lunch on Trulianne's porch, she asked if after his nap Clem could help plant them. Trulianne gave permission. So in the window boxes, which Bev had painted dark blue to match Bide-a-Wee's repainted trim and which she'd had a carpenter install on the front windows of the house and shop, Bev and Clem planted cascades of deep pink petunias. In the four cedar tubs, two in front of the shop, two beside the walk to the front door of the house, they planted matching pink geraniums, white bacopa, and trailing vinca. Out back, they replaced the plastic flowers in the burro's cart with red geraniums. She wanted to ask if Clem could come with her to the cemetery on Memorial Day, but she knew this would be pushing the family connection too far. She went alone and at the plot above the bay she planted more geraniums, in her mind talking to Mother and Daddy and, yes, dear Fred.

Family, family. The next day during lunch on Trulianne's porch, Bev put an envelope down on the table. "Another invitation," she said. "In case you didn't get the one I sent. They were created by Mimi and Lloyd." She liked to mention the children (though not Leon!) to Trulianne as often as she could, hoping to build up sneakily that sense of family.

Clem made a grab for the envelope, which Trulianne circumvented. Trulianne said, "Mom told me about you sending them one. Why did you do it, invite them? I asked her to turn it down. As for me and Clem, you know we can't come, so I didn't bother to RSVP."

Aha, Trulianne wasn't aware that Shirley had responded with a yes. Bev said, "I want you to realize that I'd love to have you there. I expected you to say no, but—"

"No," said Clem.

Bev hinted, "He'd be adorable as a ring bearer, in a little white suit." Such as the one she'd ordered, now hidden from Roger in a garment bag in her closet.

"No," said Trulianne.

That evening, burning bridges, Bev tore up her birthday card from Frankie and the past birthday cards from him she'd saved. Then, deciding that you couldn't send a Dear John letter by e-mail, she wrote him on her new office stationery, cream with dark blue lettering. Although this letter was much shorter than her letter to Ann, she wrote it the same way, fast, and didn't reread it.

> Dear Frankie,
>
> As you can see from the letterhead, I took the plunge and got my New Hampshire broker's license. Therefore, I have made the decision to stay in Gunthwaite. I am also staying with Roger, who is moving back to Gunthwaite.
>
> We'll be celebrating our 41st anniversary with a renewal-of-vows ceremony outdoors at Waterlight on June 24th. Here's hoping the infamous New England weather cooperates!
>
> It was wonderful to rediscover you at the reunion. (Roger is having his 45th next week, imagine!) It has been wonderful to discover the Southwest with you as my guide. But I'm now totally committed to New Hampshire, so I won't be back.
>
> Thank you for everything.
>
> > Bev

She quickly sealed the envelope.

On the Friday before his reunion day, Roger arrived in his

ancient black Porsche instead of the SUV, and the next morning he drove off in it from Waterlight to the Gunthwaite Conference and Convention Center to meet his committee and put up decorations. Although he didn't say that he'd be joining Gloria there, Bev assumed that Gloria had arrived from Syracuse yesterday with or without a husband, had spent the night at a classmate's or a motel, hotel, or an inn, and would be raring for hands-on final organizing of last-minute details. Yes, he and Gloria would confer and convene today.

The day was sunny, but she couldn't tend to the gardens and ruin the manicure she'd got yesterday. She should read Edna St. Vincent Millay, searching for her vow. After she started a load of laundry, she went upstairs but found herself going into her bedroom closet instead of standing at a bookcase. She carried out the carton she'd brought from Ninfield, lowered it onto the settee, sat down beside it, and opened the flaps. Lifting out the plastic bag containing her Junior Prom crown of roses that Mother had pressed, she contemplated the crumbling brown circlet, then took it out of the bag and stood up and, watching herself in the closet door's full-length mirror, placed it on her head. She picked up the queen's trophy and hefted it high. Then she crossed her eyes at her reflection.

But she decided to wear the crown a little longer. As she sat back down, she remembered the lavender gown she had chosen for that prom, strapless, net over satin taffeta. It had cost a fortune, nineteen dollars and ninety-five cents. Roger had come home from Dartmouth to take her to the prom, even though it must have seemed like kid stuff to him by then and he'd had to spend the money to rent a dinner jacket, black trousers, and maroon cummerbund from Dunlap's Department Store, as he had for proms when he was still in high school.

She next lifted out the scrapbook with the green-and-white cover Mother had woven. Opening it was torture. Torture like the oubliette Roger wanted to see at Warwick Castle. To forget. Had her essence been abandoned and forgotten as she grew up?

There must be some reason why she'd never gone to a reunion until her fortieth. She saw the clippings that Mother had cut from the *Gunthwaite Herald* about her triumphs: the Junior Prom queen photo, articles about plays and the state prize-speaking contests (the time she'd won first place in Girls' Humorous, doing a scene from *Pride and Prejudice*). The Dramatics Club had sold big nine-by-twelve black-and-white glossy photographs of play highlights and casts; Mother had bought all that showed Bev, from minor to major roles, and some had gone into this scrapbook and Bev had decorated her bedroom with others. The photographs were still starkly clear. Odd; in makeup for playing grown-ups, she didn't look the way she'd looked as she aged. No photo had been taken of the clinch with Dudley in *Our Town*. Probably that was considered too risqué, even if it was a wedding kiss.

Bev closed the scrapbook, trying to remember a poem that Snowy had once insisted she read. Philip Larkin's "Lines on a Young Lady's Photograph Album." Would there be a vow in that? But Larkin was a man, and she needed a woman poet. She opened the maroon leatherette scrapbook, the "Roger Scrapbook" she had kept. Her young self had cut out these items about his basketball team, his debate team, his prize-speaking awards, his becoming governor of Boys' State.

God, he had been gorgeous. Smart. Ambitious. Adult and worldly-wise, or so he'd seemed; she had trusted him to know everything, to handle every situation. And he had been her friend. After he'd broken up with her and gone off to Dartmouth, she had realized how much she missed him, not just as a boyfriend but as a friend.

Prize speaking! That's what their recital of vows would be like.

Should she show Roger these scrapbooks? But wouldn't he ask her why the hell she hadn't produced them earlier, for inspiration during the planning of the reunion? How could she explain the reluctance? He should understand, his aversion to reunions being as strong as hers. But now that he'd thrown himself into this reunion, wouldn't he get carried away by this scrapbook and want to show it off at the dinner?

She must save him from himself. She put his scrapbook, then hers, then the trophy back into the carton. She removed her crown and slid it carefully into the plastic bag, carried the carton back to the closet, and turned her attention to her outfit for tonight. The dress she had worn to her fortieth reunion had reminded her of Waterlight in a misty springtime dawn, pale green, its flickering tints diaphanous. The décolletage of its sleeveless bodice was another of those flattering miracles, a disguise for the lack of cleavage. To freshen it up she had bought a new pair of shoes; because Snowy hadn't accompanied her on the shoe-shopping trip she could splurge ridiculously and did so, on four-hundred-dollar strappy sandals. However, they could also be worn with the vows dress so they were almost a bargain.

Vows. She took a couple of Mother's poetry anthologies out of the bookcase and curled up on the settee.

When Roger returned that afternoon, he didn't say a word about seeing Gloria.

That evening as she rode with him in the Porsche to the Gunthwaite Conference and Convention Center, she experienced layers of déjà-vu sensations. She was wearing the same jewelry she'd worn to her fortieth reunion, the emeralds Roger had given her for their twentieth anniversary. Except for her shoes and her escort, it could be three years ago, the occasion on which she had met and renewed acquaintance with Frankie. She glanced over at Roger, who was looking quite devastatingly handsome and coolly casual in a white tattersall shirt, navy blazer, and khakis. The tie he'd chosen was one of his collection woven by Mimi. The wrap she'd brought was also one of Mimi's creations, a soft silver-threaded cloud. No, tonight wasn't three years ago. Now she was a grandmother, a broker, and in two weeks she would become a real wife again, to the man she had been going out with since she was fifteen, driving with him in the Heap and subsequent cars to movies, dances, parties, dinners, a forty-fifth reunion.

This was all too much to comprehend. Thus, when he parked in the lot behind the big brick factory whose window boxes were now planted with red impatiens, she shoved aside thoughts about the past and future and concentrated on the present. She checked her makeup in her compact mirror and prepared herself to meet Gloria.

The evening still held the day's warmth, so Bev left her wrap in the car and stepped out with only her clutch purse. Because of Roger's continuing duties they were early, but already other people were arriving, getting out of cars, calling to Roger. He greeted them back, and some recognized her and called, "Bev, great to see you here too!" She didn't recognize anybody, but she gamely exclaimed that it was great to see them. So the reunion began even before they went into the hallway, where a green-and-white sign on an easel read: Welcome GHS Class of '55.

Into the Trask Room she made her entrance with Roger. As at her fortieth reunion, the Trask Room was enthusiastically decorated with school spirit—green-and-white GHS pennants, streamers, and bunting—but since then more renovations had been made: A balcony now overlooked this space in which Trask employees had once slaved. And as at her reunion, in the front of the room there was a bar, already doing a roaring business. Beyond were round tables with white tablecloths and green napkins. Then Bev drew her gaze back from the big view and looked to her right, where beside the door a green-and-white reception table had been placed. Behind it a woman in a black silk pantsuit was tidying the name tags arranged on it. The woman glanced up and cried, "Welcome, Bev! Welcome back, Roger!"

Bev blinked. This was unmistakably Gloria Taylor, the large blue eyes, the long hair twisted up, not such a dark brown now, with graying tendrils curling fetchingly around the still beautiful face. Gloria came out from behind the table, chandelier earrings swinging, and Bev found herself being hugged, inhaling a whiff of some perfume she probably should know from the scented ads in magazines. Gloria's hug was firm. Toned, that was the word for the silk-clad body. Too late, Bev wished she'd spent more time with her weights and her Denise Austin's arms-and-bust videotape instead of reading on the treadmill. Gloria definitely had not let herself go, and in the tumult of emotions Bev was experiencing she realized, surprised, that she was glad Gloria hadn't. Would Roger succumb to her charms? Had he already? Would Gloria save her from the upcoming renewal of vows?

Gloria said, "I was so startled when I saw Roger's mustache today. He hadn't sent me a photo for the new yearbook—optional, but he should've! Doesn't it suit him perfectly?"

Roger stroked the mustache complacently. "People are arriving early. Our classmates are either very eager to see each other or to start the cocktail hour."

"Both," Gloria said. "Now, you get Bev settled and come help me hand out the name tags and yearbooks."

Whoa, Bev thought. Was Gloria going to monopolize Roger? For how long? Well, consider this a good sign, another indication that Gloria would save her. But the dismissal was nettlesome, and Bev said irritably, "Don't mind me, I can get myself settled."

They ignored the remark. Gloria gave her a tag and said, "Yours is a guest tag," and Roger pinned it on Bev's dress—at her fortieth she hadn't bothered identifying herself with her name tag, deeming it unnecessary, which it proved to be—and then he hurried Bev over to the bar, bought her a glass of chardonnay, scanned the room, and led her up the staircase to the balcony, where he seated her at one of the round tables at the railing. "Bird's-eye view," he said and ran downstairs.

He had parked her out of the way! Bev sat and fumed. She should go right straight back down there and mingle. She should find some old boyfriends; if she couldn't remember them, she hoped they remembered her. Then, toying with her silverware, she noticed how useful this vantage point was. She could clearly see Roger and Gloria working together at the reception table, greeting people, referring to checklists, handing out name tags and the mock yearbooks. Guest tags had only names; on the classmates' tags the person's photograph from the real yearbook had been photocopied. Everybody was laughing, the noise level rising to fill the room as loudly as the machinery here must once have. Was Gloria's comment about Roger's mustache a red herring, so to speak, or had Gloria and Roger really only been in touch through cyberspace and she hadn't seen him until today?

A man's deep voice said, "Gloria's administrative skills are always being put to good use."

Bev looked up to see a man too slight for that voice, with attractive crinkly eyes behind rimless glasses. Instead of a sport coat, such as most of the guys below were wearing, he wore a suit. Gray suit, white shirt, and a conservative striped tie. His name tag didn't have a photo, so he was a guest, but without her glasses she couldn't read his name, and she was damned if she was going to put on the glasses she'd brought in her purse for emergencies. Reading this guest's name tag did not constitute an emergency, did it? "Hello," she said. "I'm Beverly Lambert."

"So I gathered. They told me you were up here. I'm Charlie Thompson, Gloria's husband."

"Oh. Oh! I haven't known what Gloria's married name is." Bev twinkled at him, wondering if he was Gloria's first husband or second or more. "Yes, Gloria was running things way back in high school. It's marvelous how she's organized this reunion. Won't you sit down?"

"Thank you." He sat across the table from her, and together they looked over the balcony rail at the people hugging, chattering, guffawing, drinking.

Charlie Thompson said, "I've come to all the reunions with her, and she comes to all of mine. I gather this is the first for Roger?"

Charlie Thompson had been gathering a lot. "Yes," Bev said and didn't know what else to say about that, so she continued, "You live in Syracuse?"

"I'm from there, and we eventually settled there after a few moves."

"Ah," Bev said, assuming that this meant he was Gloria's first and only husband. "Ah, yes, the early-married moving days! Are you retired now?"

"Not yet. I'll stay as long as I'm needed."

That was an odd choice of words. Did Roger still feel needed at Lambert and Lambert?

Charlie said, "I gather that you are in real estate?"

Bev laughed. "And I'll probably never retire. Real-estate agents are apt to be like orchestra conductors and—who else? People with job longevity."

Charlie laughed too. "I wonder if Gloria will ever retire, because it's her company and she feels so responsible for everyone. She has learned to delegate, but not to that extreme."

"Her company?"

"PT Unlimited."

"PT?"

"Physical therapy," he explained, his deep voice ringing with pride. "She got interested years ago when one of our daughters broke a leg skiing and had to do PT. Gloria went back to school to become a physical therapist. Until then she had been using her administrative skills to run our household and help me, but pretty soon she had started the company."

"Oh," Bev said weakly. "Isn't that wonderful." Indeed it was. Gloria had been doing good deeds while Bev sold second homes to millionaires. She took a big sip of her chardonnay.

"It is," Charlie agreed. "The work that she does, the help that she and her associates give to people, is invaluable."

"And, um, what do you do?"

"Me? I'm just a humble parson."

Luckily, Bev had set her glass down so she didn't spill wine or snap the stem.

A voice behind her said, "Bev! Bev Colby! Remember me?"

Standing up, Charlie said to her, "Good to meet you. I hope

197

we can all talk later, when our spouses have time to relax over dinner."

"It was very nice to meet you too," Bev said and turned to a man gazing at her in astounded adoration. This was more like it! But she had not a clue who he was, and she was still determined not to put on her glasses. Then his prominent ears jogged her memory and she hazarded a guess. "Al?"

"You remembered!" Al Hanson plopped himself down in the chair beside her. He had been the program director of the Radio Club his senior year. As he proceeded to tell her all about his career as an announcer and disc jockey at radio stations in Massachusetts, she remembered that for *her* senior year she'd been the program director. But she had never thought of making radio a career, a rare thing for a woman back then. She wondered what would have happened if it had occurred to her to try to do this, and she recalled that she had never dated him because he only managed teams instead of playing on them.

Soon other people, mostly men, were climbing the stairs to the balcony to talk to her. She was holding court!

Then the cocktail hour drew to a close and Roger came to escort her down to the queue at the buffet. When she returned to their balcony table with her plate of turkey and assorted salads, she saw, amused, that the same thing had happened here as in the high-school cafeteria; there were "popular" tables where the Big Deals sat. Roger's table was the foremost, with Gloria and Charlie, the GHS '55 football captain and his wife, and Al and his wife, Al who apparently had achieved a certain celebrity and thus won a place here. Bev chatted with everybody and laughed merrily at jokes about retirement and golf, all the while watching Gloria and Charlie and sensing their contentment, watching Gloria and Roger and seeing no sparks.

Gloria wasn't going to save her from the vows ceremony.

7

"Oh," said Roger the next morning, in the hallway hoisting up his golf bag, "I think I forgot to tell you there'll be a moving van arriving from Ninfield tomorrow."

"What?" Bev followed him out the front door. "*What?*"

"Don't worry, I'll be here to oversee the unloading. You can go to work as usual."

And off he drove to brunch and golf at the country club. Bev stood there on the porch staring after him.

The day was cloudy and chilly, with a chance of rain in the forecast, so he and Gloria had been conferring last night and on the phone this morning about golf, concluding that they'd wait and see at the brunch and maybe take a vote.

A moving van.

Remember the sweatshirt, Bev exhorted herself, stamping back into the hall. Remember Roger's gray sweatshirt on our second date. Ignore the petty irritations. But an unannounced moving van? Was that *petty?* She looked wildly around, picturing movers lumbering in with the Berkline recliner. Tomorrow was Monday, housecleaning day. She rushed to the kitchen phone and tapped the number of Miranda's double-wide in Pemberton Park. She got the answering machine and said, "Miranda, this is Bev. I've just learned that things are going to be in upheaval tomorrow because of a moving van—"

Miranda picked up. "Hi. A moving van?"

"I'm so sorry not to have let you know earlier, but Roger forgot to tell me until just now that it's arriving from Connecticut tomorrow. Everybody and everything will be in your way. Would it be possible for you to come later this week?"

"When the dust settles?" Miranda laughed. "Sure, I can do a lick and a promise Thursday afternoon, and anyway, I'll be coming those three days next week to get things in shape for next Saturday."

"Thank you." Bev still felt awkward about discussing the vows-renewal preparations with Miranda, divorced years ago and then practically left at the altar last year, even though Miranda must be well aware that Bev's marriage wasn't exactly made in heaven. They'd never talked about the situation, but its difficulties must be obvious, Bev living in New Hampshire, Roger living in Connecticut. When Bev had told Miranda offhandedly that Roger would be retiring and moving here, Miranda had looked more concerned than surprised, poked her wire-rimmed glasses back up to the bridge of her nose, and commented, "That's a lot of changes for you." Not wanting to reply to the observation, Bev had blurted out the ceremony news, saying, "We're planning to renew our vows here at Waterlight, with guests, a big party." Miranda had said, businesslike, "Well, the spring-cleaning will have an extra purpose this year. What do you want done?"

Now Miranda said, "All the bedrooms will be in use, right?"

"Yes. Thank you again, Miranda."

Six bedrooms, Bev thought, hanging up the phone, and all of them would be full, indeed overflowing, so that Dick and Jessica, Leon, and Etta and veterinarian Steve would stay at Mimi's house. Bev and Roger would have their own room here in Waterlight, and his brothers and sisters would have Leon's room, Etta's room, the spare room, and the suite. Bev was leaving it up to him to decide who got the suite. Puddles would sleep on the sofa bed in Bev's office. Arriving from Ohio, Jonathan (Roger's roommate) and Jonathan's wife would be staying at the

Gunthwaite Inn, where Jonathan had stayed forty-one years ago. Cousin Elaine and her mother had also stayed there when they'd come up from Massachusetts for the wedding, but when Bev suggested it this time for Elaine and her husband, Elaine e-mailed back that her husband hated inns and bed-and-breakfasts and insisted on plain motels where you could be sure of a TV in your room and didn't have to eat breakfast with other people. So Bev had sent her a list of several and Elaine chose the Twilite Motel on the bay. Bev hadn't been able to locate Carrie, the flower girl; the only address she could find in Mother's succession of address books down through the years had been for Carrie's grandmother, who had died ages ago. Roger had tried the Internet with no luck, probably because Carrie now had a married name. Bev couldn't remember ever hearing any news about Carrie from Mother, but probably she just hadn't paid attention. The little girl in the lime green dress had vanished from Bev's life after the wedding. Bev was furious at herself for not keeping track.

Everybody else had accepted except Ann—and Puddles's husband, of course. As for Geoff, after his reaction to her broker news she assumed he wouldn't follow through on his acceptance. The guest count was now thirty-one. Thirty-three, counting the unofficial guests, Shirley and Everett.

There was some coffee in the coffemaker left over from the pre-brunch breakfast of strawberries and yogurt she and Roger had shared. Pouring another mug, she thought of Trulianne's rejection of the invitation. The phone rang. She hesitated. Snowy was still working, so Snowy wouldn't yet be phoning to get the juicy details about the reunion and Gloria. She checked caller ID. Lorraine. Lorraine Fitch, her archrival at Plumley's!

Bev said, "Hello?"

"Hello," said Lorraine. "The word around is that you've left to start your own agency. I might like to make a change. Want to have a talk?"

Flabbergasted, Bev remembered her odd vision of Lorraine working in the office of Beverly Lambert, Realtor. She tried to copy Lorraine's briskness. "Why yes, certainly. When?"

"The word around is that you're redoing part of that North Road house for your office. Shall we meet there tomorrow, ten A.M.?"

Bev thought fast. Roger had told her to go to work tomorrow and leave the moving van to him. Okay. But could she risk meeting Lorraine at Bide-a-Wee, with Trulianne there? The workmen hadn't noticed any connection between Bev and her tenants, but they were men. Well, Lorraine understandably wanted to see the office, and Bev would have to wing it. "Fine," she said, "if you don't mind the smell of paint. They're doing the finishing touches."

"Doesn't bother me. See you tomorrow."

"Fine. Bye." Bev hung up and tried to take in the possibilities. Two real-estate top producers working together. The new office might not fail after all, knock on wood. But why did Lorraine want to leave tried-and-true Plumley's? Why hadn't Lorraine ever got her broker's license? She tried to remember what she knew of Lorraine's private life, aside from the assumption that Lorraine had been sleeping with Geoff years ago. Lorraine was divorced, with two children and three grandchildren, and she lived in a nice house on the lake (not so nice as Waterlight).

Then Bev thought, chilled: I've already infuriated Geoff by leaving Plumley's. What if he thinks I've stolen Lorraine and gets even angrier, so angry that he tells Roger about our affair? Would he show up at the vows ceremony and cause a scene?

But Roger couldn't believe that she had been chaste and faithful all these years apart. Could he?

Out the windows, rain fell. If word was going around about the new office of Beverly Lambert, Realtor, she had better tell Roger soon. Even though she hadn't planned to open the office until their return from England, she ought to start chatting up her contacts, getting some listings. She reached for the phone to call Charl, who would want to hear about the reunion, anyway.

The phone rang again.

"Okay," Mimi said, "the reunion is over, hope you and Dad had fun, but now it's the countdown, the homestretch, the final details. I've finished the favors; you can check that off the checklist I gave you. I think you ought to make an appointment for a massage the day before the ceremony, the day you're having your hair done. Want me to make it?"

Bev sighed. The only checklist she was paying attention to was the one on which she had worked out the timing of the renovations and furniture. She said, "I'll do it. Don't worry; I've got everything under control, darling." Oh, how she lied!

Lists. On the fridge, under that fifties-housewife magnet, the grocery list was getting lengthy. Tomorrow would be busy. She'd better go shopping this afternoon.

She went upstairs to her office, phoned Charl and received a tip, and then spread both checklists on her desk. She added Roger's list of necessities they mustn't forget to pack for their second honeymoon, such as Pepto-Bismol.

The phone rang. She let the machine take it, but when she heard Puddles's voice beginning to list more details, details of her arrival in New Hampshire, she reached for the receiver. "Hi, Puddles, you're on schedule for Manchester Wednesday? I'll drive down and pick you up."

"Stay put. I want to have a car to use so I'll rent one. I figure I'll get to Gunthwaite about six if there aren't any delays."

"Then you'll have dinner here. I'll invite Snowy and Tom and we'll celebrate your return to New Hampshire."

"Okay, but don't wait for me if I'm late. I'll phone if there's a delay. How was Roger's reunion?"

"Al Hanson is a celebrity in Massachusetts, and Gloria Taylor has a physical-therapy business and is married to a minister."

"No shit! What does she look like nowadays?"

"Great."

"Life sure isn't fair. How are things going about the ceremony? Are you getting cold feet?"

Bev lied again. "They're toasty-warm." Then she asked, "Did you ever reach a compromise about your cheerleaders' uniforms?"

"It was an eye-opener to watch the sales rep manipulating the girls without appearing to, playing up to them so they trusted her and then convincing them that they wanted what I wanted, that simpler uniforms would let their cheerleading shine through. What we ended up with is so-called 'traditional' pleated skirts, though traditional here naturally means they're even shorter than the Gunthwaite ones we thought pretty daring, and 'traditional-cut' shells. Here's hoping it works at next year's championships."

After Puddles said good-bye, Bev looked at the lists on her desk, then left everything there and went into the bedroom to curl up again on the settee with anthologies.

An hour or so later she heard Roger call from the hallway, "Golf was rained out!"

She hadn't found her vow.

Going downstairs, she said, "That's too bad."

"Well, only the fanatics really cared. Everybody else had a great time talking, exchanging e-mail addresses, showing photos of grandchildren." She flinched, but he just continued, "It was a big success, and everyone is saying we should start planning right now for our fiftieth. So, what are you up to this afternoon?"

"I'll be going off grocery shopping."

"I forgot to get the Sunday papers. I'll go with you."

"Aren't you tired from all this? I can pick up the papers."

"No. It'll be good to wind down. You drive."

Bev had been looking forward to heating up a bowl of Progresso 99% Fat Free New England Clam Chowder to read with before she set forth, but Roger was full of brunch and not, she guessed, inclined to want to hang around while she did so. Okay, there was an emergency granola bar in her shoulder bag, should she feel faint, and of course she couldn't starve in a super-market. So off they went into town, down the Miracle Mile to Shaw's.

First, veggies. She steered a cart into the produce section. As she picked up a bag of baby greens, Roger said, "My God, four bucks for lettuce?"

Instead of smacking him with the bag, she had a brainstorm. She tore the grocery list in half and said, "Here, get a cart and find these things. We'll meet up at the front and check out together."

He looked at his half. "What if I don't know how to inter-pret what you've written? What brand?"

"Roger, you have been doing your own shopping all these years. Choose what you'd buy in Ninfield." She thought: Am I going to rue this brainstorm?

He shot her a look, then went back to the nests of shopping carts and jerked one free.

Jerk.

When she finished her half of the list, she pushed her cart to the front of the store, but he wasn't there. As she waited, she suddenly saw him in the entry-exit area past the checkout coun-ters. He was sitting on a husband bench reading a newspaper, his shopping cart in front of him filled with bagged groceries.

He was rebelling, not waiting for her.

She hoped that he had never shopped at a Shaw's in Connecticut so that when he had started checking out here and the cashier asked him for his Shaw's card that would give him a discount, he regretted his rebellious gesture, which had cost him money. Smugly she took hers out of her wallet, then realized that if he didn't have a card, he would have remedied the lack by apply-ing for one at the service desk. With Roger, you couldn't win.

205

The next day was chilly and damp. For the meeting with Lorraine, Bev decided to be casual: jeans, a pale aqua jersey (almost the color of the office walls), and a blue linen blazer. She drove to Bide-a-Wee, where Lorraine's Lexus SUV was already parked. While Bev showed Lorraine around, Trulianne stayed in the repair shop, very busy from the sounds emanating, Clem presumably with her. Whew! But there was much to discuss with Lorraine, so instead of taking the chance of lingering at the office into lunchtime, Bev suggested an early lunch at the Schoolhouse Cafe.

Over their salads, to Bev's amazement the seemingly stalwart Lorraine confessed, "I've never had the courage to start my own business. I blame this on my Depression parents. They went through life scared to death to take any risk. It rubbed off on me. Then there I was divorced, with the children, and instead of getting a job with a steady paycheck the way my parents thought I should, I opted for real estate because of the flexible hours."

Bev nodded. "Yes, that was one of its appeals for me too."

"But that's as risky as I've ever been able to get."

Bev made her own confession. "I'm terrified." She was thinking that Mother and Daddy had been of that same Depression era, but Daddy had taken risks, the chicken farm, the War. Was his risk-taking the cause of her own foolhardy courage, starting this business? Look where *his* bravery had got him.

Lorraine said, "Well, I'm finally ready for a change."

Bev waited to see if she'd reveal the nuances of her decision to leave Plumley's. The desire for a fresh start could be more keen when you hoped it would rid you of the ghosts of a long-ago love affair. But Lorraine didn't elaborate, and throughout the rest of the lunch while they discussed the new business neither of them said a word about Geoff as a lover, only as the Plumley owner who was going to be royally pissed off at the departure of his other best agent, no matter how much tact and diplomacy were used.

When Bev returned to Waterlight, she found that the moving van had arrived during her absence and was still here, backed up to the front stairs. The porch door and the front door stood open.

She got out of her car and took in the sight, remembering the moving van that had come from Ninfield thirteen years ago to the house she had rented; it had been followed by Dick driving Roger's Chevy Blazer, towing a horse van in which rode Etta's horse, Prancer, who had later accompanied Etta to Mount Holyoke and finally gone to his reward two years ago. Back on that day in 1987, she had been scared stiff, worried sick, and taking a cram course for the New Hampshire real-estate exam. Today she was experiencing the same damn emotions but she had just been discussing the potential for millions of dollars in sales with a fellow top producer.

As two huge men emerged from the van lugging the big mahogany desk she and Roger had chosen ages ago for his Ninfield den, Roger appeared on the porch looking anxious and hovered over their maneuvers, then went after them into the house. She hastened indoors to find the living room crowded with furniture ejected from the suite in addition to furniture from the Ninfield house that evidently Dick and Jessica didn't want, and cartons and cartons and cartons. She wanted to sit down and weep. She looked up and saw Leon on the balcony, coming out through the attic door. "I'm sorry," she said. "I should have called you at Heather's and warned you. Have I got her number? You're storing things in the attic?"

"Attic stuff, from attic to attic. Even a black-and-white TV. He had them bring everything Dick and Jessica couldn't use. You can guess that when I showed up here this morning, I didn't get to fixing the dock ladder as planned."

"That's okay." Bev hesitated. What to do? She was used to helping on moving days. She was used to *directing* and helping.

The movers and Roger strode back from the suite and out the front door without noticing her. She ran down the hall into the suite. Now it was definitely the den. In the sitting room were the furnishings from the Ninfield den: the oriental rug, the desk and a computer desk and filing cabinets. In the bedroom, oh God, that vast TV and oxblood-maroon recliner. Two club chairs had joined the Boston rocker at the coffee table. And still more cartons had been added to those he'd brought earlier.

She was used to helping, but this time she had a choice. She could let him handle it, or she could pitch in.

She must help. She must face the reality that Roger had moved here for good.

As she went upstairs to change into old clothes, she saw in her mind's eye her Bide-a-Wee office as refuge. She would help with Waterlight, but the office needed most of her attention.

The rest of the week she divided her time, rearranging Waterlight furniture, unpacking items she'd completely forgotten about—a hawthorn jar of potpourri still faintly fragrant; a framed photograph, treasured by Roger's mother, of Roger as an altar boy—and then at her office hanging curtains, unrolling rugs, taking drop cloths off some furniture and overseeing the delivery of the rest. Time and days seemed to be accelerating. She felt as if she were on a runaway horse, as if that Sedona horse had bolted.

Roger had indeed moved into Waterlight. He didn't drive back to Ninfield. Friday night, while he was in the suite, Bev used her cell phone to call Snowy from her upstairs office, just in case Roger might pick up the phone down there. She reported, "Roger stayed. He's settling in. He's developed a daily routine around the unpacking of his books, the hanging of his umpteen diplomas, and all that. He makes his own breakfast and lunch. I've lost control of the refrigerator. In it there's the microbrew he likes nowadays and his favorite cheeses. His Land O'Lakes real butter is crowding out the I Can't Believe It's Not Butter that Leon and I use, and I can't find my fat-free milk behind his two percent. He discovered a tennis-playing neighbor and they play here in the afternoon and then he goes for a swim. Snowy, he has *retired!*"

There was silence from Snowy. Bev knew she was trying to think up some heartening remark. Bev thought of how Snowy had moved into Tom's place, and she toyed with the idea of following Snowy's example and living with Roger unmarried. Instead of renewing their vows, they should get divorced and then shack up.

"Well," Snowy said, "*you* haven't retired. You aren't stuck at home with him all day. How are things going with your office?"

"I'll finish readying it tomorrow."

Snowy said tentatively, "I'd love to see it."

The real-estate problem between them. Just as tentatively, Bev replied, "On your Sunday afternoon off? Could you come this Sunday?"

"It's Father's Day. David has invited Tom and me on a hike with him, wife, kids, dog. But how about tomorrow afternoon? I could get away from the store for an hour. Two o'clock?"

"That would be wonderful. And Snowy, I'm panicking about a poem for the vows. I can't seem to find the right one of Edna's in anthologies. Could you bring the collected poems?"

At two o'clock Bev finished the office rooms and stood back and looked. Although the curtains and oriental rugs were subdued, the wing chair and armchairs and sofa and the seats of the conference-table chairs were not. Their pattern of big bright flowers in greens, blues, and purples had been almost too dramatic for her to dare choose it, but this was another risk she had taken. The result, the final effect, made her so happy she burst into a delighted laugh.

Then she heard a car door shut. Out the front windows she saw Snowy saw pause to admire the tubs of geraniums.

209

Bev went into the hall and opened the front door. From the shop roared the sound of an engine revving. Bev called, "Welcome to Bide-a-Wee!"

"You've transformed the place, Bev." Snowy came up the walk carrying a book. "I take it that Trulianne works Saturdays?"

"Yes. Clem is napping." Bev added proudly, "I'm babysitting," and stepped back to usher Snowy into the front room.

Snowy gasped. She seemed frozen on the threshold. "The colors!"

"The Doloffs had wallpaper and upholstery with little tiny flowers. I got rid of that and decided on upholstery of great big flowers."

"It's beautiful. And courageous." Snowy moved forward, set *The Collected Poems of Edna St. Vincent Millay* down on Bev's mahogany desk from the Pottery Barn, and touched the thistle paperweight there. She tiptoed to the wing chair and gazed at those big flowers. On she went to the curtains and touched them. "Mimi?"

"Didn't she do a wonderful job?" Bev's ears were always pricked for Clem's voice, and now she heard his "Gaga!" from upstairs. "Come see how Clem has grown." Oh, it was good to be able to acknowledge him, if only to Snowy!

So together Bev and Snowy got Clem up from his nap and took him out to the backyard, where as he played on the gym set Bev told Snowy, "I've bought him a ring bearer's suit. I went crazy. I even invited Trulianne's parents, along with him and Trulianne. The parents have said yes, Trulianne no."

"My God, Bev. Were you thinking of producing him at the ceremony like a rabbit out of a hat?"

"I don't know what I'm thinking!"

"What about Leon?"

"Since Roger's moving day, Leon has only come home to take care of the essentials, like mowing the lawn. He must be spending his time doing caretaking work at the other places he looks after, and he must be spending his nights at Heather's. I keep checking his bedroom. Those two occasions he lived with girlfriends, he took most of his belongings with him, but his clothes, his computer, his CDs, everything is still there in his room. I now know better than to try to convince him that we all three can live peacefully in Waterlight. But if he learns that Trulianne and Clem are in Gunthwaite, maybe he would move in with them at Bide-a-Wee—and maybe even get married."

"Maybe," Snowy echoed. She tousled Clem's curls. "I've got to start back. Congratulations on this place, Bev. You've worked miracles."

"Thank you for lending the book."

Miracles happen; ask the angels. That evening, up in her Waterlight office, on her cell phone Bev called Shirley. Knowing that when Shirley heard her voice out of the blue, Shirley would immediately fear trouble or tragedy, she started off with: "Hi, this is Bev and everything's okay."

"Clem is okay? Trulianne?"

"Everybody is fine. I'm just calling to say how glad I am that you and Everett are coming next Saturday. I know Trulianne has issues—" Bev paused, feeling guilty. The word "issues" was Snowy's latest pet peeve, about which Snowy was very vociferous; "issues" had replaced "hopefully," "basically," "end of the day," and God knew what else at the top of Snowy's litany of complaints about the dire state of the English language. Bev repeated defiantly, "—issues, but I can't help hoping she'll change her mind and attend."

"I know," said Shirley. "I know. I keep hoping too."

"And I can't help picturing Clem as the ring bearer, in a little white suit."

Shirley exclaimed, "Oh, wouldn't he be adorable!"

"As a matter of fact, when I was browsing in a bridal shop I saw just such a suit and couldn't resist ordering one in his size. I have it right here."

The miracle happened. Shirley instantly took over. In a firm and determined voice Shirley said, "They'll be at the ceremony. You leave it to me."

Overwhelmed by relief, Bev could only say, "Thank you. Thank you."

Shirley added, "Trulianne is coming home for a visit tomorrow, for Father's Day. We're taking Clem to the ocean. I don't want him to forget the ocean."

Envious, Bev reminded herself of Sumner Starling's theory that the lake was preferable for grandchildren. Then when they hung up she realized that Bide-a-Wee would be empty tomorrow. This was her chance. After mulling over her strategy, she phoned Mimi and said, "Would you and Lloyd be free tomorrow to meet your father and me and go to lunch?"

"I thought you weren't doing anything special for Father's Day, but sure."

Mimi, Dick, and Etta had sent him Father's Day cards. Bev was planning to buy a steak for him to grill for dinner for two. Nothing special. "It's a surprise. Could you meet us at a place on North Road, the Lakes Region Small Engine place, you'll see a sign, and then we can proceed from there to the Schoolhouse Cafe?"

"Why don't we just meet at the cafe?"

"That's part of the surprise."

"Small engines? Are you giving him a lawn mower? Leon will go ballistic. What time?"

"Eleven."

"See you then."

So Mimi would be there as a buffer.

When Bev and Roger were in bed watching TV, she said, "I'm going to do errands tomorrow. It'd be nice if you could come along."

He asked dryly, "Groceries?"

"Always groceries. But first, something else."

"What?"

"A surprise."

Intrigued, he said, "A surprise? For Father's Day?"

"Well," she said, "partly, and let's call it partly a Husband's Day surprise."

He looked even more intrigued.

The next morning Bev busied herself watering the house-plants and doing laundry until ten o'clock. Then she phoned Bide-a-Wee and got Trulianne's answering machine. This meant she could safely assume they had left for Eastbourne. She returned to laundry chores until she couldn't stand the suspense of waiting any longer. She sought Roger, found him at Leon's workbench in the cellar, and said, "I'm ready to leave now."

"Will Leon continue to do his disappearing act?"

"He needs time to adjust."

"He needs to clean this cellar. And can we count on him to get the lawns and gardens shipshape for next Saturday? I doubt it."

"Come, Roger, let's go. The surprise awaits."

They went outdoors into the sunny morning. In the garage, the Porsche seemed very much at home sitting there beside her Outback. Dick would drive Roger's SUV up next Friday, while Jessica drove her car for their transportation back to Ninfield after the ceremony. Bev knew that the Porsche would live on protected in the garage, while the SUV braved the elements in the driveway. Or would Roger suggest expanding the garage to hold three vehicles? She asked, "Which car, mine or yours?"

Roger said, "Better take yours, more room for two cartloads of groceries. I'll drive."

Bev ignored the shopping-carts gibe. "Fine." As she got into the passenger seat, she inhaled a deep breath and said, feeling as though she were jumping off a very high diving board, "We're going to the Gunthwaite end of North Road."

"That's a clue?"

"You'll see," she said, wondering how she could change her mind now. She couldn't.

He drove to North Road. Too soon she saw the blue sign ahead: Lakes Region Small Engine Sales & Service.

She said, "There, pull in there."

He looked startled, but did so. "You're giving me a chain saw for Husband's Day?"

213

"Park in front of the house."

He read aloud incredulously, "Bide-a-Wee?" and parked.

Taking the keys out of her shoulder bag, she went up the walk to the front door. She unlocked it, stepped into the hall, and threw open the door to her office. The vivid colors again made her laugh with delight. She looked back at Roger. "Do come in."

Cautiously he entered, then stared.

She hurried over to her desk, against which leaned a big rectangle wrapped in brown paper. Ripping off the paper, she held up the white sign with black lettering on its two sides: Beverly Lambert, Realtor. "I haven't had it put up yet. I'll officially open the office after we get back from England."

"This is your office?"

"I'm a broker now." She had decided not to mention the exam, not to brag about passing it, because real-estate exams and their results were such a sensitive subject between her and Roger. She was praying he wouldn't say the wrong thing anyway.

"You've left Plumley's?"

"Yes. I'm going into business for myself. The way you did. I'll have one agent working for me, for starters."

He walked over to a window, but instead of admiring the curtains he looked out at the view of the repair shop. "This location doesn't seem exactly your style, to put it mildly."

She set down the sign. She did not have to justify anything to him, but she couldn't help saying, "It was an excellent deal."

He walked on into the former dining room and looked at the office machines and the conference table. "You're renting?"

"I bought the property. The mechanic is renting the rest of the house and the shop from me."

"You could have had an office at Waterlight."

"It's too much off the beaten path. I have to be on a main road. So. Well. Anyway, this is the surprise." She felt both deflated and relieved. Roger's reaction wasn't what she'd hoped—awe, respect—but it wasn't what she'd feared, belittling mockery.

He walked back into the main room, surveying everything.

214

"Funny, your mother did all that terrific weaving but she didn't give a damn about what her house looked like. You've got her artistic eye, but for rooms."

Bev wasn't sure she heard him correctly. "I certainly haven't inherited her talent. Mimi's the one. She made the curtains." Bev then did hear a car. She rushed to a front window and saw confusion. Lloyd was stopping the Weaverbird van in front of the repair shop, while Mimi was pointing to Bev's car in front of the house. "Mimi and Lloyd are joining us, and we're all going to lunch. That's the Father's Day part of the surprise." She ran into the hall and called out the front door, "Over here!"

Lloyd swung the van over to the house, and Mimi jumped out saying, "Bide-a-Wee! Mother, what are you up to?"

"Come see." Bev herded them into her office, watching for the expression on Mimi's face.

To her joy, Mimi started laughing, just as she herself had. "Wow! What *is* this place?"

Roger said, "Hi, kids," and held up the sign before Bev could. "Your mother's new office. She is now a real-estate broker."

Bev felt anger flood her entire being. Last New Year's Eve he had apologized for his blunder with her real-estate certificate, but didn't he realize he now was doing a version of that, stealing her thunder, making her accomplishment his?

Mimi and Lloyd said, "Congratulations!" and Mimi ran to a curtain, saying, "So these weren't for Waterlight!"

Roger asked Bev, "Where's the signpost?"

She said tightly, "Stored behind one of the sheds behind the house. Until we get back from England."

He said, "Might as well put the sign up now and start advertising. Is there a shovel in the sheds?"

She wanted to scream at him. She said, "Yes, there is, but I've arranged to have the sign put up *after* our return." How many times did she have to tell him? A zillion, but he still wouldn't listen. She said, "Anyway, we're going out to lunch now. Digging a posthole will take forever."

"Come on, Lloyd," Roger said, handing him the sign. "Let's get the post and see where Bev wants it placed, and then we can come back and work off lunch putting it up."

As Roger and Lloyd left, Bev clenched her fists, and Mimi said, "Why did you keep this a secret? I could have helped."

In her frustration, her towering rage, Bev almost unburdened herself of the big surprise, Bide-a-Wee's tenants. But she said to Mimi, "You've got enough to do at your shop, darling, and you're helping so much with the ceremony."

"Does Etta know? Leon? Anybody? And why this house? Does the engine shop go with it?"

"When I stumbled upon this bargain on this wonderful main road, I snapped it up and rented out the shop and most of the house. Now that I've finished fixing up these rooms, I'll be telling everyone about my new office."

Out a window Bev saw Roger striding down the driveway toward the road, carrying the L-shaped signpost and a shovel. She realized her fingernails were slicing into her palms, so she unclenched her fists. Okay, she told herself, this was another part of his reaction to her news, and although it was insensitive and misguided, it was also practical.

That evening, the phone rang when Bev was upstairs in her office and Roger was downstairs in his den. She glanced at the caller ID and grabbed the phone, saying in a rush, "Hi, Shirley, we're having phone problems here, let me call you right back on my cell." She hung up fast. There had been no sound of Roger picking up his extension; he must be engrossed in some TV program. On her cell phone she called Shirley and apologized, "I'm sorry about the confusion. Did Clem enjoy the ocean?"

"That he did," Shirley said. "And afterward I gave Trulianne a good talking-to. I reminded her in no uncertain terms that she was brought up to have manners. She and Clem will be at your place a half hour before things begin. I figured it would be best if she puts him in the suit there, not at Bide-a-Wee, so there'll be less chance of him getting it dirty. I know from experience with

216

my sons, and you must know from yours, that you can't take your eyes off boys for a second or they'll be filthy."

"Thank you," Bev said. "Thank you."

Puddles walked with Bev and Snowy down the sloping lawn toward the lake and said, "Usually places don't live up to their photographs, but Waterlight outdoes the ones you sent. Oh, I can't believe I'm here at last, up north!"

Bev thought that Puddles looked as if she had completely forgotten her New England roots. She was wearing a halter dress in strident shades of fuchsia and salmon, with pink flip-flops on her long narrow feet. Bev and Snowy were wearing jeans; bare legs weren't a wise idea during bug season. Over her dress Puddles had put on a white cardigan because her system had thoroughly adapted to the South and she'd grown chilled, though nobody else had.

"Home," Puddles said. "I'm home."

Puddles had arrived from Manchester on time for dinner with Bev and Roger and Snowy and Tom on the back porch, a meal of New England treats in honor of the occasion, lobsters from the fish market and strawberry pie from Indulgences where Bev had a final conference about the catering. During dinner, Roger announced that Bev was now a broker with her own office. Bev had forewarned Snowy by a phone call Sunday night saying that Roger and the children now knew about this. Snowy and Tom acted surprised. Puddles was properly surprised and demanded to see the office tomorrow before she went to Woodcombe to see Snowy and Tom's apartment and businesses.

And at the moment Roger and Tom were loading the dishwasher while Bev showed Puddles the backyard with Snowy.

They reached the shore, the beach and boathouse, and stepped onto the dock.

Puddles said, "Remember all the sunbathing we did on the public beach? We were doing it for beauty but we also thought it was healthy. It's a wonder we don't look like beef jerky these days."

Definitely not, Bev thought. Puddles had always been pale; she was paler. In the year since Bev and Snowy had seen her at Hilton Head, Puddles had aged slightly in a way that Bev couldn't quite put her finger on. Puddles hadn't gained back the weight she had lost. Indeed, she looked cheerleader-coach fit despite her arthritis. Nonetheless, she seemed, well, *faded*. Her short brown hair was fading more than graying. Her brown eyes were faded too, almost bare despite mascara. Because Bev saw Snowy often, she couldn't gauge how Snowy was aging. If Puddles noticed changes in Bev's appearance, Puddles would probably remark on them—or had she learned tact at last in her sixties?

Puddles turned her gaze from the beach to Waterlight. "Remember what they used to say in the olden days about big houses, that if you took a laxative in the front room it would be working by the time you reached the backhouse?"

Unfazed, Bev laughed affectionately.

"Guess what," Puddles said. "I won't be dining here tomorrow night. I have a date."

If Puddles had hoped to shock them so much they'd fall off the dock, kersplash, she was disappointed. Bev asked, "You got in touch with Norm?"

Snowy asked, "You've been e-mailing?"

Puddles looked smug. "Uh-huh. Dear old Norm Noyes."

Bev asked, "Where are you going, the movies and Hooper's?"

"And parking?" asked Snowy.

Puddles said, "As a matter of fact, we're having dinner at Hooper's. After he gives me a tour of the changes in town. That's all."

218

Bev glanced at Snowy, knowing they'd both love to be flies on the wall during that dinner. However, Bev thought, because Puddles was a nurse and Norm a reconstructor and investigator of car accidents, the subjects of their conversation were sure to be ghastly enough to make even Snowy lose her appetite.

The next morning as Bev was toasting a bagel, Puddles came down to the kitchen from a night on the sofa bed in Bev's office wearing white shorts and a short-sleeved shirt swimming with a tropical-fish design, her feet slapping in the pink flip-flops. She carried a small square package wrapped in wedding-present wrapping paper. "You said no presents, so let's call this a hostess gift. Go ahead, open it. I'll make my own bagel."

Bev obeyed, then started laughing. It was a travel first-aid kit. For a wedding present forty-one years ago, Puddles had given them a terrifyingly huge first-aid kit. Bev said, "You remembered!"

Puddles said, obviously enjoying the moment, "*You* remembered!"

"That big one came in handy through all the children's scratches and scrapes. Thank you, Puddles."

After breakfast, they drove in separate cars to Bide-a-Wee and Bev showed the office to Puddles. As she'd hoped, Trulianne and Clem were out of sight in the shop. Puddles said, "Well, the interior of your office suits you, but the exterior sure the hell doesn't." Then Puddles drove on to Woodcombe, and Bev sat down at her new desk at her new computer and tried to work on real estate, but the ceremony was too close, too intrusive. For the millionth time she clicked on the weather report. Saturday's forecast was still sunshine. On TV this morning, the weather forecaster had said there wouldn't be any "precipitation issues" this weekend, a phrase that would make Snowy foam at the mouth. Sunshine. The ceremony wouldn't get rained out. She couldn't take a rain check.

Since Bev and Shirley's talk on the phone last Sunday, during lunches on the back porch Trulianne hadn't said a word about her mother's orders, so Bev didn't know if she'd actually follow them when the time came. Trulianne didn't say anything today, either. After Clem's nap Bev took him back to Trulianne, to the play area in the shop, and then returned to Waterlight and helped Miranda by polishing silver. In the mail was a present from Ann, who like Puddles had ignored the no-gifts note on the invitation. It duplicated the wedding present Ann had given her forty-one years ago: a set of monogrammed green bath towels. Bev wept over the present, pulled herself together, and that evening after dinner she did some more second-honeymoon packing and then waited up for Puddles, doing paperwork, but Puddles hadn't returned by the time she started nodding off, so she joined Roger asleep in bed, trying not to feel like an anxious parent. She thought of Guy, Puddles's husband, alone in their Hilton Head house. Who the hell was she to judge?

The next morning she fully expected to discover that Puddles hadn't come home at all, but lo and behold the door to her office was closed so Puddles was in there, asleep, and heaven be praised, this meant that Bev couldn't use the treadmill and had another reprieve, as she had yesterday. Anyway, according to Mimi's checklist this Friday morning was supposed to be devoted to pampering. Then Roger's sisters and brothers and spouses would be arriving. Roger had decided that the suite should go to Pauline, the older of his sisters, and her husband, who'd had a coronary bypass operation. At Mimi's house, Dick and Jessica and Etta and her veterinarian would arrive this evening, at the Gunthwaite Inn and Twilite Motel there'd be the best man and the bridesmaid—

She wanted to go back to bed and pull the covers over her head. Roger had got up early and gone off somewhere, so she'd have the whole bed to herself. Did this qualify as pampering or was it sheer panic?

She took her shower. Returning to the bedroom, she heard the lawn mower and went to a window. Hooray, Leon was at work! She dressed in jeans and a jersey, and downstairs in the kitchen she delved into the fridge. Amid the supplies for guests' breakfasts she found the cartons of Egg Beaters and made an omelette to keep her strength up.

"Hi," Puddles said, appearing in the kitchen doorway. Instead of tropical attire, she was wearing jeans and sneakers and had acquired a Lake Winnipesaukee T-shirt to display her famous breasts. "Don't bother about me, I'm having breakfast at Norm's. I'm meeting him at his house and we're going to Portland. I'll show him what I remember from my early years."

"House?" asked Bev, scenting possibilities.

"Oh, it's the one he grew up in. On Bridge Street. He inherited it."

"He lives there alone? A single man rattling around in the family home?"

"You won't be selling him a condo, Beverly Lambert, Realtor, or getting your paws on the house. He's having a grand time whatchamacallit, rehabbing it."

"I suppose you won't be back for dinner?"

"No. Norm Noyes. I can't believe how age has improved him, his personality, his looks. Even his Adam's apple isn't so noticeable." Then Puddles gave Bev her clinical scrutiny. "How are you feeling?"

"Well, today's schedule is: massage, hair, manicure, pedicure. Mimi has everything under control, and I'm supposed to relax."

"Yeah, right. I figure the best way I can help is to stay out from underfoot, but is there another way? I can always break a date with Norm."

"You did that enough in high school. Run along, Puddles."

Soon after Puddles left, Snowy phoned from work and asked, "Did Puddles come home last night?"

"She did, and today she and Norm are off to Portland. If she's showing him her childhood, is it serious?"

"With Puddles, who can tell." Then Snowy said, "How are you holding up? Do you need any last-minute help?"

"Everything's fine." Bev heard her voice quaver, but she

continued, "Everything is all under control and under way. I'm being pampered today. I don't have to cook or anything. Tonight there's the dinner at the Gunthwaite Inn that we're hosting for the people who've come from afar for the great occasion." She swallowed a sob.

"Oh Bev," Snowy said. "You can call a halt, you know. That's a rule that keeps agoraphobics such as I am from going to pieces. We tell ourselves we can always leave, turn back, though I admit I've found turning back impossible after the point of no return on some hikes."

"I'm okay," Bev lied. Then she wailed, "The collected poems, there are too many, I can't find one for tomorrow!" She knew Snowy would think this was just like the occasions in school when Bev had left her homework to the last minute. "I'll take the book to the beauty parlor this morning, but . . ." She trailed off.

After a moment, Snowy said, "In your anthologies, have you looked at Christina Georgina Rossetti?"

"No."

"Try her."

Bev reached for the kitchen memo-pad pencil. "Give me the name again. Do I remember it from senior-year English?"

"Yes, we read one or two of her poems then. Christina Georgina Rossetti. Her name is a poem, same as Edna St. Vincent Millay."

"Thank you!" Bev jotted the name down, hearing Miranda arrive for the final preparations. "See you tomorrow." In the front hall she told Miranda, "There's coffee in the kitchen."

"Thanks," Miranda said.

Bev hurried on down the hallway to check the suite. It had occurred to her that Roger would never think to clear his things out of the top couple of drawers of the bureaus in case Pauline and her husband wanted to unpack, and sure enough, he hadn't. She lifted up some winter sweaters to shift to a closet shelf and saw a manila envelope underneath, a nine-by-six envelope addressed to Roger on a computerized label. She remembered finding this envelope in yesterday's mail along with Ann's present and junk mail, supermarket flyers and such. She had left it for him on the hall table.

She picked it up. You could snoop in your children's rooms, but in your husband's den?

No return address. The postmark was blurry.

Roger had slit the envelope open. She tipped out the contents. Photographs. There she was, sightseeing in Santa Fe and Sedona.

The weather did hold. The next day was sunny and lovely, and as she tended to last-minute details throughout the morning, Roger's relatives kept saying to her, "Happy is the bride the sun shines on!"

She hadn't had a moment alone with Roger except in bed last night, but there he'd immediately fallen into a real or fake sleep. After discovering the photos, she had walked in a trance to his mahogany desk in the sitting room. Gone was the mesquite desk set she had brought him from Sedona. Had he, enraged, swept the pen and pencil and letter opener off onto the floor, thrown them away? In a paroxysm of fear and guilt, she finished clearing out the bureaus' top drawers, then rushed upstairs with the envelope to hide it in *her* bureau where, oh irony, she had hidden those birthday cards from Frankie.

To her pampering session she had taken Mother's copy of *The Oxford Book of English Verse*. Reading Christina Georgina Rossetti's poems, she found her vow at last. She copied it into the real-estate notebook she carried in her shoulder bag and began memorizing.

When she'd returned home, she kept waiting for Roger to

confront her, but he was occupied with the final preparations, overseeing the putting up of the canopy by the dock, ushering his relatives to their rooms. She kept telling herself the photos were not incriminating evidence. She wasn't doing anything in them except gawking at scenery.

But she was the daughter of a poultry farmer, and she knew that the chickens had come home to roost.

Roger's sisters were still floridly brunette and pretty, spread into comfortable matronly shapes. His brothers were gray and wiry. While Roger had shown them and their spouses around Waterlight, Bev could hear his siblings kidding him about living on the lake like a summer complaint, a summer person. He kidded right back. But he kept his distance from her. Then they'd all gone on to the Gunthwaite Inn and joined roommate Jonathan and his wife and cousin Elaine and her husband for dinner. At the original wedding Elaine had been a sinewy athletic girl; forty-one years and two children later, she was just as sinewy but resembled the beef jerky about which Puddles had spoken. Jonathan looked like what he was, a close-to-retirement private-school history teacher and football coach. Roger had laughed at the toasts and jokes and not caught Bev's eye once.

Puddles hadn't returned last night. Bev tried not to worry about traffic accidents, tried to imagine instead Puddles and Norm spending a romantic night at a Maine seaside inn. Midmorning, Puddles phoned and said, "After seeing Portland and my old house, Norm and I drove down east, down the coast through towns so picturesque they'd make you sick if you weren't wishing you lived there. We got back awfully late, and I knew I'd wake up your household coming in so I stayed here at Norm's. I used to keep peeling his hands off me in the movies. Well, he sure has improved in this department too. But nonetheless, I insisted on spending the night in his guest room."

"You did?" Bev said. "Really?"

"Yes," Puddles said, sounding confused, "I surprised myself.

Thinking of Guy. But Norm and I did have a great time, sight-seeing and reminiscing about high school. We remembered crazy trivia; he stopped smoking a year ago, thank God, so cigarettes are still on his mind, and he remembered the Lucky Strike slogan, L.S.M.F.T., remember, Lucky Strike Means Fine Tobacco, and I reminded him how we used to say that instead it meant Loose Sweaters Mean Floppy Tits. And he said my sweaters were the tightest in the whole school and he went on some about my boobs. But I stuck to my guns about the guest room, and he was a gentleman. I guess I'm glad about that. How are things there?"

"Everything's fine."

"We're having a late breakfast. I'll be back in time to change."

"Fine."

"Happy is the bride the sun shines on! Bye!"

Time sped faster. As Bev arranged the flowers that a clean-shaven Leon had cut, and as she fussed over the florist's flowers and did a thousand more chores, she wondered if, like Miranda, she would be left at the altar. Would Roger get revenge by not appearing for the ceremony, by moving out of Waterlight, by filing for divorce? She couldn't cancel the ceremony and thus avoid humiliation. Too late. The party had, to all intents and purposes, already begun. The house was in an uproar, the Indulgences catering crew and servers had taken over the kitchen and dining room where they were readying scallops wrapped in bacon, mushrooms stuffed with crabmeat, a mountain of shrimp, platters of prime rib, grilled chicken, poached salmon, and Mimi and Etta were zipping around everywhere—and then she saw Puddles hurrying upstairs in yesterday's jeans and a new T-shirt emblazoned with: Maine, The Way Life Should Be. Bev looked at her watch. Eek! One-fifteen. She glimpsed Roger walking down the hall. He had changed into a white shirt, khakis, a Mimi-woven tie, and his navy blazer with a small white rose in the buttonhole.

225

Mimi grabbed her. "Mother, why aren't you upstairs changing? Go!"

Bev chased after Roger and said, looking at his hand, not his face, "Give me your wedding ring, it's a surprise."

Without a word, he wiggled it off and placed it on her open palm. Then he went on down the hall.

Bev raced upstairs to her office and tapped on the door. Puddles opened it, adjusting a pink sundress that made her pale skin flushed—either the dress or the excitement of the event that had struck her and Snowy so funny at the outset of plans. Puddles asked, "Isn't this better than those lime green dresses?"

"Puddles, could you go down to the front porch and keep an eye out for a young woman with a little boy and bring them up here to my bedroom?"

"What's all this about?"

"Hurry!"

When Bev was dressed and examining her reflection in the full-length mirror, the iceberg green jacket, lace shell, and long straight skirt, the emeralds, the strappy sandals, she heard a Puddles-peremptory knock on the door and in came Puddles shepherding an apprehensive Trulianne wearing the first dress Bev had ever seen her in, a polo dress that looked like a belted navy polo shirt that reached to her knees, carrying Clem who wore jeans and a Red Sox jersey, over her shoulder the teddy-bear tote bag out of which a dinosaur and a fire engine reared. Snowy followed in a pale blue pantsuit that Bev remembered Snowy buying a year or so ago at the Liz Claiborne Outlet in North Conway. Snowy gave Bev a slight shake of the head; Snowy hadn't identified Clem to Puddles.

So Bev made introductions. "Puddles, this is Trulianne Hughes and her son, Clem. My grandson. Trulianne, thank you for coming. This is my dear friend Jean Cram, aka Puddles."

Riveted, Puddles goggled at Clem. She breathed, "Jesus H. Christ."

Bev hastened into the closet and brought out the white suit

226

and the ring cushion. "Clem, we're going to be playing a new game, and you get to wear this costume for it."

Puddles breathed, "Leon."

To Bev's amazement, Trulianne laughed and asked Puddles, "Is that a wild guess?"

"The resemblance," Puddles said. "I see it now. Can't miss it. For years Bev sent Christmas cards with photos of her kids. This kid's a spitting image, if you'll excuse the expression."

Trulianne set Clem down and unbuttoned his jersey. "I knew the minute I saw Leon that he had good genes."

Bev wanted to protest that there was more to Leon than sperm, but Clem began to protest instead, unwilling to relinquish his jersey, so she and Trulianne and Puddles and Snowy all had to persuade him into the white Eton jacket and short pants, white socks and shoes, and then Charl tapped on the door and looked in and said, "Mimi sent me to tell you we're here and Dudley can begin whenever you—oh, who is this, oh, a ring bearer, isn't he the *sweetest!*", so Charl was the next person to be introduced to Clem, as Trulianne whipped a comb out of the tote bag and fluffed up his curls.

"Now, watch!" Bev said to Clem. With her beautifully manicured old-lady grandmotherly hands she used the pearl hat pins to affix Roger's wedding ring and her own to the cushion. "This is the game, holding the cushion level like this, walking straight ahead." She paced with exaggerated care down the length of the room and back, then hitched up her skirt and knelt to coach him. He kept alternately scowling in concentration and giggling.

Trulianne asked him, "Do you have to go potty?"

"No," he said.

Puddles plucked the bouquet of white roses off the settee and handed it to Bev, singing, "Here comes the bride, fair, fat, and wide, see how she waddles from side to side!"

So they were laughing as they began leaving the bedroom. Bev cast a look back at her reflection, realizing that nobody had commented on her outfit and that she was upstaged by her grandson. She didn't give a damn. Then she remembered her vow and snatched the piece of folded notebook paper out of her bureau and put it in her jacket pocket.

"Trulianne," she said, "do please stay with us when we walk outdoors, to help get Clem down the steps and keep him happy."

"Okay," Trulianne said.

A phone was ringing in Bev's office. "Hell," Puddles said. "I forgot to turn off my fucking cell phone. I'll be down in a sec." She dashed into the office.

Down the staircase the rest of them went into the hallway, and halted. Charl ran off to alert Dudley, Roger, and Jonathan, and Snowy went to round up Elaine. Bev saw that a few people were chatting in the living room, where the French windows were open onto the porch, but most people were outdoors on the back lawn. She felt that she was in a trance, waiting in the wings in a coma, waiting to see if Roger would still be here to be found by Charl.

From the living room Shirley, in a yellow dress with perhaps too many ruffles, came hurrying into the hall, Everett behind her constrained in a buttoned collar, crooked tie, burgundy blazer, and sharp-creased pants. Shirley knelt in front of Clem. "I won't cry. I won't, but isn't he adorable?"

Clem explained earnestly, "Have to keep level, Gram."

Snowy brought Elaine, followed by Mimi who said, "So this is the ring bearer," then did a classic double take and dropped to her knees beside Shirley to gaze at Clem, speechless. And then Puddles came hurtling down the stairs, suitcase in one hand, car key stabbing forward in the other, her shoulder bag soaring behind her.

Bev said, "Puddles, what on earth—"

Puddles gasped, "Guy has had a heart attack. That was Amy on the phone." Amy, her daughter the doctor. "I'm flying back."

Bev looked at Snowy, remembering how Puddles had got them to come to Hilton Head by telling them her husband had had a heart attack, which he hadn't.

Snowy asked Puddles, "Is this the boy who cried wolf?"

"It's real," Puddles said, pushing open the front screen door, dropping the car key, catching it. "I didn't pack, I threw, I've probably left stuff, send it to me sometime, I'll phone you after I get home."

Bev asked Snowy, "What do we do, what do we do, is she in any shape to drive, should I drive her, yes, I should drive her to Manchester—"

Mimi said to Clem, "You're Leon's, aren't you." She apparently was unaware of Puddles's departure.

Clem asked impatiently, "When walk straight ahead?"

Snowy said, "Mimi, go tell your musicians to start."

"What? Oh, oh yes." Mimi jumped to her feet and ran out a French window.

Shirley asked Bev, "Your friend's husband has had a heart attack? How awful. Everett, he's had an angioplasty, and it taught us how short life is, just like they say."

"A heart attack," Bev said to Snowy.

"Real," Snowy said.

Bev heard the flute and guitar begin to play the song she had chosen instead of the wedding march. Her cue. To "My One and Only You," she followed Elaine and Trulianne and Clem out a French window onto the porch. A quick survey of her audience—Tom; Ruhamah and D. J.; Darl and Bill; Harriet and Jared; Elaine's husband; Jonathan's wife; Roger's relatives—showed her that Geoff had indeed decided not to attend. The photographer and videographer were aiming lenses at her. Then she saw Roger in a group waiting under an oak, Roger and Jonathan and Dudley. He hadn't left her at the altar! But would he turn his vow into a scathing denunciation, a public flogging? Ahead of her, Trulianne lifted Clem and carried him down the stairs to the lawn, then set him on his feet again and pointed him toward the group, which Bev now saw included Dick and Jessica, Mimi and Lloyd, Etta and Steve, and—

Starting down the stairs, Bev almost fell flat on her face at the sight of Leon standing in this family group with Miranda, his arm around Miranda's waist. When Bev had given him his invitation, she had explained that he could bring Heather. In the storm of wonderment—had there ever been a Heather, had Leon helped Miranda through her cancer treatment after Miranda's fiancé fled, and how much older was Miranda anyway, ten years?—Bev recognized ruefully that Leon had inherited some of her flair for the dramatic, so while she was planning to spring a surprise on Roger and on Leon, Leon had been planning his own surprise. He didn't seem disconcerted by the presence of Trulianne and Clem. Had Trulianne invaded his space by phone or e-mail to forewarn him?

And now Bev saw that Roger was staring at Clem who stumped onward across the lawn, more or less steadily, the cushion wobbly. Roger's head snapped toward Leon, who observed Clem's progress with a half-smile. Roger looked again at Clem and back at Leon. But Roger could not throw a fit in public. Could he?

Bev glided up beside Roger and whispered, "This is our grandson, Clem." To Clem she whispered, "You did great, darling. Now the rest of the game is to stand beside your mother until we need the rings."

Roger whispered, "His mother?"

Bev whispered, "I'll introduce you after." Then she couldn't resist adding, "He calls me Gaga! What do you want to be called?"

Dudley cleared his throat. "Welcome, everybody, to this beautiful occasion on this beautiful day. Forty-one years ago, Beverly Colby and Roger Lambert exchanged their marriage vows. Today they are renewing their bond of love, with special new vows. Bev?"

Bev watched her shaking hands pass the bouquet to Elaine and take the folded paper from her pocket. She had planned to recite "A Birthday" by Christina Georgina Rossetti while gazing meltingly into Roger's eyes, only referring to the paper if she went blank. Now she lost her nerve. But she'd forgotten to bring her glasses! She held the paper far out and began to read. Her voice was shaking, too. Her memory supplied those words she couldn't see.

My heart is like a singing bird
    Whose nest is in a water'd shoot;
My heart is like an apple-tree
    Whose boughs are bent with thick-set fruit;
My heart is like a rainbow shell
    That paddles in a halcyon sea;
My heart is gladder than all these,
    Because my love is come to me.

If she were at a prize-speaking contest or in a play, her stage fright would have ended by now. But her voice and hands continued shaky as she read the last verse.

Raise me a dais of silk and down;
    Hang it with vair and purple dyes;
Carve it in doves and pomegranates,
    And peacocks with a hundred eyes;
Work it in gold and silver grapes,
    In leaves and silver fleurs-de-lys;
Because the birthday of my life
    Is come, my love is come to me.

When she did look up into Roger's face, she saw tears shimmering. She almost didn't understand that they were tears, because she had never seen him cry during all their years together.

Clem said imperatively, "Go potty!"

With a swift motion Trulianne picked him up, and turning toward the house she loosened the cushion from his grip and passed it off to Leon before she broke into a run. Guests were smiling, murmuring.

Dudley said, "Roger?"

Out of an inside pocket of his blazer, Roger took a folded sheaf of papers. Bev's fears were confirmed; he was going to be long-winded. But had he changed his vow to a denunciation?

Then he shoved the papers back and said to Bev, "That song and that poem say it all. My one and only you."

Dudley wasn't thrown by this change. Smoothly he launched into, "Will you, Roger Lambert, have this woman to be your wedded wife, to love her, comfort her, honor and keep her, in sickness and in health, and, forsaking all others, keep thee only unto her, so long as you both shall live?"

Listening to the words, Bev thought how far she and Roger had strayed.

"I will," said Roger.

Dudley turned to Bev. "Will you, Beverly Colby, have this man to be your wedded husband, to love him, comfort him, honor and keep him, in sickness and in health, and, forsaking all others, keep thee only unto him, so long as you both shall live?"

Bev said aloud, "I will," and added silently: This time. She realized that Leon was walking up to stand beside her. He held forth the cushion.

Roger gave Leon a penetrating look, then suddenly grinned. "A son?"

Leon nodded.

Roger unpinned the smaller ring and slid it onto Bev's finger. She slid his ring onto his.

Dudley said, "I do hereby pronounce you renewed husband and wife."

They kissed.

232

Bev typed:

Dear Snowy,

We have found an Internet cafe in Warwick and are having our tea here after touring the castle. We had lunch at the castle, a cottage pie of minced beef and mashed potatoes, which we split, thank God. I belatedly realized that I should have waited to eat any morsel until after we'd visited the dungeon, which made me want to vomit as we descended those dark narrow stairs into that terrible cave with the oubliette and torture devices. Men's horrible ingenuity.

Of course for me the best part of the castle was the rooms with waxworks portraying "A Royal Weekend Party, 1898," the glamorous guests in their gorgeous clothes, the waxwork maid filling a tub with real water.

In Stratford, at the Shakespeare Centre the best part was the costume exhibit—especially the codpieces! I embarrassed Roger with a giggling fit. Then in the garden at Anne Hathaway's Cottage I embarrassed him again by automatically pulling up a weed. He thought I'd be arrested by the Shakespeare police.

But we are having fun. And from this distance Roger can view Leon's unconventional situation with some detachment and equanimity. Besides, as you saw, Roger has already fallen in love with Clem. We're going to have to buy another suitcase to bring home all the toys Roger is buying. They include, of course, a red double-decker bus and a London taxicab for the vroom-vroom gene.

I like Miranda so much that my hopes for Leon and Trulianne aren't so dashed as they would be otherwise. It was nice of Miranda to apologize for going along with Leon's deception. His reason seems to have been a desire for privacy—as if I would've raised a ruckus about the age difference and any other reservations I might've had! (Okay, I realize he knew that even if I wasn't voicing an opinion I'd be fretting over these things in silence.) He'll have moved in with her properly now, and I think she'll become the go-between that will get him involved in Clem's life.

I wonder what Puddles will do when things settle down after Guy's death.

Tomorrow we drive on to stay in Chipping Campden, from which we'll take trips to Blenheim Palace and Oxford. Yes, it's fun (except dungeons, etc.), and the climate is marvelous for my skin (as you said, it's like walking around in a vat of moisturizer), but I keep thinking about site fidelity.

Love,
Bev